PRAISE FOR RICK MOODY'S THE ICE STORM

"THE ICE STORM is a powerful indication that the art of the novel is in the best of hands with the younger generation. A remarkable work, full of wit and drama." —**George Plimpton**

"Packed with keen observation and sympathy for human failure."
—***Chicago Tribune***

"A remarkable, brave, and beautiful book. With intelligence, restraint, and without sentimentality, Rick Moody has created a moving portrait of a nuclear family meltdown."
—**Jeffrey Eugenides**

"Moody is a stylishly clever writer. . . . A deft second novel."
—***TIME***

"Insightful and convincing." —***Publishers Weekly***

"Moody's poignant tale of that night's turbulent events places him in the tradition of such other suburban WASP authors as Cheever and Updike. But by focusing on the children of these confused adults, he puts a distinctly nineties spin on what might seem familiar territory." —***Vogue***

"Rick Moody writes exquisite, word-smitten prose." —***Elle***

more . . .

"Should appeal to readers who lived through the '70s and to members of Generation X, who seem to be fascinated by the decade of their birth."

—*Hudson Valley* magazine

"THE ICE STORM works on so many levels, and is so smartly written, that it should establish Moody as one of his generation's bellwether voices. . . . Builds toward a remarkable scene that will change everyone's life forever."

—***Hungry Mind Review***

"One of the wittiest books about family life ever written."

—***The Guardian***

"A dead-on portrait of wayward teens. . . . Brilliantly captures the era's oversexed sorrow."

—***Mirabella***

"It is beautiful, in the strange way that tragedy can be—heartrending, awesome—and it resonates deeply long after the reader is finished with the book."

—***Fairfield County Weekly***

"Excellent . . . Moody's second quirky novel is a huge '70s nostalgia trip, a litany of kitsch, a mountain of memorabilia as the backdrop to a bittersweet story of suburban America."

—***Time Out***

"A blackly funny, beautifully written novel . . . remarkably mature, containing far more insights about family life and far more wisdom than any 29-year-old author should reasonably possess. Moody is clearly a writer to watch."

—***The Sunday Times* (London)**

"Elegant, moving, and regenerative." —**Donald Antrim**

"Remarkable . . . at times the author's exploration of human frailty is profound. . . . A fine novel."

—***The Economist***

"THE ICE STORM is reminiscent of Cheever and Updike in the best of ways. Rick Moody comes off as the true heir, the next generation. His is an often elegant, if unsettling, view of family life."

—**A. M. Homes**

Also by Rick Moody

GARDEN STATE

THE ICE STORM

RICK MOODY

WARNER BOOKS
A Time Warner Company

I need also to acknowledge some people and institutions who have made the composition of this possible: Fishers Island Colony, Yaddo, MacDowell, Michael Pietsch, Malanie Jackson, the Count de Cenci, D. A., Helen Schulman, Dan Barden, John Crutcher, N. B. W., Shrug, Jack Moody, Angela Carter, and especially Jules.

Warner Books Edition

This Warner Books edition is published by arrangement with Little, Brown & Co., 34 Beacon St., Boston, MA 02108.

Warner Books, Inc., 1271 Avenue of the Americas, New York, NY 10020

A Time Warner Company

Printed in the United States of America

First Warner Books Printing: August 1995

10 9 8 7 6 5 4 3 2 1

Library of Congress Cataloging-in-Publication Data
Moody, Rick.
The ice storm / Rick Moody. — Warner Books ed.
p. cm
ISBN 0-446-67148-7 (pbk.)
1. Family—United States—Fiction. I. Title.
[PS3563.05537I24 1995]
813'.54—dc20 95-11750
CIP

Cover design by Julia Kushnirsky
Cover photograph by Amy Guip

For Hy,
Peggy,
Meredith,
and Dwight

I

SO LET ME dish you this comedy about a family I knew when I was growing up. There's a part for me in this story, like there always is for a gossip, but more on that later.

First: the guest room, with the orderly neglect of all guest rooms. Benjamin Paul Hood — the dad in what follows — in the guest room. In the house belonging to Janey and Jim Williams, just up the street from Hood's own comfortable spread. In the most congenial and superficially calm of suburbs. In the wealthiest state in the Northeast. In the most affluent country on earth. Thanksgiving just past and quickly forgotten. Three years shy of that commercial madness, the bicentennial.

No answering machines. And no call waiting. No Caller I.D. No compact disc recorders or laser discs or holography or cable television or MTV. No multiplex cinemas or word processors or laser printers or modems. No virtual reality. No grand unified theory or Frequent Flyer mileage or fuel injection systems or turbo or premenstrual syndrome or rehabilitation centers or Adult Children of Alcoholics. No codependency. No punk rock, or postpunk, or hardcore, or grunge. No hip-hop. No Acquired Immune Deficiency Syndrome or Human Immunodeficiency Virus or mysterious AIDS-like illnesses. No computer viruses. No cloning or genetic engineering or biospheres or full-color photocopying or desktop copying and especially no facsimile transmission. No perestroika. No Tiananmen Square.

Much was in the recent past. Jimi Hendrix, Janis Joplin, and Jim Morrison were in the recent past. Four dead in Ohio, one at Altamont. Nixon had shipped arms to Israel for the '72 war, but slowly, slowly. The Paris Peace talks had lapsed; Kissinger had become Secretary of State — in September. (No Nobel Peace Prize for 1972.) China had joined the U.N.; Nixon had gone to visit.

In the recent past, buildings had already been occupied and abandoned at Columbia and Berkeley and everywhere else. Now Abbie Hoffman was in hiding. Now Jerry Rubin was writing for the *New Age Journal.* Angela Davis had been acquitted. The Beatles were recording solo albums. The war in neutral Cambodia was heating up. (The Khmer Rouge would take Phnom Penh. Lon Nol would soon be deposed.)

The energy crisis was getting under way.

Rose Mary Woods had just *accidentally erased* eighteen and a half minutes of a subpoenaed conversation. (The White House released a photograph: Woods reached for the phone while absently stretching to depress an erasing pedal.)

None of this, though — not the Watergate Hotel and its palette of hypocrisy, coercion, and surveillance, not Jonathan Livingston Seagull, whose movie had just opened, not transactional analysis or Gestalt therapy — troubled Benjamin Hood's sanguine and rational mind. Hood waited happily for his mistress. In her guest room. In those dark ages.

Billy Jack was the most popular film of the year.

Imperiously, Janey Williams had strode from the guest room to install her birth control device. Imperiously. With a subliminally pervasive trace of something like resentment. It was the bum note in the sweet song of this tryst, but Hood didn't notice it. His thought was this: with all this innovation, with the simplicity of the birth control pill and the reliability of the IUD, why persist with that rubber stopper?

Well, the delay had its pleasures. It conjured dirty and agreeable fantasies.

The plaid flannel comforter on the bed in the guest room was mussed with the recent tangling of neighborhood kids. An amorous tangling, Hood thought, an adolescent hunting and groping. The sheer, white drapes in the guest room were limp as the bangs of a sad schoolgirl. The dresser drawers were empty but for a skittering mothball and an ancient box of disposable douche. Guest room furniture reminded Hood — as he opened and closed drawers — of the cutaway sets of television soundstages. It was ugly and impermanent stuff. The shag rug, for example, was mustard and forest green. It concealed remnants of cheese bits and bland, tasteless crackers. He might himself have been the culprit here. For there had been one prior encounter with Janey.

On the bedside table a perfect bottle of perfect Finnish vodka glistened perfectly. He had been in this house a hundred and fifty times since the Williamses had moved in. A hundred and fifty times before he ever sought this refuge, the refuge of the guest room. He was grateful and ashamed both. He wished he had stayed at his end of the street. But he was helpless before the itch. This was one way he accounted for it. He had been lonely even in his wife's arms, lonely in crowds, lonely at meetings, lonely throwing tennis balls for his dog, lonely playing *Operation* with his kids. He had been lonely during commuter conversations, lonely during late-night heart-to-hearts with old fraternity brothers. His dad, living alone up in New Hampshire, made Hood lonely. The severe landscapes of November made him lonely. Only Janey, for reasons Hood wasn't likely to analyze, distracted him from this isolation. He was aware that this was a temporary situation, but he felt bound to look into it.

There was more to it than that. In the mirror over the dresser he looked good for forty. Almost forty — next March. Wait a second. His skin was stretched over his paunch. As if someone had cellophaned a constrictive packaging over the youthful Benjamin Hood, soft even then. He was mottled and patchy. He needed a new coat of semigloss. His hair was going. He had worn it short all his life — he had never seen it, really — and now it was gone. His glasses were perched on his tiny, crooked nose like a large, barren tree on a granite outcropping. His minuscule eyes were the color of antifreeze. Okay, he was forbidding to behold. He resembled a longtime funeral director or a salesman of bogus waterfront property. He knew this. He tried to make up for it with kindness and fidelity. He tried.

His erection was subsiding. Right now. His bejeweled weapon of persuasion was subsiding where it used to beckon, at his boxer shorts.

Once his dreams had been songs. He'd been a balladeer of promise and opportunity. The corridors of the financial industry were *his*. Once he had been the filly before the first race, the cadet before the invasion. He had advanced in the direction of his dreams. But by 1973 desire surprised him at inappropriate moments: during television broadcasts of

Southeast Asian massacres, during the Frazier/Ali rematch, when Archibald Cox was fired, when Thomas Eagleton admitted to shock-therapy treatments.

Hood was not here, in this guest room, because he perfumed himself, because he was sunny and joyful. He was here, he opined, because his touch could be cruel. He was masculine and magical and mystical. He was a swordsman. Janey Williams brought it out in him. Having a mistress was like discovering, as an agnostic, the consolations of religion. It was like caving in and having a stiff drink right at the moment the clock strikes four. He felt no need to probe new ways of lovemaking now that he had come out of retirement from love. There was no need to express his *feminine side*. He preferred the conventional posture. Janey wanted him as he was. (And he heard her footsteps, now, going down the staircase. Perhaps in search of a candy to feed him during the act.)

So he had a little trust. A little trust wasn't much, but it was something. Trust never overpowered him. Hood was full of dread. And anxiety. Any change in his environment — the failure of Bob's Stationery in town, for example, or the relocation of Bruce Abrams to some distant Shackley and Schwimmer branch office — filled him with dread. The small failures of life brought him, inexplicably, to the verge of tears, though he always managed to step back from that precipice. He could see desire had grown subtle and strange in the years since he had learned about it. Desire wasn't about large breasts in Cross Your Heart brassieres anymore. It was about hunting for comfort.

This was perhaps a useful moment to fix a drink.

Because of anxiety, he suffered the following: a mild case of eczema, which broke out all over his body, mostly in winter, and which turned his skin a patchy orange; piles, because he could move his bowels only after a comfortable day at work and these were now few; a duodenal ulcer, which he treated with liberal doses of antacids and by eating primarily foods that were *white* (rice, oatmeal, Cream of Wheat hot cereal, white bread, potatoes, the occasional glass of milk or slice of American cheese); a swelling in his feet which he imagined was gout; a noticeable enlargement of his liver and pancreas; and canker sores.

Most of all he suffered from canker sores. The very survival instinct of his cells seemed to have failed in the small pursed region of his mouth. The cells there no longer cohered; they opened up crevices and left them open. Hood's canker sores tormented him constantly. He often had two or three a week. On occasion he had more than a dozen *at one time*. Most prominently, these occasions were (1) during his second year at boarding school, (2) in the weeks of college after he broke up with Diana Olson before he began to date her roommate, now his wife, Elena O'Malley, and (3) during Lent of 1971, when he had given up tobacco, caffeine, and alcohol.

Benjamin Hood believed himself to be a record-holder among those afflicted with mouth sores. He got canker sores on his lips, in the back of his throat, on this tongue. He got long, narrow ones in his gums that looked like irrigation ditches.

Citrus, ketchup, spices — these were all contraindicated. As was the act of speech.

Yes, there was a shadow urge behind his pox, and Hood could pinpoint it. The imprecision of speech, its risky improvisations and inventions — it was best to shut himself and his canker sores out of all regrettable conversations.

Had he not as a young man abandoned a career as a radio broadcaster for the more concrete world of securities analysis? Was it not language and its insidious step-relative, sentiment, that so destroyed his mouth?

Ridiculous. He could remember his first canker sore, sometime in the midst of WWII, and it had nothing to do with speaking in class or with being seen and not heard. Nothing to do with speech at all. Born of Yankee stock, and that was all, born of farmers who spent whole afternoons on the porch without directing a word at their people, born of Yankees who would invite any stranger to their homes for Thanksgiving and engage them in conversation not once.

He just didn't feel like talking.

Where was Janey? It was after four. Dusk had fallen. Anxieties clamored in him. The cures for canker sores, the charlatanical cures, the sorts of American Indian mystical stuff his wife might have suggested — lecithin, yogurt cultures, vitamin B_{12} in large doses, nuts, citrus, prayers to St. Christopher — he enumerated these, as he also considered the performance, in light trading, of the entertainment stocks he analyzed for Shackley and Schwimmer.

The Williamses had moved in about the time his own son, Paul, had gone off to school. Three years ago? The Williams boys — Sandy, thirteen, and Mikey, fourteen — were just behind Paul and Wendy, sixteen and fourteen, respectively, but they were all friends anyway. This didn't mean that Hood approved of the situation. Janey's kids were inferior company for his own. Mike was a dim, sinister boy, graceful as an aluminum baseball bat. And Sandy was genuinely creepy. A scheming and reticent cynic. Sandy marketed incorrect answers to math tests, just for fun. He would grow up to own one of those stores that sold telephone bugs, high-powered telescopes, and other surveillance devices. He would drink and watch neighbors masturbate.

Jim Williams, their father, did nothing particularly. His work consisted entirely in dreaming up half-baked investment schemes, the sort that required willing suspension of disbelief. Williams was an early investor in those little Styrofoam packing curlicues and a videotape gizmo with which star athletes could review their own performances. Especially with this device, Williams seemed to have *defined a need.* That business school stuff sank right in with him. The videotape machine generated both capital and notoriety. Williams brought home professional athletes Seaver and Koosman to meet his boys. The urchins of the neighborhood hovered out in the street, on their banana-seated Schwinn Typhoons, to watch the progress of superstars.

Williams's professional sloth didn't seem to bother anyone but Benjamin. Hood believed in the stolid riders of the New Haven line, those grailing knights, legendary heads of household whose leadership was marked chiefly, though not entirely, by intimidation. Jim Williams, on the other hand, purchased Marimekko place mats. He purchased a water bed and Cadillac sedan. He said *far out* occasionally. He disappeared on obscure business trips for several weeks at a time. He was a golden retriever in temperament — a slobbering, friendly type — but he was also a liar, a teller of fish tales. The way he told it himself, Williams paddled through the white water of 1973 and it was just a charming shallows. He never had bad luck. He never had a bad day.

But his worst crime was this: he didn't prize his wife. Jim Williams. A good guy.

The vodka catalyzed this vengeful litany. Hood looked at his carefully folded trousers, his checkered cardigan sweater — they were piled on a wicker chair under the window — and wondered if he should dress, if Janey was waiting for him to dress so she could disrobe him all over again. *Maybe that was it. It was some sort of erotic game. Of course.* Like teenagers arriving for strip poker in thirteen layers. Hood wouldn't convert to nudism — there were no nudist beaches in Fairfield County anyway — but he liked a game.

It never did to compare your wife and your mistress, because your wife always won, the way the classics were better, the way the jazz standards had nuances no other songs had. Still, those pop ditties of the moment could sometimes get stuck in Hood's head. Sometimes they articulated a whole season of trouble at the office. Sometimes they articulated the sorrow in a stalled marriage. His loneliness. Then the strings swelled in the bridge and those songs weren't so bad after all. He and his wife were well suited to one another, really. For example: in the cessation of all intimate contact. They didn't make love anymore. For almost two years, it hadn't occurred to them.

Family, what a flawed system of attachment! Stalin took children from their parents and raised them as wards of the state. Love, according to Mao's little red book, was no excuse to procreate. These weren't such terrible approaches to the problem. Here, in the Northeast, you ran off with your mistress yet still loved your wife. Because you hadn't yet comforted your mistress in sickness and she hadn't yet seen you cry over a blowout or strike your own son. And she hadn't grown tired of your two poorly articulated philosophical positions (that a stint in the national service builds character and that no man should ever teach secondary school) or happened upon your concealed hatreds of certain ethnic groups. In time, though, she and your wife grew alike — maybe they even became friends. Then you fell for a new mistress.

Elena had been shy and beautiful and stoic and brilliant. He knew this the way he knew that certain films were great because he had adored them when he was young. Now he might sleep through these same films on television, but he loved them still. Elena had been shy and brilliant and beautiful and impossible to talk to.

At a party in 1956, where there had been a competent jazz band with a locally prominent drummer, a party where conversation had lurched and turned awkwardly and no one seemed to be setting their feet down exactly in time, where Benjie Hood was drinking away the remorse of romantic failure with Diana Olson — she was present in the room and dancing with some other guy — at a party while cold rain and snow pelted the greater Boston area, Hood had first plied his suit. Maybe it wasn't that evening itself that he remembered now, maybe it was only the stories of that evening, but he hung on to those stories anyway. He told and retold them.

Elena seemed to recognize something about him right away, he had thought, and it was something she didn't like. This would give her some work to do. What Hood was concealing — remorse, canker sores, lack of athletic prowess — was apparent to Elena. Maybe she had heard about it from Diana.

The complex rituals of civilization fell away from him and he was immediately uncovered for her care. He couldn't hide it. He had changed elementary schools once too often. He had fallen from a railroad bridge, into a swift river, while being carried by his father. Almost drowned.

His parents had rancorously parted. He told her all this. He couldn't remember which story he had used. He couldn't remember much in the way of specifics except a dim, smoky room, the warmth of tweed, the excess of that drummer, the swift tempo of a new attachment.

— You should read ———, was what Elena first said to him. Some mystic. Emanuel Swedenborg. Or Mme Blavatsky. She said it smilingly, flirtatiously, the way other people winked and said *nice tie*. He hated her for it; he hated that he didn't recognize the name. Had she been a guy, Hood would have spit his rye in her face. Nevertheless, he was deep in conversation, drunkenly rambling. Talking about that railroad bridge again. He was uncomfortable with her and that seemed to be a part of things from the beginning.

Fraternity brothers happened by, eased in and out of the conversation. Dances came and went. Long clarinet solos. The drummer had them all applauding. That drummer scattered himself around the kit as though the story of that evening, the story of that party, were his responsibility. As though he had to be sure to pass through ever percussive mood, every tonal color, before the evening could pass away. It was a race against time signatures. Anything could happen in the world, Hood was telling his future wife. Profit and loss. Communism and capitalism. It didn't make a bit of difference. He could be accepted at the training program at Chase Manhattan or First Boston or he could not. The notches in a whaling harpoon, the destruction of northeasters, the tedium of duck blinds — he couldn't decide which opinion to give first. All that counted was a flashy car, a girl who would wear slacks and wasn't afraid to smoke.

Elena didn't say anything. She was as easy to read as

some German theological tract. But she didn't chide him either. She didn't mention his weight and she didn't muss his hair. It broke his heart in the end how she just kept listening and listening and he kept saying things he didn't want to say.

In this way, Hood figured out that love was close to indebtedness. In settling this debt, he married Elena O'Malley. Family was a bad idea he got because there were no other ideas in those days. It was the outer margin of one little universe and nobody knew what lay beyond it. There were years full of evenings when the habit of marriage astonished him, when its repetition comforted him like nothing else ever had. Then this period came to an end. He had two kids, a house and a lawn mower, a Pontiac station wagon with simulated wood paneling on the side, a new Firebird, and a Labrador retriever named Daisy Chain.

He loved his wife and children, and he hated all evidence of them. The noise of children, and the terrible quiet just after, which augured — always, every single day — some broken heirloom or injury: it squeezed the life out of him a little bit at a time. His worry was ceaseless. His son, Paul, had picked his little nose and grabbed at his crotch in public. His daughter had exposed herself to a boy at the country club. Almost any life was feasible at his salary, but this was the one he had. It was seventeen years since he had met his wife, and in seventeen more years it would be 1990 and his son would be thirty-three and he would be fifty-six. Until recently he had believed that the elderly were born that way, unlucky. Now he knew how effortless that transformation was. His son would be there to remind him. In 1996, Paul would be his present age, thirty-nine, while he would be sixty-two, his mother's age at the time of her death. His wife would be sixty, and she would be remarkably skeletal. Her church attendance would be regular.

—Janey!

Hood draped his prim, salmon-colored button-down shirt around his shoulders. He pocketed an escaped collar stay. Whose? His? In one hand, the bottle, the other, the drink. His vodka. A mourning dove was complaining out in back of the house. A car passed on Valley Road. Hood was sad. He opened the door. At the top of the stair, he called her name. Janey had assured him that the house was empty, that Mikey and Sandy were over with friends for the night—committing acts of vandalism, probably, ringing doorbells and running—that Jim was in the city for a week. Still, Hood thought he heard voices.

He fled back into the guest room and sat in the uncomfortable wicker chair. He zippered his pants, pulled on his socks.

He married Elena and they had the kids in '57 and '59 and they traded up in houses and they traded up in cars. To afford the family car, the Corvair, in '63, Hood had been forced to trade in the Jaguar he had driven in college. It was all economics now. Or maybe he overlooked the subtlety of feeling that hid beneath economics. Beneath math. He made $48,000 a year not including the annual bonus. Income from stock held by Elena, $3,600; income from his own bad investments, a little less. Savings account. Joint returns. Public school meal allowance. Power boat. Life insurance. (His father had sold insurance.)

He had wanted another sports car ever since. And the first blossoming of adultery took place along precisely this vine. It was as humdrum as it could have been. He actually picked her up at the office Christmas party. This woman.

Not at the family office Christmas party, to which he had taken the kids when they were young, but the interoffice Christmas party.

There was a drunken urgency to the event, an atmosphere of fear and need. He felt he *had* to say shallow, boorish things to this girl. There was no surprise in the way he complimented her *knockers* and her *tush*. He descended into vulgarity the way a buzzard locks in on some morsel of decay. He gorged himself on his discomfort. He had spilled a glass of wine on himself while trying to dance to a rock-and-roll song, and the spill, on his white shirt, resembled a chest wound.

He fully intended to drive her back to her Village apartment and then to get on some wide avenue north. It was uppermost in his mind. Instead, though, he found himself in his pathetic Karmann-Ghia, chauffeuring her around the empty west side of Manhattan, past the prostitutes and strip joints, through the haunted industrial quarters of the city. He pulled over, in his station car, in the meat-packing district. In front of a loading dock. He began to tell her stories, fabricated stories, about some past full of good humor, full of fraternity pranks and sex with girls in fast cars. And then he simply put his face in her lap, right in the middle of her lap. His nose and cheeks abraded on her wool skirt. He began to tongue the spot on her skirt where he imagined his disgrace might concentrate itself.

—Ben, she said. Take pity on me. I can't even see straight. Come on.

He wouldn't talk to her though. He was pulling off the lingerie under her skirt. She was still sweating from the dancing and he could smell it on her. She sighed. The lights of passing cars had a metronomic regularity. He maneuvered around the stick shift and the emergency brake to get his face between her legs. His pinstriped ass was up around the steering wheel. He was doing his best to feel bad. It didn't matter that she had not bathed that morning; they had an arrangement now. Soon she was holding up her end. She was grunting softly, almost protestingly. He'd never heard such a thing before. Sounded like a swallow trapped by a barn cat.

— Ben, Ben, she whispered, let's move. This isn't the right place. You know that.

He pretended she meant *to the back seat.*

Hood banged the back of her head on the rearview mirror as he was swinging her around and trying to carry her to that tiny storage area behind the front seats. He was close to tears now, though he was determined to go through with it.

— Take them down, she said, take down your trousers. I want to see you in full. If it's going to be like this.

She worked the zipper herself. She didn't require his help.

He remembered her kneeling across him. His suit pants coiled around his ankles like shackles, around his cordovans. His tie was loosened, his shirt unbuttoned, the tails of his shirt flapping around in the midst of their efforts. It was cold in the car, he could see his breath.

— Get on board, he said. C'mon.

He had never spoken during the act before. The words sounded to him like an impropriety. They were like an ethnic slur. They were like talking about money in public.

She sat on his impoverished penis.

Hood thought of Elena, of course. How could he not? And of Paul and Wendy and how they would feel when they found out. The look of inconsolable shame and remorse with which they would greet him. Something led

Hood these days into degradation. There was some tug, some mournful and beckoning melody he followed.

In fact, Melody turned out to be the girl's name, and she was better at it than his wife. She was fortissimo — *ff*, when scored. What was upsetting about Melody was what was good. He thought about prostitutes and group sex and transvestites and sadomasochism and he could see the lure of the alien, the lure of the barbarous sexual act. As she rocked, she banged her head again. On the ceiling. He came. All the life went out of him. And then the moment turned. Really. For a second everything smelled sad and good. Like after a heavy rain. He held her in his arms. Melody from the office, whom he would have to see again right after the family ski trip to the Berkshires, right after he saw his dad, his lonely dad, right after he relaxed for a week. He would have to see her and he wouldn't know what to say. He would forget he had been happy right then, for a moment.

— Should we get a drink?

He hoped she would decline. He was a little scared.

— You have to go back to your wife, fool, she said quietly. You'll be folded up on some lane divider if you have another drink.

— I can make my own decisions —

— Well, I don't want another drink with you. Even if I do appreciate the company.

They didn't talk anymore after that. He dropped her off at her apartment.

The trip home was an adventure into the northern wastes. He drove erratically, despondently, dangerously. He sped, tailgated. Back at his house, in the master bedroom, he splashed water on his penis. He bathed the site of his transgression with a violet shell soap.

— What are you doing? Elena called sleepily as he dried himself off in the bathroom. Never coming enough out of her unconsciousness to see it.

— Oh, just brushing my teeth, Hood mumbled. Didn't want to wake you. Just brushing.

Nine months later. A full gestation period after Melody, he began to execute his affair with Janey Williams.

Their kids and his kids got along famously. This provided the opportunity. The kids were like some suburban gang of Sharks or Jets. Slovenly, affluent kids from the suburbs, staying out late to shoot pellet guns at the Van Dorens' rottweiler, to smoke marijuana, or to get into one another's pants. Mikey Williams and his friends had begun to call each other *Charles* all the time — this was part of how Janey and Hood had grown close, one night, talking it over. Hood had asked Mikey, taking him aside brusquely one night at a dinner party at the Williamses, what the hell *Charles* was all about. Short for the opposition in the Vietnam conflict? Nickname of Manson? Name of a perfume? Nah, Mike told him sullenly, Charles, like Charles Nelson Reilly. From *Match Game*. The one, Hood surmised, with the incredibly long microphone.

Wendy was the only sensible kid on the block.

The wind gusted fiercely, wailing its dissonances, turning the corner around Janey's house, around the guest room, passing into the valley below, over the Silvermine River — a creek, really — and into the forest. The weather report was bad. Rain, rain, and then turning sharply colder. It was coming down in sheets now and mixed with harder stuff.

Kids, that was how it happened. They had a laugh over *Charles*. It was Halloween night and their kids, his daughter and the Williams kids and Danny Spofford from up the street, were dressed up, along with every other kid in the neighborhood, as *vagrants*. Decked out in rags with mud and tar and eyeliner speckling them, with penciled-on boils and gin blossoms and dead teeth. Dressed like urban flotsam. Benjamin Hood had driven the half mile to fetch some forgotten culinary item, a cup of milk or some Tang or something. He sat for a moment on the couch next to Janey. They rated the costumes of their beloved vagrants. The further the distance from their cushy lives, the higher the rating.

It had to do with kids and Halloween. With this mythology of the holiday. The carnival of sleep and death. The ghosts of the past, the ghosts of all his mistakes, crowded the earth, reminded him of the folly of his best efforts. Regrets. Hood turned the other cheek: he permitted the kids to carry shaving cream and soap and raw eggs out into the street. *Go ahead,* he laughed. *Go fuck each other up. Doesn't matter in the long run. Doesn't matter what the hell you do.* The kids froze, stunned by the oath.

Then they piled out the door, to menace the neighbors.

Janey Williams's lipstick was a chocolate color, a real earth tone.

The long flat stretches of matrimony were over. He was thirty-nine and balding and unattractive and his children wanted to be nothing so much as vagrants.

—Let's *fuck,* he desperately proposed to his neighbor. He drained a highball.

—So romantic, she said. But I think you might have another engagement.

—Oh, Janey, he said. You know what I mean.

—Boy, do I, she said.

—Tell me I'm totally wide of the mark, he said. Tell me it's all in my head.

Janey smiled sadly. She had her own problems.

He made it back in time for dinner.

The erotics of adultery are well documented. In the guest room, thinking back, Hood drank again. Maybe he honored his wife in this way; maybe it was *for her*. Maybe he fucked against the notion of family, to escape its constraints. Maybe he adultered because of his keen appreciation of beauty. Maybe he celebrated the freedom of the *new sexuality*. Maybe he did it to abase himself. Maybe he did it to hurt Janey Williams, or to injure her husband — they were more attractive than he was, they were more at ease. Maybe it was her husband he wanted to fuck, and it was such a terrible, dark secret that it was secret even from Benjamin. Maybe he wanted to get caught. Maybe he did it to escape, from his job, his anxieties, his psychosomatic complaints. Maybe he did it because his parents, too, had done it (or so he supposed) and the desire to cheat boiled in his genes. Maybe, at last, he did it simply because he wanted what he couldn't have.

Touching briefly — in the guest room — on this shortage theory of adultery, Hood arrived at a brilliantly incorrect understanding of Janey's absence. He believed suddenly that he understood the afternoon. Of course! He was supposed to look for her! In the overdecorated chambers of her house, he was to embark on a quest, a Buzz Aldrin or Neil Armstrong sort of a quest. He would have to work for this oblivion he wanted. He was dressed but ready to disrobe. He poured a fresh tumbler of vodka and set off on the tour.

— Janey . . . ? Janey . . . ?

To the right lay Sandy's room. Jim and Janey's prized, brainy, creepy son. The jigsaw-puzzling son. The son who did puzzles of popcorn — just popcorn, or just M&M's.

The brainy son who memorized Nolan Ryan's E.R.A. going back into the late sixties, who explained the physics of curveballs and kept track of the dead in Vietnam. He wouldn't permit his photograph to be taken. He was afraid of water.

Sandy's room was tentatively decorated, as if he suspected he would be moving soon. A lone Yale pennant was tacked up over his bed. It served only to confirm the emptiness of the space. There was a bookshelf full of strange-but-true baseball stories, strange-but-true ghost stories — *The Thing at the Foot of the Bed* — and the 1972 edition of the *Guinness Book of World Records.* (Heaviest man, Robert Earl Hughes of Monticello, Ill., who achieved a peak heft of 1,069 pounds. Buried in a piano case.) On top of the bookshelf, several small fish tanks full of Magic Rocks.

— Janey! Hood whispered, in the center of this unnaturally clean space.

He slid back the door to Sandy's closet. A mound of dirty laundry piled there. No Janey, though, crouching, in lingerie, waiting.

Back in the hall, Hood headed for Mike Williams's room. He was sure the doorknob would be rigged with home electronic alarms. The apparatus for this alarm would be arranged on the floor just inside the room, rigged with pipe cleaners and roach clips and a nine-volt battery he had lifted from somebody's automatic garage opener. Mike liked whoopee cushions and rubber dog excrement. He often wore a Nixon mask.

And he also had a fondness for the crank telephone call.

— Hello, is your refrigerator running?

— Why, yes.

— Well, I guess it must be, because I just saw it run by my house. HA! HA! HA! HA! HA!

— Hello, is this 655-FUCK?

— Hello, is this 655-SHIT?

Paul had told him all this one night. One of those frail dusks when father and teenaged son share a good laugh over something. Few and far between were these days. Hood found these calls hysterically funny. Perhaps this was the day that Paul told him about his own crank phone calls, and about the bizarre miracle of their own number, 655-4663. The last four digits actually rendered their name. 655-HOOD.

Mike's doorknob released no shock, however. It sent up no electronic squeak. (Alarms were never activated for the real intruders.) The room belonged to Hood, the interloper. Black-light posters and tapestries covered the walls, tapestries that, in light of the dim table lamp Hood switched on, were full of burn holes and unidentifiable stains. A water pipe the size of a barber pole stood in one corner. Janey permitted this behavior? With more time he might have extended the search. No doubt the traditional pornographic magazines were concealed between his mattresses, along with socks crusty with his dried seed. The shame and resourcefulness of the masturbator coming into his craft! No fabric or substance or receptacle was beyond being tested. Mike's laundry was probably welded together with his semen.

Imagine the sheer volume of it at single-sex schools and in penitentiaries. Consider how often the average American male masturbated in 1973. That year there were, say, 100 million American men, two thirds of whom were capable of achieving orgasm. At once a week, that meant approximately 3,432,000,000 ejaculations in the calendar year. At ½ ounce per ejaculation, that's 1,716,000,000 ounces or 13,406,250 gallons. Larger than a very large oil spill. Where to put all that waste sperm? All across the vast land, in the suburbs, in the rural and forested regions, in inner cities, guys were coming into rags, into sinks, onto their own bodies, outdoors in the alley or upon the earth. How many thought about disposal?

He had tried to explain self-abuse to his son once, and this was one of the conversations that did not go well. He sat the boy down in the bedroom one day and asked him not to do it in the shower, because it wasted water and electricity and because everyone would expect it of him there anyway, and not to do it onto the linen, and not to do it with his sister's undergarments or any clothes belonging to his mother, and not to do it with the dog. The best time was when he was certain no one else was in the house. The best place was into the john, where it would cause no trouble and mix with the other sad waste products of America. If he became concerned about any sign of perversion in his habits, he should feel free to come forward and discuss it. Together they could consult a medical text.

At the close of this monologue, Paul looked as though he had just learned of his family's financial ruin.

Every man lusted to renounce masturbation once and for all, to cease from those tepid orgasms whose only novelty lay in the freedom to invent that they encouraged (Janey in crotchless hot pants presenting her ass to him while sucking on her third finger). Inventions that were otherwise shameful to harbor. Yet Hood himself had not found occasion to give it up. Sometimes he even had to masturbate while lying next to Elena. He imagined, he hoped, he relied on the fact that she slept through these nocturnal abasements.

Hood left Mike's room. He stood at the top of the banister and looked down. He leaned over it and felt the cool of the polished wood on his abdomen. Why dwell in the illusion that Janey was waiting for him here? She had left, of course. The conclusion was unavoidable. She had released him to the inevitability of his marriage, to confession and inadequate apologies. He could hear the rain and sleet pelting urgently against the windows of the second floor. It was only a half mile or so to his house, along Valley Road. In minutes, he might be settled in front of a fire in the library, contemplating the oblivion of fires.

He headed for the Williamses' bathroom. One last look. A survey of the medicine cabinet. He wanted to see if there was a diaphragm in there at all, to see how deep the slight ran. He wanted evidence.

Where would Janey have gone? To the A & P to find something to go with turkey leftovers? To purchase beauty aids in pıeparation for the Halfords' party that evening? Maybe she had gone to his house, to rifle his own medicine cabinet?

Hood set the bottle of vodka on the speckled, beige, faux-marbleized countertop and poured some more ambrosia. Then he began to peruse the remedies on the other side of that mirror: Cover Girl Thick Lash mascara, Revlon Ultima pancake, Max Factor lipstick (chocolate), Helena Rubinstein Brush-on Peel-off Mask, Kotex tampons, Bonne Bell Ten-O-Six lotion, Clairol Balsam Color (blond, although she frosted her hair), Summer's Eve disposable douche, Spring Breeze. Valium, Seconal, tetracycline, the first of these in a renewable prescription.

No diaphragm case.

In a tiny space at one end of the top shelf, Jim Williams apparently kept a few things. The Dry Look, Old Spice deodorant, Noxzema Shave Cream, Water Pik teeth-cleaning system. Vicks VapoRub.

It was an L-shaped bathing suite. Hood drained his glass and ducked into the alcove where the toilet and shower were shrouded in darkness. On top of the toilet, Janey had piled Clairol Herbal Essence shampoo, Clairol conditioner, and Tegrin medicated shampoo.

She had taken leave of him at this spot. This was where she left behind her evidence. A black lace garter belt and stockings had been draped across these hair-care products. Like some waterfall of loss and eroticism, the stockings swept down over the closed lid of the toilet.

Meant for him. Hood marveled at her boldness. And having completely surrendered to an appreciation of her tactics, he decided he still couldn't forgive her. Her flaws sprang to mind: her stretch marks, the port wine blemish on her left thigh, her lipsticked teeth and inexpertly manicured nails. She had left him in the guest room with his trousers around his ankles. She had sealed him down like a bank vault. He was an empty parade ground, a shuttered theater, an abandoned roadside attraction. Janey had information on him.

He liberated the garter belt from where it was anchored by the dark green shampoo bottle, and the stockings from the garter. And then he flung back the shower curtain, hoping one last time to see her there, grinning, shivering, perhaps stretching out one hand to him, the other on the hot water spigot.

Realizing, of course, that abandonment titillated him, that he was mildly aroused, that his beleaguered *member* thrived under bad circumstances, he unzippered anew his flannel slacks and, using the garter belt as a spur to his isolation and arousal — as a dressing gown for his hard-on — in flagrant violation of the precepts of autoerotics as he had explained them to his son, he began to stroke himself. Always practical, Hood secured the door as he worked.

Must we always imagine a woman to accomplish the deed? It was less hurtful to women and their history to imagine them this way than to violate and oppress them. Hood recognized and was proud of his own technique — above all he wished to hurt as few people as possible. Yes, he himself had eliminated the problem of representation entirely.

In the fifties, back in Hartford, Conn., where his father's insurance business had temporarily been located, and where Hood's testes had first erupted, he had been able to ejaculate simply over the word *bosom*. He had also managed to fashion an orifice for himself out of a pliable old feather pillow. The pillow took him all the way to college, where the abundance of breasts lingered in his imagination like some divinely inspired thought, like the perfection of harmony and meter. But then he had fallen on hard times. In the company of the marriage neither breast nor ass nor the vesuvian moisture of down below on its own moved him. The contemplation of body parts was no more fascinating than a grocery list.

At last, in his early thirties, only true pornography would do it. Solitary orgasms were like sneezes or yawns. He imagined women in hot pants and leather goods. He kept *Playboy* around. (In this month's issue there was a first-rate short story by Tennessee Williams.) He imagined devices. His cheeks flushed.

What a blessing when oblivion descended on these exercises. Masturbation was a falling sickness, with the emphasis, these days, on the sickness part. But at least he didn't have to think. At least he was granted a moment without Benjamin Paul Hood and his fiscal responsibilities, without the lawn, the boat, the dog, the medical bills, credit card and utility bills, without the situation in the Mideast and in Indochina, without Kissinger and Ehrlichman or Jaworski or that Harvard asshole, Archibald Cox. Just a little peace.

He groaned dully as he issued forth, firing with unusual range and payload onto the shag throw rug, as well as onto the garter belt itself. With the soiled garment, he swabbed and dabbed at the spot on the rug where he had splattered. Sighing, he refixed his trousers. Sighing, he unlocked the door.

Where to stow the evidence?

The garter belt was an empty snakeskin, a stately and somber artifact of his failure, a sort of Shroud of Turin. In the hall, with it balled in his fist, he turned first left and then right. Like a ghost, he ventured into Janey and Jim's bedroom and gazed sadly upon the pacific waters of their waterbed.

He thought to set it right upon their pillow, but he couldn't do it. Scruples.

In the hall, though, he found himself again at Mike's door. Impulsively, he entered with his death shroud, with Mike's mother's soiled garter belt, and stuffed it in the back of Mike's closet. The kid would never even know he had been framed.

Then with a lightness of heart, a relief at folly alleviated, Hood started down the stairs. He thought about riding the banister, but the newel post had a sort of asparagus bulb at the top of it, one that must have neutered generations of banister-riders. Unable to leave the premises, he toured the first floor. Possession was the larger part of ownership. Fluted crystal, lace napkins, the finest eight-track stereo components, all the Williamses' personal property belonged that afternoon to him.

At the front door, however, the last of Hood's resolve failed. He was a spook, a fool, a voice from the beyond, a housebreaker, and it was time he faced up to these things. His wife took no notice of his comings and goings, his mistress abandoned him in her own house, his children wouldn't speak to him. Only the back exit was fit for Benjamin Paul Hood. He would leave by the servant's entrance, with imperceptible footfalls. On tippy-toes. Like a Plumber, an official burglar.

Then, at the top of the basement stairs, having opened the door already, having opened the door absently, he heard laughter. The laughter of teenagers. That hard, bitter, revenging laughter of distrust and disillusionment. One way out! One way only!

NEW CANAAN was tiny already, but as Wendy got older it seemed to be shrinking, too. It was vanishing, maybe. Its avenues were like the crosshatching on a legal tender dollar bill. You could read Wendy's town with one of those beginner microscopes that Paul had gotten for his birthdays from three or four relatives. Next to New Canaan, a black ant was like a Cadillac or like an armored personnel carrier; a housefly, the Huey helicopter. Shag carpet was like an Asian rain forest.

One time she had cut her wrist lightly — just a scratch: long sleeves to school for a while and no one knew any better; later you couldn't even tell — so that she could look at her own blood under the microscope. Just the usual traffic and hustle, though, these globs of color overtaking these other globs.

In New Canaan, there was one high school, one junior high, four elementaries. No school bus more than fifteen minutes from its destination. This meant that you could know everyone in your demographic category by the time you started high school. So Wendy Hood knew everyone. One movie theater. One grocery store. Churches were Protestant. Neither snow, nor rain, nor gloom of night stayed

New Canaan's relentless progress toward neighborliness.

The girls took home economics and the boys took shop or else risked civic humiliation for the rest of their lives. Wendy took home economics but she hated it. Best thing about it was its resemblance to sorcery. Between cooking and science, she had learned all the fundamentals of poisoning. Eagerly she imagined dispatching a loved one, or altering her own future, or turning her father's SX-70 camera into a twisted sculpture of metal and plastic.

To class she wore ponchos and handmade sweaters, and her blond hair tickled the top of her butt. She had toe socks and clogs and painter's pants. Wendy's Tretorn tennis sneakers were filched from Mike's Sports not two days ago (the day before Thanksgiving) and now the patent leather gear she was supposed to wear for the holidays was safely enclosed in a Tretorn box on the 5½ shelf in the back of the very same store. Wendy wore the uniforms other kids wore, but she thought a lot about black gowns and putting spiders in the pockets of her girlfriend's hip-huggers. She wanted to smoke pot and take sleeping pills (she had located some prescriptions in her parents' bathroom) and fondle the one sad-looking boy in the special-education class. Fondling she had learned precociously like everything else, in conversation with her brother, from her mother's copy of *The Sensuous Woman,* and partly from her own imagination. Sometimes it was hard to understand the descriptions of this stuff in books. You had to use the wilder senses.

Only one place in this desolate village interested her really. She was lucky enough to live beside it. Silver Meadow! A private residential psychiatric facility. A drying-out joint, her father called it. Funny farm. It was marked off as precisely as a crossword puzzle on the hillside beside their house — neat little footpaths, neat architecture, neat bowling alleys and auditoriums, pools, saunas, paddle-tennis courts. Precisely landscaped shrubs and evergreens. Benevolent security personnel roamed Silver Meadow and they recognized in Wendy Hood a local sylph whose comings and goings were not averse to the therapeutic process.

What did it mean to dry out? She had seen the lonely and decrepit emerging from the Mercedes and BMWs. They wore suede and fur and bangles or matching denim suits; they checked to be sure the car door was locked because issues of security were important to them. They tried to memorize their spot in the parking lot and failed. She saw them walking aimlessly around the parking lot, forgetting. What they had in common besides their wealth were their anguished faces. They had rings and minks but they were worn out and desperate. You could tip them over just by blowing hard. And they weren't violent or criminal. They were just people. As far as Wendy could tell. No hardened serial killers sodomizing young girls and leaving their bodies in rural creeks. Wendy was among her people here on the premises of Silver Meadow. From all around the country, from New York and Cleveland and Athens and Dallas and Las Vegas, they came to Silver Meadow for the cure of folly. She didn't want to overstay her welcome here — she didn't want to exhaust its riches — but she liked the place better than her hometown. And that was why, on Friday afternoon, she was here waiting for Mikey Williams.

Rain. Some fat, smiling weatherman would say it was *raw*. New Canaan was maybe a single degree about freezing. Surfaces contracted. There had been hail, too. Her poncho didn't keep out the cold, but she withstood it, shivering, because she was precociously brilliant — everyone said so — and impractical. Anything was better than the homely, pink ski jacket her mom had bought her.

Originally, it wasn't Mike Williams but his brother, Sandy, with whom these trysts had taken place. He was a jumpy, quiet boy and Wendy liked how he was shocked by her, how he was always a little bit uncomfortable when she was around, how he didn't want to kiss with his mouth open; she liked how he was always skulking off to work on a model airplane, one of those monuments to futility and boredom. He was a challenge.

One afternoon she successfully persuaded him to let her enter the bathroom with him. It was just the sort of pastime they got into over the years. Wendy had wrestled with him at touch football; she had eaten the sandwich ends he left behind — cream cheese and jelly, Fluffernutter, deviled ham; she had shared her Mountain Dew with him and tortured insects with him. Though Sandy didn't talk much, Wendy thought what he thought and knew what he knew. Until that time in the bathroom.

The Williamses' downstairs bathroom was wallpapered in a velvet floral print. As Sandy unzipped his tiny shorts (this was the summer just past), and squatted down over the toilet, the absolute *nakedness* of his skeletal body struck her. There wasn't a fold or pouch on him. He was like a little *National Geographic* photograph — the wise villager struggling against famine.

And then there was his dick. It was no more than a little outcropping. It looked like the end of a number-two pencil, the part you throw out because it would be too short to extract from the sharpener. Not a hair surrounded this appendage. Sandy was as blank as a newborn, as simple as one of those modern pictures — all black or all white or all red — that any kid could do. He reposed on the toilet like a little girl, and began to empty himself. But then the enormity of being observed in this private ritual, this ritual of cleanliness messed him up. It was like she had stumbled into his sleep and learned all about his nightmares. Immobilized on the commode, he started to shout:

— What do you want? What do you want? Get out! Get out of here!

His usually peaceful face became twisted and raw as he rose up toward her. Brass-colored urine trickled lazily down his thigh — under his bunched, unfastened safari shorts — onto the throw rug. No girlish smile was going to get her out of this.

Mrs. Williams must have heard the commotion. She pulled Wendy out by the ear. But because Mrs. Williams was *cool* and because she approved of the basic changes brought about by *young people* in the last five or six years, she let Wendy off with just a few cautionary words. A person's body was his temple, Mrs. Williams had said, and it was his decision when to worship there and when to fast or rest. Did she understand? A person's body was his first and last possession. We come into this world alone, Mrs. Williams said, and we permit this aloneness to be understood by another maybe once or twice in a whole life. And in adolescence, which Wendy probably knew about from her own parents, our bodies betray us. They grow strange. That was why, Mrs. Williams said, in Samoa, and in other developing nations, adolescents went out into the woods on foot, unarmed, and didn't come back until they had learned a thing or two.

Sandy hated her after that, as Mike and Sandy hated each other. Wendy knew already how boys fought when they were close. They fought the way families fought. The explosions and the affections came out of the same place. She had seen Mike chase Sandy with a fire iron one day, fully intending to put out his brother's charcoal eyes, the next day volunteering to write Sandy's poem for English class. They were more alike than not, those two boys. She watched Sandy and she learned how silence could conceal all kinds of high jinks. Still waters ran organized criminal networks and spearheaded new pornographic markets. Mike and Sandy were the same way except Mike was loud about it. They called each other *Charles* (and it was a term of respect) and they never went in the other's bedroom, but the loved each other and would die inside when they parted for good.

An example of their unsavory entrepreneurial activities: Mr. Williams had negotiated a deal with the folks at Topps Chewing Gum. What the deal was, nobody could ever explain to Wendy. She wasn't sure Sandy or Mike understood it either. Bazooka gum, among the principal product lines of Topps, was a factor in the deal. As a result, the Williamses ended up with several large crates of Bazooka. These crates were warehoused in their basement. Bazooka, which was like a gold standard at Saxe Junior High and at New Canaan High School, was thus available to Mike and Sandy in gross quantities for use at school. With it, Mike was able to produce an impeccable collection of the 1973 New York Mets baseball cards (which didn't help them win the World Series). With Bazooka Joe he had also procured fake vomit, a T-shirt that said *Enjoy Cocaine* in the same letters as the *Enjoy Coca-Cola* commercial, many types and varieties of firecrackers, such as M-80s and ladyfingers and bottle rockets, and a red Flexible Flyer sled. Sandy had turned his gum into currency, for a price slightly above retail, and filled a gigantic change bank with the money. He just liked to count the stuff.

How Mike bested Sandy in the battle for Wendy's body, a prize she was pretty willing to give up anyway, isn't much of a story. Sandy wouldn't look at her after the bathroom incident, and there was no one else suitable within a mile or so with whom to lock arms and make flimsy vows. She missed Sandy, but she was always missing something, and that little naked spot wasn't going to be filled by him or by anyone else on Valley Road. It was through the chewing gum, ultimately, that Mike had lured her, alone, into the basement with him. She had walked among those boxes as carefully as if this were some vast arms shipment. The sheer amount of gum dumbfounded her! What kid in their age and class would not kill for a twenty-four–count box of Bazooka rolls? Who cared about the endless fillings, about the horror of dentistry? Today a kid is here, tomorrow she is grown! Gum! Give us gum! We are hungry for gum!

And Mike was prepared to honor her wishes. He popped a piece in his mouth right then. She could smell it. She could taste the taste — amusement park and industrial cleaning agent. Together — shoulders brushed up against one another like they were already pledged to troth — they read the comic, laughing at how Sandy was like the guy, Mort, who always wore a turtleneck up over his mouth.

— Seriously, Mike said. Do you want gum?

— Of course, you jerk, she said. Why else would I be here?

— Nasty mouth, he said. Well, there's gonna be a little, you know, opportunity cost here. It's a cost-of-doing-business–type thing.

— Huh?

— You know, Charles. Pussy.

The word fell from his mouth like the name for a particularly dull frozen vegetable. Twat, pussy, cunt, muff, slit, pudenda. There were no good words for the anatomy of girls. Why were the words for beautiful things — orchids, gables, auroras — so beautiful? Would her pussy, if it were named after one of these, still sound so homely?

— You want to get into my pants, Mikey?

And this turned out to be the right way to approach the issue. At the invitation, he got all panicky. She could see him freezing up. She had been wearing shorts with little floral suspenders that day. Suspenders were in since *Godspell.* Some frilly, lacy shirt. A trainer bra. Mike had never bargained on cooperation. Boys thought of girls the way they thought of particularly good careers, things to work toward. Or as fine objects: they wanted to haggle and get a good price. Wendy thought she was the first fourteen-year-old in America to fully understand this point.

— What's my payment, Mikey? If you want what you want, you gotta put your cards out on the table.

The opportunity to fool with the boxes of gum afforded him the time he needed to think. The Williamses never understood *people,* really. That's what Wendy thought. They fooled around with enterprises. Her mother had told Wendy this. It was one of her mother's very firm points of view.

Mike brought two gross boxes from one of the packing crates and placed them at her feet, like he was one of the wise men in the school Christmas pageant.

— Not enough, she said.

— No way, Wendy. My dad'll see. You know? He's keeping an eye out —

— So he chews it too?

— It's not that, it's —

— Mikey, you're making me mad. Forget it. You're insulting me. I want the whole thing. I want a whole crate full.

He couldn't. He just couldn't. In Wendy's social studies class they were doing skits about *ethical dilemmas* in November, and this would have made a fine one. Wendy did hers on President Nixon's agonizing decision about whether or not to burn the tapes rather than turn them over to the special prosecutor. What Mike didn't realize was that Wendy would have done it for nothing.

Now, in November, it was wet and cold and he was late. He should have had time to stow his soccer clothes and make it to Silver Meadow. He should have had time to put everything else out of his mind except her, except the things about her — her hair in the wind, the way she hugged harder than anyone else, her devotion. In summer it was easy, and just a look at her body was enough to get him to put aside boyish things. The moment came, that first moment, gratis, at the country club.

They were behind the snack bar, about to go their separate ways, to their separate bathhouses. Such a small parting. But she felt as though she were losing an heirloom at that moment, as if the memory of her lost grandparents had vanished somehow, or a friend who died in childhood of leukemia had just been laid to earth, so she held him by his shoulder and with one hand tugged down the bottom of her American stars-and-stripes two-piece bathing suit and revealed the blond, almost hairless pubic bone underneath.

Because the town was as barren as a rock face. Because

her family was chilly and sad. It had come over her that fast. That's why she did it. Or if love existed, it was buried so far down in work and politeness that its meager nectar could never be pumped to the surface. She had never seen her parents embrace. Her mother had actually once denied loving her father — she'd said she *liked him all right*. Her dad said these were subjects for encounter groups, for religious cults, and for the inmates over at Silver Meadow, but not for families. Wendy yearned for vulgarity, for all this sloppy stuff. She yearned for some impolite rustling or a torn piece of fabric; for some late-night moaning, for some Swedish Super-8 movies: *Biology Class* or *Madame Ovary*. For anything that didn't have the feelings bleached out of it. She would have made out with their retriever to learn a little bit about love. Please God, Wendy thought on the stately paths of Silver Meadow, not another winter night of New Canaan conversation . . .

So, back at the country club. Mike gazed at her vagina — its concealments and complexities — and froze. The sounds of the country club swept over them like an orchestral tuning. She could hear caddies suggesting a particular iron, kids arguing about who got to go off the high dive first, mothers hurrying children up to the snack bar. He smelled like coconut. She smelled like sweat and chlorine and generations of good breeding. The day smelled like hot pavement.

Then Mike Williams untied the knot in his maroon swimming trunks and revealed his own inheritance. He was no more like Sandy than she was. It was a big, sprawling thing, a garter snake coiled in his swimming trunks, or one of those Fourth of July snakes, the kind that unfurled themselves — from a little black chip — in a thick, stinky, sulfuric haze. A small down of auburn hairs adorned its base where the little fellow was now swelling forth as though she had used its secret name.

— This is it, Wendy, Mike said.

They embraced. And parted. Wendy laughed and laughed and laughed.

For a couple of weeks after that Mike was pretty shy. Well, she gave him the benefit of the doubt. Watergate was heating up. Saturday Night Massacre. Wendy had started watching Watergate more closely than even *Dark Shadows* or *The 4:30 Movie*. She liked to see Nixon sweating under the cameras; she liked the relentless glare of network news. But Mike came back eventually, like he was coming up Valley Road, now, on his Fuji bicycle.

Finally, she had led him from his chewing-gum counting house and down to the little graveyard on Silvermine Road, where lost souls from the nineteenth century slept fitfully — Sereno Ogden, Capt. Ebenezer Benedict, and S. Y. St. John — where none came to mourn, where kids practiced their French inhaling. When the dizziness from their own pack of Larks was too much, Wendy lay across his chest. And he held her there.

She could see his erection in the tan corduroys, straining like the kid in math who always had the answer. And they undressed there in the graveyard, their clothes piled neatly on some family mausoleum, and then they stopped just short, each with the other's smell on his or her hands, each like an overwound watch. They just stopped. Who knew why? So the graveyard, for Wendy and Mike, inaugurated the tradition of dry humping.

— Where have you been? she called across the gloomy landscaped expanses of Silver Meadow.

— Something with my mom, Mike said, hauling his bike

alongside him. She was getting out of the house in a hurry and I was in the driveway trying to get the chain back on the bike, and then, because of the rain, I went back in the garage —

Mike pointed at a spot on her chest, right in the center of her poncho, and she looked down. He chucked her under the chin with his index finger. HA! HA! HA! HA! He always did that.

— Freezing my ass off out here, she said.

— Don't bum out. Charles.

The light was failing. The precipitation had turned to snow. Or something close to it, fierce nuggets of precipitation. Precipitation like an insult. But the anticipation of licentiousness thrilled Wendy, worked that tantric magic on her. Winter didn't trouble her. She could have waded miles in the slush and ice, like a superhero.

The basement of the Williams house was unused and lonely. She had seen, in the frugal architecture of local churches — Congregational and Episcopalian and Presbyterian; her mom could never make up her mind about denomination — those small altars where just prior to communion the minister arrayed himself in his professional garment, and where the sacred vessels moldered. Sacristy? This was how she thought of the Williamses' basement, as she straddled the seat of Mikey's bike (he pedaled standing up), and held fast onto his waist.

It was an uphill ride and they left her own house behind — on the far edge of Silver Meadow — that ramshackle place of dark brown, full of drafts and ancient hinges, the former home of Mark Staples, Republican assemblyman and Episcopal minister of New Canaan from 1871 to 1879.

And then up the hill, up the hill. Mike downshifted

angrily, as though the incline were a challenge to his burgeoning manhood.

The Williamses' place was white and squarish with columns in front. An American flag usually hung limply there, but not this afternoon. Mourning doves wailed in the backyard. The steep backyard that tumbled headlong down into the creek there. (Down where Wendy lived the creek ran right under the living room patio.) There was always wildlife strutting around Mikey's backyard — raccoons, muskrats, and rabbits. The wildlife of the suburbs. It was practically like *Mutual of Goddam Omaha* back there. The Silvermine River teemed with inflatable canoes.

Mike dumped his bike on the grass by the garage door, never mind the rain. They snuck in through the porch, downstairs.

In the ritual of their congress, Wendy insisted on silence. No getting-to-know-you chatter. Some conversation was inevitable, the table-setting, the hors d'oeuvres, but a silence was more dignified. Around them, the dusty packing crates full of gum were like the faceless sentries that protected some imperial decay, like the Easter Island statues in this book the boys at school had lately been passing around, *Chariots of the Gods*. The Bermuda Triangle. The basement was a neglected precinct of the Williamses' place. The Ping-Pong table sagged in the middle of the room, like a rotting sea vessel. The power tools hanging on the wall were instruments of torture. The dart board had a woman's face, torn from a magazine, stuck upon it.

The other book everybody read at school was *Go Ask Alice*.

Were Wendy to peel off the layers, the painter's pants, the turtleneck, the toe socks, she would also have to shed the church-going, cheerleading Ivory Soap girl. She would have to reveal to Mike the depths of her complicated feelings. But this was not her gig. This was New Canaan, after all. Her idea, instead, was about putting on more roles, more deceits. On the platform at the end of the room, on the beanbag chair that faced the television set, they positioned themselves.

And Wendy began reluctantly to confide in him her instructions. They played the roles, that afternoon, of corporate managerial type and assistant. Mike was coming to her house one afternoon, one weekend afternoon, to deal with a crisis — yeah, that was it — a crisis concerning some stocks, and he needed her help. He needed her.

— And I'm just lying here, Wendy said. I'm just lying here and something's really wrong. I'm crying, sobbing maybe, because I'm alone, because my man has gone or something, and you come in and try to comfort me.

— But —

— I'm in the middle of some really awful heartbreak.

On his knees, with the clumsiness of a boy who would never appear on stage in his entire life, he mimed the adjustment of his necktie. He set down his attaché case by the magazine rack. Wendy put a finger to her lips and the performance began in earnest. In the half-light.

A long afternoon was over at the office, Wendy thought. The daily political struggle was over. He brushed back her hair. Who was he and why did he understand so well how to console a woman? The loss of her husband, the estrangement of her children — she had been judged unfit — her inability to work. She had only the properties and income that the divorce settlement deeded her. Not enough to live in the style she was accustomed to.

— Baby, Mike said. Our waiting is over.

From the beanbag chair, Wendy slid to the floor. She

rolled across Sandy's battered pocket calculator. Her turtleneck rode up and the pale spotless area under her breasts was visible. She arranged it that way, just like Willie Mays arranged for his cap to fly off in pursuit of the long fly ball. Mike pinioned her — one arm under the beanbag, the other under a green leather footstool. A *TV Guide* with *Sanford and Son* on the cover was only inches from her face.

— Maybe we should turn on the television, Mike whispered, in case someone comes along.

— Don't be silly, Wendy said.

She dragged his hand along her stomach, and he climbed up on top of her. It was a sort of desperate embrace. Stuff was going to get into her hair, bugs and crumbs, and old pieces of gum that had been stamped into the rug.

— Tell me your long-range plans, Wendy said. Tell me that you aren't going to leave. Tell me that you aren't like all the others. Read the awful parts of the *Old Testament* to me. Would you harm people for me? Would you give me your most expensive possession? Would you be on call twenty-four hours a day? Would you leave the church of your birth for me? Would you give up weekend sports activities, including touch football? Would you do my laundry, including the very personal items? Would you take responsibility for filling my prescription of birth control pills? Would you grow your hair or go to a group encounter session or visit Nepal? Would you swing?

Their hips locked together uneasily, like mismatched pieces of a jigsaw puzzle. They ground themselves against one another slowly. She grazed the part of his jeans where the monstrous thing had swollen again. It looked as though it was bent uncomfortably toward his right pocket.

— Have you forgotten everything? Mike said.

— What do you mean, my darling? Wendy said.

— I gave you work for the weekend.

— I'm afraid I don't understand the assignment. I'm going to need an extra help session.

The quiet was funereal. Wendy slowed to a stop. Mike had transformed himself entirely into the unforgiving executive of her dreams. The guy who would look after drug and alcohol procurement. She could smell it on his breath, and his tongue had a taste it never had, a medicinal taste. Her needs were going to be met. She grabbed the back of his ass. It was loose and boyish. Just bones and jeans. Nothing more. He wrestled with her as though she were a sailor's knot he had never learned.

— C'mon, he said.

— You mean the tapes, Wendy said. You mean the tapes you wanted me to look after. You want me to fast-forward —

Mike grunted.

— C'mon —

— I'm afraid there's been a problem. There's a problem in processing —

— Wendy, Mike said, you gotta take off your pants.

— No way, not until I'm fifteen.

— It's not . . . you can't do it like this. You have to take off your pants.

— No way.

He caught her by the wrists again. He let go and got up on his knees. He began to fumble with his belt buckle. And then with the zipper.

— Okay, she said. Okay. I'll touch it, but that's as far as it goes.

Mike shoved his jeans down around his knees and lay down on her again. Goosebumps. His briefs were tangled in his pants. They reminded her of nothing so much as a diaper. Her turtleneck was still bunched up around her breasts, and he set his penis on the unnavigated terrain there, on her belly. It felt like a salamander to her. It felt like a salamander scampering across her.

Then the door at the top of the stairs opened.

The light when the door opened! That splendid bad news! Wendy never knew that a door, so imperceptibly ajar, could promise so much. It was like the climax of a fabulous chorale. The thrashing of Mike's salamander recaged, the unknotting and refastening of shirts and pants. Instantaneous. No soldiers anywhere were ever quicker to arms. The two of them were like some undercranked silent movie, like Keystone Cops at a laundry line.

She knew, somehow, that it was her dad who descended those stairs. Before she even heard his tiresome, methodical steps she knew it was him — the incongruity of him didn't strike her until a long time after. By the time she could see his face she and Mike had been through all the unspoken strategies and cover-ups — they could presume he didn't know what was going on, they could lie about it, they could tell the truth and hope for the best. Mike found a fourth option: he seized another *TV Guide* — Gene Rayburn on the cover — and studied it furiously.

— *When Worlds Collide,* he muttered.

— Huh?

— 4:30 movie.

Her dad had reached the bottom of the stairs with the sort of exaggerated drama that marked all his paternal moments. It was fake. There was something fake about him. He stood with folded arms among the Topps packing crates.

— What the hell are you kids doing down here?

His face was scarlet. Not the color of drinking, which she knew pretty well, but the scarlet of shame and rage, the color of a baby's face when, smeared in its own poop, it is left in a parking lot with a note pinned to its breast. Wendy had seen her dad like this only a few times and she didn't like the memories.

— What do you think we're doing, Dad? she said.

— What do *I* think? I think you're probably touching each other. I think you're touching that reckless little jerkoff, for God's sake, and I think he's trying to get into your slacks. I think, at fourteen goddam years of age, that you're getting ready to give up your girlhood. And I can't believe my eyes —

— Hey, hang on there, Mister Hood —

His shirt wasn't buttoned properly. Wendy's ordinarily immaculate father, her father, the Mike's Sports mannequin, the L. L. Bean dad, had misbuttoned his shirt so that an extra inch of fabric on one side was mashed around his scarlet jowels. He was chewing the air, like he needed its nourishment in order to get fully into his elaborate condescensions. His shirt was luffing.

— Don't you direct a single word at me, Mike. I don't want to hear it. I will be speaking with your mother and father about this situation very soon. Bet your ass on that, son. I can't believe you two have any idea what you're doing here! I'm shocked to think you're so misguided, that this seems to you like the best way to spend the Thanksgiving holidays. This is just shameful, you kids, shameful.

Mike wasn't going to take this last speech too well, Wendy could see this. She knew him well enough. He was considering some harsh rejoinder. It was fight or flight time. If it developed into a fight, she figured that she would root for Mike. Because her dad outweighed him by probably 140 pounds. It was only fair to back the underdog.

But Mike hung his head with barely concealed rage. He didn't say anything.

— Young lady? Her father looked her over.

— Talking to me, Dad?

— Who else would I be talking to?

— Well, then forget all this stern dad stuff.

— I'm not interested in your smart-ass remarks right now, lady. Let's go. Right now. You and I can discuss it on the walk home.

At the mention of the walk home, at the mention of pedestrian conveyance, Wendy began to crack. The regret began to creep in like the bad colors in a bad sunset. She started to feel ashamed. She had curled her hands around Mikey's almost concave stomach as she rode up on the back of his bike and it had been a cool ride. Something about the fact that her father was here without a car, that they were gonna have to walk back to their house, walk along the roads of New Canaan, in the heaviest weather, like people who couldn't manage car payments, it embarrassed her. And she would have to defend her virginity to him. It was a *burn,* as they said at Saxe Junior High School. This was a burn. It was going to be an awful weekend. It was going to be a holiday weekend. There were going to be lectures and long, cruel silences. It would never end. She curled her tresses around an index finger — as she stood silently next to Mikey — and squelched tears.

— Well, her father said.

She joined him, didn't say anything, looked back one last time at Mikey. In his haste, Mike had zipped his shirttail up in his fly. She thought of his beautiful red and brown pubic hair, the color and consistency of a baby's first tangles, and her worries diminished. Love was bittersweet. Then, on the way by, she thrust a hand into one of the packing boxes and came up with a half-dozen loose pieces of Bazooka.

— Services rendered, she called back to Mike.

Her father sighed.

They closed the Williamses' front door behind them. Evidence of night was everywhere. The freezing rain fell horizontally. It was ten or fifteen degrees cooler than when Wendy had waited down at Silver Meadow. Sleet and freezing rain. The mixture fell threateningly on her and her father as they made their way, skidding and cursing, down the walk and into the driveway. She began to shout a feeble and grateful apology to her father, but it was hard to manage with the wind and the rain. You couldn't hear.

On Valley Road, an emergency snow truck lumbered past them, hissing and spitting sand on the accumulating slush. Its yellow strobe lamp swiveled on top.

Wendy's father took her arm roughly at the shoulder.

— Baby doll, he called, and his voice seemed to come from some beyond.

— Baby doll, don't worry about it. I really don't care. I'm just not sure he's good enough, that's all. We can keep this between us.

She didn't get where he was coming from. She could hear the apology.

— Huh?

— I mean, he's a joker. He's not serious. He'll end up living off Janey and Jim, you watch. He's just not worth it. And that's not a family you want to be part of.

— Dad.

They walked in cinnamon slush. They sank deeply into it. The precipitation fell with a relentless uniformity. On nearby communities with less affluent tax bases — Stamford and Norwalk — as well as on New Canaan's wealthy. The sleet ruined Wendy's toe socks and her father's cordovan loafers and at the same time, across town, it ruined the orthopedic shoes of Dan Holmes's sister, Sarah Joe, one of the special-education kids at Saxe Junior High. Sarah Joe's heart was all battered and worn, and she seemed to know it. But she managed to trudge along. The kids said that she would sleep with anyone. Wendy wondered if Sarah Joe had any instincts about positions and sex, if she knew about the myth of the vaginal orgasm, or if she felt somehow intuitively that her sexual fumblings were more gratifying with someone she loved. Sarah Joe, laboring up Brushy Ridge Road herself, through the slush, walking up that hill that all the boys careened down in tenth gear.

Somewhere the popular girls were trapped indoors with their ephemeral crushes, the infatuations they shared with no one. And elsewhere the half-dozen poor boys of New Canaan High, whose fathers would have to go out into the snow and run the plows, watched TV from couches covered in flame-retardant vinyl. The sleet and snow turned the last light a sullen yellow. The sky looked awful, nauseating.

Wendy wanted to know why conversations failed and how to teach compassion and why people fell out of love and she wanted to know it all by the time she got back to the house. She wanted her father to crusade for less peer pressure in the high school and to oppose the bombing of faraway neutral countries and to support limits on presidential power and to devise a plan whereby each kid under eighteen in New Canaan had to spend one afternoon a week with Dan Holmes's sister, Sarah Joe, or with that other kid, Will Fuller, whom everybody called *faggot*.

Wendy wanted her father to make restitution for his own confusion and estrangement and drunkenness.

So when he asked how cold her feet were and then hoisted her into his arms for the last quarter mile, past Silver Meadow, down the embankment, through the thicket of barren trees, across the circle in the driveway, the driveway covered with frosted maple leaves, maple leaves, maple leaves, where a single lonely soccer ball lay buried in a crater of slush, the soccer ball Paul had been kicking around despondently before going into the city — when her father carried her close to his chest in silence, she thought it was fine. She would put off her journey to the Himalayan kingdom of the Inhumans. She would stay with her family for now.

MORE OF SAME — or worse. That was the weather report. The mercury would retreat into its little bulb. The heavens would open. Elena foresaw glazed and treacherous roads. Ski jackets with fur fringe. Hats with pom-poms. And this wasn't all bad. Any excuse to avoid the Halfords' party was a blessing.

She was in the library. Cross-legged on the sofa. Her home was silent as a library. Reading was a brave spiritual journey for Elena Hood, and little piles of books were for her like the stacks of rubble — the Tibetan prayer walls — that marked the progress of pilgrims. There was a warm force field, an invincibility, around her in the midst of this reading journey, no matter how conventional it was by 1973, no matter how trammeled, shopworn. She cherished the *I Ching* and the tarot deck, though she told no one in the suburbs; she believed her decisions were mapped by unseen cartographers. She purchased books from the occult and religious studies sections according to their spines, or if she overheard talk about a title, or if it was advertised in *Psychology Today*.

In her library, in firelight, she read, in silence. Her hair was frosted blond. Her glasses were thick, but she wore them only for reading. The rest of the time she squinted.

She wore amber wool slacks and a wool sweater she had knitted for herself and Hush Puppies. Elena was always cold. Her college textbooks were relegated to a low, dusty corner of the shelves, below the Book-of-the-Month Club selections — glossy, hardcover editions of current fiction that she ordered for her husband, who neglected them.

She was reading about impotence in older men. She had opened Masters and Johnson, *Human Sexual Response,* to the very page. According to the experts, the chief cause for the diminishment of intercourse in middle-aged couples was a single incident of impotence. This initial crisis, whether caused by the traditional drinking — *provokes desire but affects performance* — or by anxiety or other mental factors, so frightened men that thereafter they frequently inclined toward celibacy. In their indignity and remorse, they claimed to be uninterested.

The very page she turned to. She enjoyed Masters and Johnson. Much better than Havelock Ellis, the grandfather of sexual studies, who was big on examples from country life — hairpins removed from teenaged girls' vaginas, accounts of couples unable to uncouple afterward — but short on the pathos of unhappy marriages. Much better than Kinsey, that precursor, with his quaint, polite view of sexuality — mouth-genital contact may not be, after all, a strictly homosexual practice — or Krafft-Ebing's monumental *Psychopathia Sexualis:* the hallucinatory and dangerous cousin to Reich's *Function of the Orgasm.*

There were some sensational pictures in here. Like the diagram of the penis, scrotum, anus, and prostate. All neatly inked in. The prostate intrigued her — that little walnut the urologist was always wringing out. Men sheltered it away. So much, in the end, was done in deference to the prostate. When it strangled off the urethra in older men, it struck the famous and unknown with the equanimity of a plague. They all stood shaking out meager drops at the urinal.

And there were graphs, too, graphs that rendered, in seconds, the likelihood of nipple-stiffening and muscle-shuddering and labia-moistening. This was up-to-the-minute stuff. For example: in New Canaan, suddenly, women were familiar with the term *labia*. They had strong opinions on the vaginal orgasm. She could recall any number of recent afternoons when she had overheard Dot Halford and Denise Blackmun — or somebody — trading theories over a glass of carrot juice: *Dot, I'm aware of how the clitoris functions when I climax, but I'm just not sure, when he's wombing me, that my vagina has a role in it. I'm just not sure.* Anxiety etched in their faces.

Elena and her husband were not truly middle-aged. They hadn't sagged that far yet, but they *had* experienced *the initial trauma of impotence.* They had felt its clean incision. Both of them. Yes, she had felt it, too: "The inhibitions of the upper-level female," as the experts had it, "are more extreme than those of the average male." It was something like eighteen months. Eighteen months since then.

Whether Ben's drinking had brought on his impotence, which had in turn brought on the drought in their connubial relations, she couldn't say. But when she saw his penis now, as he showered or dressed for work, she felt no more for it than she felt for any plucked and headless game bird. It was a quaint reminder of another time, an antique, a curio. A reminder of Ike's stroke or the Berlin crisis. And the worst thing about it was she felt the same way about herself. The fertile spot in her, the mandala in her belly was shut down, stored away.

The way she saw it, the drought led straight to Benjamin's unfaithfulness. Masters and Johnson had no good advice here. The plain facts hadn't dawned on Elena suddenly. There had been no painful encounter with evidence — stained shorts or lipsticked collars or perfumed envelopes. It just struck her at a party one night — a party was the natural place to learn these things — that this was the logical next step for him. This was the narrow channel at which they had arrived.

So there they were, Janey Williams and Benjamin, at this party, sunken into a couch without any kind of back support. Buried in throw pillows. Janey Williams, miserable, desperate Janey, whose husband no longer comforted her. There they were, Benjie and Janey. Getting sloppier as they moved toward one another. Their expressions were mournful, their drinks were frequently empty. They inched around each other like porcupines, closing in for warmth, then stabbing one another and moving off.

The idea of betrayal was in the air. The Summer of Love had migrated, in its drug-resistant strain, to the Connecticut suburbs about five years after its initial introduction. About the time America learned about the White House taping system. It was laced with some bad stuff. The commodity being traded was wives, the Janey Williamses of New Canaan. The payoff was supposed to be joy, but it was the cheapest approximation of exalted feeling. It was just a demonstration of options, nothing more. From her meditative position on the couch, in her unflattering slacks and Hush Puppies, Elena felt she could judge the motives of New Canaan, Connecticut. Because she had permitted her own options to dwindle. Time sputtered and flickered and consumed the comedy of her efforts.

Elena read. She roused herself now and then. For dinner: Green Giant frozen peas in butter sauce, leftover stuffing, and leftover turkey. This parsimonious and homely table awaited her husband and daughter.

It was monks who first taught the art of reading in silence. During the Dark Ages. Augustine, perhaps, was first. And silence was a tongue Elena understood. Silence was her idiom for support and caring. Silence was permissive and contemplative and nonconfrontational and there was melody to it. It was both earth and ether. When Paul hinted that he had been experimenting with drugs, Elena said nothing. When Wendy boasted of her first period, Elena said nothing. Later she placed on her daughter's pillow the box of Kotex, with the instruction circular removed and placed carefully beside it. Silence suited the complexities of these passages — the initiation in yajé, and in the lunar calendar. If you were an American Indian, you went off into the bush and hallucinated on your own. And if you were a Druid girl, a marriage would be prepared for you, and this very effluent would be a condiment at your feast. We would drink your menstrual blood, and later, eat your placenta.

Elena said nothing about this or other matters, and not just because she had found in this village of Republicans — Republicans all the way back to Garfield — that she couldn't articulate her own opinions without appearing foolish, but because she came by this silence through experience.

Her Irish forebears went from the kind of trash you eighty-sixed from a riverside saloon to the sorts of people who repealed the Volstead Act. They folded rags-to-riches fabrications so deeply into their recollections that they believed their own public relations. Or that at least was her father's way. Her father had been a newspaperman, a publisher of cheap tabloid philosophies. He had worked his way through a Midwestern journalism school moonlighting as a soda jerk. He had hopped a freight train east. Started in the mail room. He had married his high-school sweetheart.

The strain of bearing up under this tabloid myth led to the mute intolerance of her father's household. You could take the Irish out of the saloons, but not the saloons out of the Irish. Their hearts were caves of doubt. Edwin O'Malley was a two-fisted drinker, a collector of fine wines, but his wife, Margaret, Elena's mother, slipped behind the curtain of alcoholism before Elena even graduated from elementary school. Margaret couldn't communicate in the palaces and mansions that the O'Malleys frequented during the Depression. Her tongue was tied. Chat failed her. She was like the rat balking at the maze.

Her father didn't mince words: *You look like hell. Jesus Christ, you look like hell. Why bother to come down here? You can't even walk — how are you going to feed yourself. You're drunk and you can't even walk. You're a disgrace. Damned disgrace.*

It seemed to Elena that she was always waiting for her mother to come downstairs. Her parents had separate rooms, of course; they never slept together. When her mother limped downstairs for dinner, it was often the first they had seen of her that day. Elena hid behind servants and furniture and she listened. She stored away the results. She repeated phrases of affection and hatred alike, until she couldn't tell one from the other, couldn't tell derision from respect, a beating from a fond hug. Once, a friend of her father's visited: *Oh, Margaret, lovely to see you, you look marvelous.* To which her father had replied, *Jesus, Karl, don't you have eyes?*

That was her mother. Her mother fell down the staircase and they left her there, at her father's instructions. Her mother disrobed on the front lawn. Her mother locked herself into a shed, looking for stashed treasure. She might have stayed there for days, if it hadn't been for the gardener.

Margaret O'Malley lost a little bit of herself every evening. She turned to climb the stairs again, after each episode of humiliation, until there was no dignity left, no character to assassinate, until she no longer had to climb because it was too dangerous. A primitive home escalator was installed, at great expense.

Her father made sure Elena knew about her mother's condition. He called her down from her room to witness each infraction against him, against his success. So when she was a child and her mother tried to take her own life with sleeping pills, he induced vomiting, called for an ambulance, and then brought Elena into the bedroom. Margaret O'Malley was soiled and unconscious. Shit and piss and bile puddled around her, in her linen, spattered on the rug. *This is your mother. Go ahead. Look.*

It was the holidays that always brought her back to this past.

She had left home with the mixed feelings anyone might have. By the early sixties, her mother often threatened to take her own life. Elena calmly woke Benjamin and, as the sun rose, she caught the first train to New Haven, to the airport there. The threats had always evaporated by the time she arrived. Her mother was asleep, or on her bed, placidly doing a crossword puzzle, drinking gin and smiling.

They dried out Margaret and then released her to the world. Dried her out and released her again. It was like any annual occurrence, like a harvest or saint's day. They dried her out, and all were hopeful for a couple of weeks, even her father would seem to be of good cheer, and then her mother would drink again — sometimes she would even toast returning to the house — and soon it was back to the weekly delivery of cases. Elena's father paid for her detoxifications and for her wardrobe and the tabs at each and every liquor store and for the long-distance telephone calls, and he paid extra to have her bathed and cared for at home. All the bills were paid.

Had it been just the three of them, there would have been cause enough to leave Weston, Mass. But she had a brother, too. A carbon copy of his father — as stable as some inflammable gas — full of impatience and hate. And he drank like his mother. He was the most difficult man Elena had ever met. He actually argued about the weather. His sense of rectitude was so finely tuned that he lay awake nights ordering and enumerating worldly infractions according to a code he could never observe himself. Billy O'Malley was ten years older than Elena and he had taken her education entirely into his own hands. He claimed even to have named her himself, according to rules of prosody. Two bacchic feet. Elena O'Malley. No middle name. She'd just get rid of it later. He'd named her for Bacchus. Her parents were mostly busy anyway.

Instructing her in water safety, he had pushed her, as an infant, into the swimming pool. She sank. Instructing her in etiquette, he had removed her elbows from the supper table with the sharp side of a steak knife. She took a number of stitches. Instructing her in respect for her elders, he'd dangled her by the ankles from a third story window. Instructing her in the management of local mass transit, he'd abandoned her blindfolded in downtown Boston.

Elena had been a good student.

Thanksgiving dinner at the O'Malleys, as Benjamin had often pointed out, was like waiting for the end of a cease-fire. Billy and her father would assume a guarded silence until the first drinks had been consumed. Then Billy would launch into his list of dissatisfactions beginning with, say, her father's *preposterous* support for the House Un-American Activities Committee. Open disgust was not far away. Elena tried to interpret, mediate, and assuage; she tried silence and she tried slipping out to chat with the staff in the kitchen. It did no good. And then her mother would appear for dinner, having spent hours arranging herself, balancing between the spot where she couldn't button a button because of tremors and where the double vision got the best of her. Elena's mother would descend and the evening would really get under way. *Holy mother of God, why did you even bother to attend? Will someone call for a bib, please? Or a stretcher? Maybe a stretcher is in order. Could we have a stretcher, please?*

At which Billy would fly into a rage. Because Billy and Elena's mother were attached by more than drink. They were attached by their sadness and their lying and their self-pity. They died in the same year, the way lovers of long standing did. Margaret O'Malley's liver succumbed, and Bill went down in a plane about six months later. Plaques commemorating their unhappy terms in this life adorned the stone wall in a lonely New England churchyard. And these plaques had been joined recently by one bearing her father's name. He had supported Nixon right through Checkers, but the flimsy valves of his heart — tinkered with by the eminent cardiologists of the day — couldn't survive Watergate. He died the day Cox was appointed special prosecutor, April 17.

When Elena was small, she had played in her mother's dressing room, where two mirrored walls faced one another. The reflections traveled back ceaselessly in that space. When Elena stepped into the purview of these mirrors, she too was reproduced innumerably. She was always trying to catch a glimpse of her incalculable selves. She stretched, she sensed, toward the origin of her family, into its pedigreed peeves and illnesses and delinquencies. But no matter how she tried to sneak around the margins of her reflection, to see the edges of that parade, her mirrored self shadowed her. In silence.

So: Paul and Wendy and Benjamin. And Daisy Chain, the dog, presently sprawled — licking himself — on the library carpet. This little family had tightened around Elena. She put aside Masters and Johnson, marked with a New Canaan Bookshop bookmark — at the page concerning the onset of menopause, just by chance — and repaired to the kitchen. She threw light switches up and down the hall. Because of the oil embargo the British were working a three-day work week, but Elena was uncomfortable in darkness. Duraflame logs. She needed more. The President was pondering special powers to ration electrical resources. Sunday leisure driving was officially discouraged. The market had plunged fifty points this week. *Three percent,* Benjamin had said, *only three percent.*

She thought of Janey Williams's breasts, the perfect way she presented them, in a brassiere that probably carved tracks in her shoulders. Her breasts were large and rounded. This you couldn't miss, through her lacy, flimsy chemises. Ripe and properly displayed, the way the men of Elena's acquaintance liked them. Janey was not afraid of presentation, while Elena was, on the other hand, small and compact and reserved. But she was sexual and capable of abandon. The mistake Benjamin made — in assuming she was only one kind of person, a virgin bride of the Eisenhower years, a daughter of gentility — brought her as close to outrage as she came. She had read widely on the subject of personal growth. She wasn't impervious to change. There was growth left in her. To pin her down, wriggling like a butterfly specimen, was a kind of violence.

Still, when she had to be, she was a chef. She filled a saucepan from the tap, set it on the range, and immersed in it the brick of frozen peas. They were frozen into a small rectangular pool of yellow simulated butter. Then she exhumed the turkey carcass from its tomb in the fridge and set it on a cutting board. As dispassionately as any butcher, Elena aligned the hewn strips of turkey on each of three plates. Turkey the day after was the most heartbreaking protein she could imagine.

In the den, the screen door opened. The announcement of bad conversation. The gales had begun to whistle around the side of the house and over the creek. As her husband slid the door closed, this howling hushed briefly. Shuffling into the kitchen, Benjamin and Wendy muttered hello like late arrivals at church.

— Ten minutes, Elena said.

These estimates were almost always folly.

— Go dry off, Benjamin said to his daughter.

The two of them, Ben and Wendy, were peeling off their footwear. The puddles extended around them in rivers across the kitchen floor, back toward the hall carpeting. They carried their drenched garments around the sink to the laundry room. Wendy stripped off her poncho and her pants and shook out her hair. In her panties, she stood dripping. It was one good thing Elena had done, she remembered; she had given birth to a great beauty.

Ben followed Wendy back toward the stairs, and Elena followed Ben. They climbed the stairs in this order. Wendy commandeered the bathroom right away. There was the firm *ping* of the push-button lock.

The hall was blue-gray and the master bedroom was blue-gray and the rug was a deeper shade of blue-gray and the curtains were a sort of blue-gray. The bedspread on the master bed was blue and red, checked. The light outside was blue-gray, and when Elena switched on a light by the bed it hardly did the trick. Benjamin had the last of his clothes off quickly. He piled them on the chair where he hung his suit pants overnight.

Elena watched him from the edge of the bed.

— Never guess where I found her, he said.

He disappeared into the walk-in closet. The sound of his voice was husky among suits and gowns.

— In the basement over at Janey and Jim's. With that creep. Not even a television on. And they're on the floor. Kid's got his trousers down — I can see his little white cheeks pumping away. Got his pecker out there and everything.

The Benjamin's voice was muffled. The smell of naphtha and dry-cleaning chemicals. She could tell he was nervous.

— He's only partly on top of her, though. He's partly on top of her and partly off. She's still dressed. He's flopping around like a fish on the deck and she's just lying there.

Benjamin poked his head out of the closet now and looked at his wife. She admired what was left of him, couldn't help it, what was not consumed by uncertainty and heavy drinking and the ravages of adulthood with little exercise. In many ways, he was ugly, scaly, even repulsive. When he smiled, the effect was almost always lewd. It was getting hard to locate her affection in the midst of all this noise and dissolution and thoughtlessness, but she liked him sometimes anyway. It was hard to live next to someone and not come up with a little respect.

— Should I dress for the party now, or should I dress after? Give me your —

— Up to you, she said. I'd like to go early, though, and leave pretty soon after that.

— I get you loud and clear. Your signal is coming in. Anyway, I don't know what was in it for her, because she wasn't giving him . . . she wasn't giving him a hand job or anything.

— Do you have to be so graphic?

— I'm just telling the story, baby doll. She's not giving him a hand job and she's not, you know, grappling with the situation herself either. Probably too shy to do it to herself in front of the creep. I guess we should be glad about shyness. And I come down the stairs and I pause dramatically, like I'm the prosecutor or something, and then I really let him have it. You've never seen anyone rearrange their clothing so fast in all your life. Kid's got the pants hiked up around himself, shoes and socks on, shirt carefully tucked in before I can say a word. Shirt sticking out of the fly and everything. He's pretending to be absorbed in the *TV Guide.*

Benjamin laughed. He was searching far and wide for a laugh.

— Hey, you look nice, he said to her now, fixing a paisley ascot around his neck, zippering the blue-and-gold–checkered pants. She knew she looked anything but nice. Familiar, maybe, kindly.

— And?

—And Wendy's out of the way. She squirms away on the floor, puts some distance between her and the creep. So I started to yell and I called the kid I-don't-know-what, told him I'd personally separate him from his manhood if I ever caught him with her again and that sort of thing. Wendy came home peacefully.

Another laugh. A party laugh, trailing off precipitously. Elena watched him in the bathroom now, straightening the ascot. She waited a while before asking. She let it hang in the air with the menace of a grave diagnosis.

—So what were you doing in the basement anyway?

Only a slight hesitation:

—Just dropping off a coffee cup. Jim left it, last time he was over. It was on the dash of the car. You were, you know, reading. I was just dropping off the cup.

Benjamin emerged from the bathroom. Smiled. Spread wide his arms to announce his arrival.

—Let's eat, babe. I am cool. I am ready.

She lifted herself, as though it were the greatest chore, from within the fold of the comforter at the end of the bed. It diapered her. And this was a great chore, too. Being lied to required such work.

—Oh, right, she said. The mustache coffee cup. The one that was sitting on the dash.

—Yeah, sure, he said. That's the one.

—That one.

Benjamin nodded vigorously.

—That one.

Her husband simply laughed. As if the flimsiness of his deceits wouldn't adhere to him.

So they were back in the kitchen. Disappointment in the room like a sullen dinner guest. The peas bobbed in their sulfurous oil slick. All was ready. Wendy appeared behind Elena, wearing another pink turtleneck and corduroys. Without prompting, Wendy searched the long, narrow drawer by the range for a wooden spoon with which to disembowel the turkey of its stuffing. She set the spoon at the edge of the serving platter. Then, in the cupboard by the refrigerator, Wendy found three glasses, the ones with the decorative blueberries painted on them. The really good holiday finery would wait.

In the den, Ben had vanished to fix himself another drink. Absences of this sort Elena knew intimately. Soon, according to habit, there would be the sound of ice hitting the bottom of a tumbler and the sudden swelling of show tunes from their new high-fidelity stereo system.

Richard Kiley was going to dream that impossible dream again.

Elena spooned the peas onto the plates Wendy provided and then went to help her daughter fold the napkins and arrange the cutlery, turning a knife here so that the sharp side faced in, adjusting the glasses so that each was at the right-hand corner of the plastic place mats. The dog trotted in from the den, decelerating as he rounded the sink, spinning in circles before settling under the center of the table. And behind him came his master, whose beverage — its tinkling melody — announced his entrance.

They each stood around the remains of the turkey, spooning carbohydrates onto their plates beside the peas. The order of it was impeccable. First Wendy, then Benjamin, then Elena carried her plate to the table and returned to the refrigerator in search of a beverage. After a long, fruitless investigation, Wendy settled on pasteurized, homogenized, vitamin D–enriched milk. As Wendy held out the milk carton for her father, who accepted it and poured himself a glass — it would sit next to the scotch-on-the-rocks — Elena concluded that her daughter and husband each looked into the refrigerator in the same way. Hopefully. While she and Paul recognized what limited offerings were concealed there.

The sleet or slush or whatever it was against the kitchen windows. Elena couldn't see beyond the driveway, where a light on the house threw a dim glow against the sheets of precipitation. No one in New Canaan would really want to stay home on a Friday night in heavy snow. No one would want to stay home with their children. The party would go on.

And the turkey was no longer moist. This conclusion was unavoidable. Above all, she and Benjamin agreed on the necessity of moist turkey. This was an area where progress had certainly delivered miracles. And yet this moist quality seemed to last through the first serving only. One had to guard against dryness in leftovers. One had to reheat gravy. And Elena had failed here. She knew that if she ever suffered a real and debilitating mental illness, its onset would not be the result of a failed marriage or because of twentieth-century spiritual impoverishment; it would be caused instead by these details, by a pen mark on the designer pantsuit she'd bought for the holidays, by the slight warp in her Paul Simon album, or by the acrid taste of old ice cubes. These small things led to a bottomless pit of loneliness beside which even Cambodia paled.

She rose again from the table and flung her napkin on the chair. The dog struggled up immediately after her, betting on plate-clearing. She patted the flat spot on his head, where he might have had a brain, before locating the leftover cranberry sauce in the Frigidaire. Wendy and Benjamin greeted the bowl of jelly with smiles, with mouths full.

The dog trotted back to his spot.

Elena circulated the jelly, but it was too late. Wendy was almost done with her turkey. Benjamin was concentrating mostly on his scotch. So there it was. There were automatic appliances of every kind now — washers and dryers, dishwashers and ice-makers, juicers and electric grills. There were moon shots. But still there was the conundrum of day-old turkey.

Twenty minutes now without a syllable of conversation. It stunned Elena as she was corralling a half-dozen peas against a mound of stuffing. She had felt the obligation to create conversation for years, perhaps for a lifetime. That is, she had felt the obligation when she had not felt the contrary one, to refuse all conversation. It was her duty to take charge. Words that soothed and were inoffensive. Words that bore up wounded hearts. Maternal language. But she had seen how these *bons mots* were ineffective. She had seen Benjamin, as she had seen the men in her family, bristle at some mild word of kindness.

On the paddle-tennis court, recently:

— Benjamin, she said to a doubles partner, has a serve like a howitzer.

At once, he called to her across the court.

— Don't be a dip shit, baby doll.

His face like a red balloon, swollen.

To start a conversation was to be the messenger of ill. She would no longer feel obliged. She thought about her daughter in the Williamses' basement. She imagined Wendy with a skirt hiked up, imagined the precise curve of her buttocks, the tuft of blond pubic hair. Wendy's calves already had a perfect feminine knot, as though she had been wearing high heels for years, and it was clear from the early protrusion of her breasts that she wouldn't have the small, insignificant bosom that her mother needlessly restrained with under-wire support.

Wendy didn't seem ashamed in the aftermath of this contretemps. She seemed, on the contrary, emboldened by being caught. In secret, Elena admired her daughter's pluck. Lost in affection, she missed the opportunity to chastise Wendy — who hadn't asked to be excused. Her daughter was poised at the fridge again, having left her plate and glass in the sink. Again the fridge disappointed Wendy. She turned instead to the cupboard where the cookies and candy were stacked haphazardly. She selected a box of Hot Tamales, a candy that was left over from her Halloween basket. Maybe her final Halloween basket — she was old now for that kind of dressing up. Then Elena's daughter slunk out of the room. *Dulcinea! Dulcinea!* was replaced in the library by the distant sound of the television, leaden and excruciating. That it was already time for *A Charlie Brown Christmas* seemed intolerable to Elena.

She and her husband rose together from the table. The dog trotted after them to the sink.

— What's for dessert? Benjamin said.

— See for yourself.

— No advice from the experts, huh?

— Don't expect me to amuse you tonight, Ben.

He idled in the center of the room.

— Sounds like we're in for a good time.

His plate slipped out of his hands and into the trash. He fished it out, set it on the counter.

— Party time, he said. Kinda wow —

— Don't start, Elena said.

— You think I —

— I have no idea —

She set her plate in the sink a little gingerly. It had a dramatic crash to it she hadn't intended. The *Peanuts* theme song — that happy and melancholy piece of jazz — filled the next room.

— What's on your mind? he said. Don't —

— It wouldn't make it a pleasant evening, she said, if that's what you're after. I don't want to talk about it.

Furiously, Benjamin reached into the cupboard, into Wendy's cache of Halloween treasure and filched an Almond Joy bar.

— Well, let's not talk then.

— Surprise, Elena mumbled. And then: — Stupid mustache cup.

Wearily, he said:

— What do you mean?

— Don't be dim.

— I don't know what you're taking about.

— I'm not surprised, Elena said.

Hood pointed half an Almond Joy bar at her.

— Listen, honey, if you're gonna pull that passive aggressive stuff on me again . . .

— Your *unfaithfulness,* she said. That's what I'm trying to talk about. Your unfaithfulness, your betrayal. Your *dalliance*. Okay? And you won't do me the dignity of being up-front about it.

Hood went pale. He was frosty and blank and empty.

— Am I unfaithful? Is that what you're trying to say? Is that what you're trying to accuse me of?

The conversation got quieter and quieter.

— It's a starting place.

— Well, what kind of faithfulness are you after? he said.

— If you're going to insult me with —

— What else could I be? Hood rushed on. What else could I be besides unfaithful? We're not living in the real world, honey. You're living out of some fantasyland from the past. You're living out some advice from the fancy psychotherapists. There are some hard facts here.

A room full of silences.

— Look around you, anyway. It's the law of the land. People are unfaithful. The government is unfaithful. The world is. Look at those two guys on the Yankees, for God's sake. And you saw that movie. Nothing is the way we think. Everything is diluted. And I'm not having any fun at it, I can tell you that. Look, it's all bruises, baby doll. And I'm not . . . I can't wait for us to heal up forever, you know —

In the library, the television grew louder.

— Oh, lord, Elena said. You think I'm so dense. And now you want to be seen with your dense wife at the cocktail party. You want to wear your ridiculous ascot out to a cocktail party. That ridiculous ascot that doesn't go with those pants at all. You want to wear that out, and you want me to shake hands with your friends and make conversation. And you want me to dress up in some outfit that shows off a lot of cleavage. And you're not even going to accord me the respect of talking honestly about this.

— At least we can get out of the house, he said. At least we can get some air. Let's just go and try to be part of the neighborhood. Let's just throw in with the rest of the people for the evening, honey. I don't want to spend the night reading in separate rooms, you know? Let's have a good time, run with the pack.

He threw the Almond Joy wrapper on the counter and stole into his daughter's plunder again. Charleston Chew.

— You don't really know what this feels like, Elena

said. You haven't considered that. You never do. And when you finally do —

— Sure I do, Benjamin whispered. Do I know what loneliness feels like? I sure do. I know a lot about it, if that's what you're saying.

— Benjamin, she said. That's supposed to explain it?

— All I'm saying is that loneliness is the music of the spheres around here. That's all I'm saying. And as a result I have fallen into some things I regret, baby doll. I have regrets, I will tell you that.

He seemed to grow tired suddenly. He walked into range, into her reach. She certainly was not going to embrace him. She certainly was not going to assume the posture of the vulnerable. They were apart, attracted and repelled. The moment passed. Elena thought practically about turning up the thermostat, and of reminding Wendy about the Duraflame logs. Her mind was deflected from her own predicament. She was sad, but she refused any responsibility for sadness. Was there enough newspaper by the fireplace?

They parted, to regroup. Hood closed himself into the hall bathroom.

Elena wiped her face with the dish towel. The dog stood expectantly in front of her, its windshield-wiper tail going back and forth.

In the library she found Wendy engrossed in her ninth or tenth encounter with Charlie Brown's morose little Christmas tree. Elena leaned over the back of the Naugahyde recliner and buried her hands in her daughter's hair.

— We're going to the Halfords'. The number is on the calendar in the kitchen. We should be home around eleven.

— Is it a big party? A big neighborhood party?

Wendy's eyes never strayed from the screen.

— I suppose, Elena said. Why?

— Just curious, Wendy said earnestly. If there's a problem, I guess I'll just call you there to interrupt.

— What sort of problems are you planning exactly?

Elena kissed the top of her daughter's head, right at the part. Wendy's concentration didn't ebb.

— Thought I'd steal the station wagon, go joyriding, and then drive up to a commune. Or enlist. Or set the house on fire. You know.

— Just bundle up, Elena said. Extra blankets in the linen closet. We'll see you in the morning.

The hall bathroom door was open. The toilet tank was filling. Elena would not change her Hush Puppies or paint her face. She searched the front hall closet for the right kind of rain gear. The journey was about a mile, door to door, and they would travel by car. Still, Elena took the light-blue raincoat she had purchased on sale at Lord & Taylor in Stamford.

Through the narrow windows by the front door, she peered out at the sleet. It had begun to collect on the lawn — what there was of a lawn there — and in the brush and fallen leaves around their house. The roads would be full of treachery. They would be slick and undependable. The maintenance crews would be laboring, again, up to the top of the hill, spilling rock salt and sand, casting floodlights to and fro.

Outside, Benjamin was going around and around in the circle at the end of the driveway. She called good night to Wendy and got no response.

Peanuts music again. Then she closed the door behind her and skipped through the first inches of slush on the flagstone. In the car, she and her husband were silent.

In college, she had often announced her love for Benjamin to the back of his head, to the back of his tweed suit, to his retreating figure. Only to find that it was not him after all, that it was simply some look-alike. Sometimes it was even a redhead or a black man or a *woman.* She had so much affection for him that it spilled over everywhere.

Or she called his fraternity — *Darling, I'm looking forward to seeing you tonight!* — and found herself connected with a brother posing as Benjamin. *Oh, Elena, sweetiekins, my little lemon tart! HA! HA! HA! HA!*

This period of farce, culminating in the day on which Benjamin proposed — out of lack of imagination, it seemed now — was also characterized by calls she meant to place elsewhere — to Diana Olson or to Billy O'Malley, for example — but that ended up ringing at Benjamin's fraternity house. She would get him on the phone and believe him, at first, to be someone else. It was as if she couldn't have any other relationship, as if there were no other calls left for her to make. Back then, she had loved all of them, all those who resembled Benjamin Hood and even those who did not.

So love was mistaken identity. Erich Fromm and C. S. Lewis and Paul Tillich all agreed. Love was scattered on the winds. It exceeded its targets. So maybe Benjamin was right and the adults of the seventies had good cause to misplace their affections among phantoms and strangers and memories of desire. This man driving the car picked his nose in the same way as the man she'd married, scratched his ass in the same way, and took incredibly long showers, but he was not the same man. She remembered things about him he would never know again. The way he started to cry over a run-down petting zoo they had visited with the kids in Bridgeport; the way he had loved reading *Breakfast at Tiffany's;* his bewilderment at his mother's stroke. His smile was full of cheap sunsets and lonely Christmases. His rage had sharp angles. She'd remember all this stuff. She cheated on Benjamin with his own lost youth.

And Benjamin had his perceptions of her as well. Chief among his criticisms of his wife, she knew, was her failure to make small talk at parties. In the car there was a moment to bone up. Since the market had fallen off, since the government had recently revealed that it had both lost and erased important sections of its own secretly recorded tapes, since the Arab nations had effected an oil embargo against Western nations that supported Israel, and since the U.S., therefore, would likely be rationing petroleum in the near future, current events were not an appropriate topic of conversation at the party. They were all trying to forget current events.

It was late autumn, and the country club had been closed for three months, so no one had much played tennis lately. Or golf. A few, maybe, had played paddle tennis. But there was touch football and high school football and college football — which would be televised all weekend — and these were effective subjects, as were the professional sports. The Giants were again failing to live up to their promise. The Mets had been good until the series, and the Rangers were said to be excellent this year. See what you can learn from a quick glance at the second section of the *Stamford Advocate?*

Theology was out, of course, except for the practical issues at any given parish. Was anyone doing anything about the winter clothing drive? Who was supposed to make coffee this Sunday? Complaining about sermons was also a fine thing to do. Or about the rector at a church. And then there was popular religion: *Godspell* was a hit.

Jesus Christ Superstar was a hit. *Jonathan Livingston Seagull* was a hit. (And the film version had just opened, featuring the songs of Neil Diamond.)

Likewise, there were the P.T.A. and local property taxes and the selectmen and the cessation of town meetings. But these were topics that would go only so far. What were you to do during the long, sprawling, drunken turns, when you were pinned to the wall by a bearded man with pinkeye who wanted to discuss two-headed dildos in African art or the bisexuality of higher mammals. What were you to say to him?

There was one man who had cornered her at parties in the past, who had gone through a sort of Gestalt-therapy cult where they made you sit still for three days in a windowless conference room and listen to convolutions about the universe, which would, it was said, improve your productivity at work. But this man was rarely invited to New Canaan parties anymore, and the fact that she had met him at the post office and later arranged to see him at a diner in Norwalk, well, it was probably just as well. Wesley. They'd had a vague, abstract sort of conversation and nothing had come of it anyway. Maybe that was how these things were supposed to turn out.

The only right and true subject for party conversation was gossip. The more tawdry the better. Elena had gossiped like anyone else, about friends checking themselves into Silver Meadow, about breakdowns and cheap affairs and white-collar crime. And Elena realized, of course, as Benjamin eased the Firebird up the hill toward the Halfords' house, that she was now the subject of this gossip. She was appearing in public with a man who was no longer faithful to his wife. And the question in some circles would be whether or not she, Elena Hood, knew herself to be betrayed. She was like a lonely spinster now, a lonely spinster in a riverfront town, who wore, as perfume, her own urine.

On the other hand, maybe Benjamin Hood was right and everyone was a cuckold. Maybe the nature of marriage was to be both cuckolded and cuckolding, adulterer and adulteress. Yes, the thing to do was to relax into this deterioration, to recognize that we could still live in these calm and lovely homes and still make ourselves beautiful on occasion and still love our children and lavish them with the opportunity and affection that we never received. We could spill the wine and dig that girl.

HARD TIMES at the Baxter Building. Bleak House. Heartbreak Hotel. Is life not ironic? If nothing else? As Annihilus remarked back in issue #140. Love and work had come between the Fantastic Four, America's greatest superheroes. For almost a year — a year in real time, a year in Paul Hood's whirlpool teens, but a few days, no more, in the motionless, imperceptible time of Marvel comics — Sue Richards, née Storm, the Invisible Girl, had been estranged from her husband, Reed Richards. With Franklin, their mysteriously equipped son, she was in seclusion in the country. She would return only when Reed learned to understand the obligations of family, those paramount bonds that lay beneath the surface of his work. In her stead, the Medusa had joined the Fantastic Four. Medusa: Tibetan-born Inhuman and cousin of Johnny Storm's paramour, Crystal, the Elemental. Medusa: her tresses had a life of their own. Once a sworn enemy of the Fantastic Four, a member of the anti-F.F., the Frightful Four.

The mood in the Baxter Building was grim. Besides the Richards's marital problems, Crystal had recently chosen to marry Quicksilver instead of Johnny Storm. Sue was worried about Franklin's trances; Reed was worried about

Sue; Johnny was worried about Crystal; Ben Grimm was worried about himself.

It was a good period for readers of the F.F. And Paul Hood was a compulsive reader of comics. Still, the magazine would never equal its first eighty issues, when its creators, Stan Lee and Jack Kirby, were at the helm. But it was pretty cool. Twelve years ago, exactly, in 1961, the first issue, with its chronicle of the battle with Mole Man, had appeared. Paul's sister, Wendy, was almost the same age as the book. Fourteen years ago his family had arrived at its tetragonal shape. In fact, if you thought about it, it was possible that his sister, Wendy, was *born* during the creative gestation that led to the Fantastic Four. Where had Stan Lee been in those two years? The Hoods trailed after the implications of these characters as if Stan himself pulled their strings.

At a newsstand in Stamford, at the train station, Paul was perusing the squeaky spin rack in the rear, near the pornography, where the comics were nestled. Number 141 beckoned to him. It boasted, unsurprisingly, *the end of the Fantastic Four*. On the cover, a deeply perturbed Sue held in her arms her irradiated son: "Little Franklin is glowing like an ATOMIC BOMB!"

Sure, Paul had tried D.C. Comics. He had read *Batman* and *Justice League of America*, and he had followed some of the other Marvel titles, too: *Spider-Man, Iron Man, The Incredible Hulk, The Avengers*, and *X-Men*, and especially those titles that were F.F. spin-offs, *The Silver Surfer* and *The Sub-Mariner*. He had tried them all. He had ranged far and wide. But he kept coming back to the F.F. Batman was cool: his skills were not supernatural. He was just smart and rich. Superman was a moral force. The Hulk had hubris. Silver Surfer was definitely created by a mind on psychedelics. *Thor* was the comic you read if you wanted to work for one of those touring Renaissance festivals, if you wanted to wear a shirt that was called a *blouse.*

So why the Fantastic Four? First of all, Paul couldn't shake the uncanny coincidence that his father had the same first name as Benjamin Grimm, the Thing. When he was younger, he actually thought of his father as the Thing: chunky, homely, self-pitying. When Paul was a kid, his dad raged around the house like a pachyderm taking down underbrush. His father would find a damp towel clumped on the bathroom floor and sprint to Paul's room to accuse him. His father would lay in wait for the tiniest noise, the scantest footfall, and then he would howl from the bottom of the stairs. But his dad was always coming around to apologize, too. He couldn't terrorize with real commitment. He was like the Thing. He hated the world, hated mankind, hated his family, but loved people, loved kids and dogs.

And his mother was the Invisible Girl. Although, on the other hand, sometimes she was like Crystal, the Elemental, a prophetess, a seer. And sometimes his dad was Reed Richards, the elastic scientist. And sometimes Paul himself was Ben Grimm, and sometimes he was Peter Parker, a.k.a. the Spider-Man. These models never worked exactly. Still, the F.F., with all their mistakes and allegiances, their infighting and dependability, told some true tale about family. When Paul started reading these books, the corny melodrama of New Canaan lost some of its sting.

By the way, corny melodrama: Tuesday night, only three nights ago, they were all watching television in the dorm. At St. Pete's, where Paul was incarcerated. It was the last night before Thanksgiving vacation, and he was in the common room. *Rudolph, the Red-Nosed Reindeer* on the box.

Seemed like every year they started these Xmas specials earlier and earlier. Someone had turned off the lights. They all cozied together in the dim, flickering images of holiday myth. Didn't matter who was there. Paul had been lucky enough to score some Thai weed from some math club guys who doubled as drug dealers. He had just smoked it.

One problem he had was that drugs had sort of stopped working for him. When he had stuffed his head for the first time, he had felt his teen death sentence lift temporarily. He had felt the kindness of inanimate objects, the kindness of trees, the kindness of old dormitories. He had found brilliant comedy in the connections between things. He had talked to girls and told them that he didn't want to go home, he didn't want to go home, he couldn't talk to anybody, he couldn't talk, oh, he didn't want to graduate, *ever,* and these girls had cupped his forehead with their palms and held him tight.

But lately these drugs had not been working. Lately, nothing made it through his paraffin shell. His skin crawled. And that night, Tuesday, after smoking the Thai stick, no matter where he looked he saw red dots. The screen was all red dots, shifting patterns of red dots. Like a pestilence of ladybugs. Rudolph made no sense at all. The story of Rudolph was menacing. In Rudolph's ascendance to lead reindeer, Paul sensed the machinations of thought control and government intrusion. He kept coming out of his hallucination to find the abominable snowman threatening the town. He had tried to cheer himself up by singing along with "Silver and Gold," but it didn't do the trick.

—Hood, someone said. Hood, something wrong?

—Don't interrupt. Concentrating.

Or maybe he was feigning romantic transportation.

Suddenly. Because the Bear, Carla Bear, not only a fan of Rudolph and his cousin Frosty the Snowman, but the kind of girl who could quote from *Miracle on 34th Street* and dance along with the Hallmark Hall of Fame presentation of *The Nutcracker,* was sitting next to him. And yes, he realized that the Bear was trying to calm him down. Carla Bear, one of the intrepid first women of St. Pete's. She had enrolled as a third-former in 1971, the first year of coeducation. She was leaning against him on the gray synthetic banquette and comforting him. And during a sequence in which Rudolph was being ridiculed by the other reindeer, or was it later, he encircled her in his arms. It overcame him. He yielded.

— It's okay, kiddo, she said. It's okay.

She had a big maternal heart.

— I hate Thanksgiving, too, kiddo, she said. Who wouldn't? Why would you want to go home? On the other hand, staying here isn't so great either, y'know?

And Paul was sure she was telling the truth. St. Pete's was where the affluent families of the East unloaded their heirs, where they penned them until college. The Bear knew, because, he had heard, her own mother, her single mother, was ill. Dying. Tumors. Cancer of some kind. There were kids at St. Pete's whose parents would be removed from this very Thanksgiving table to have their stomachs pumped of sleeping pills. Whose siblings had hanged themselves or gassed themselves or who had driven expensive cars into the ocean. There were kids here whose only relative was a trust-fund officer. These were kids from devastated families. Devastated and wealthy.

— Shut up, someone said.

Paul couldn't hear the program. He had his arms around Carla. A little elf cheerfully rode a Norelco cordless razor across a snow-covered landscape. Over a mogul, into the air. Paul wanted this embrace to work magic. He was dimly aware that the common room was full of writhing embraces. He was seized with laughter. Something wasn't working.

So Paul put his hand inside the Bear's pink button-down shirt and felt the lace margins of her brassiere. There was an overpowering gentleness in the space close to a woman's heart. He was drawn to it, but at that moment he couldn't possibly say why. Carla the Bear neither encouraged nor denied. In the next stillness, during the next commercial break, he let his hand stray even further, to her breast — small, serene, and comforting. Not sexy so much as reassuring. She clamped her hand around his wrist. She restored it to his lap. All around the room — the room swimming in red dots — girls were clamping their hands on the wrists of boys. The whole thing messed with his high. His eyes were occluded by irritations.

— I know, kiddo, the Bear was saying, shoving his hand back down into his lap. I know, I know.

So he did the only sensible thing. He fled the common room. He waited for the drug, and for his shame, to pass. He fled.

That story was connected to this one just as events were linked in the world of Marvel Comics — where *The Sub-Mariner* #67 was folded between two panels in *F.F.* #140, which itself contained information primarily available in *F.F.* annual #6. This imaginary world and its inhabitants coexisted with the so-called real inhabitants of the so-called real world in just the way the dead saints of antiquity were supposed to be frolicking around him — right on this platform at the Stamford Conrail station. In the world of Marvel, his parents were off exposing the malfeasance of a local political figure whose daughter was the girl Paul would one day marry, while his sister, meanwhile, was seducing an art collector and amateur nuclear physicist who would one day be Paul's employer. This physicist just happened to be a part-time Balkan spy raised from the dead who was working on the *Apollo-Soyez* mission and carrying out, on the side, a high-level conspiracy to destroy Benjamin Hood's business. All these things were happening at once, simultaneously. In the world of Marvel, Carla Bear might show up on the train, in the seat next to him, to say that she had always loved him. The train would then be attacked by hordes of spear-bearing Connecticut Indians. Or this train would lead into the main action of *Rudolph, the Red-Nosed Reindeer*. Where Paul would engage in hand-to-hand combat with the abominable snowman, until Richard Nixon appeared, in person, to plead for peace, as he had done in *F.F.* #106.

Paul's dad hated comic books, of course. The idea that hard-earned Schackley and Schwimmer dollars might trickle down into the hands of the Marvel Comics Group needled him. Maybe it was because he and Ben Grimm were too much alike. Neither of them wanted to be reminded of it. But it wasn't only the comics that his father disliked. He disliked Paul's helmet of long, wavy hair, and his loneliness, and his lack of athletic prowess. Radio club and chorus and recreational tennis failed to impress Paul's dad.

So Paul had given up trying. He hung out with the stoners. Paul was a garbage head! A loser, as they were called among stoners. Paul bought oregano and thought it was good shit. He borrowed nutmeg from a master at school, hoping to catch its buzz. He had smoked a Quaalude; he had overdosed on cold pills. Paul Hood, eater of morning glory seeds. Decipherer of obscure lyrics. He and his roommate had parakeets named Aragorn and Galadriel. He had pored over *The Chronicles of Narnia* and the pronouncements of Michael Valentine Smith. He had black-light posters and tapestries and he burned incense and wore wire-frame glasses and played military strategy games. He managed to keep one shirttail untucked at all times. His tweed jackets and khakis looked as though he had slept in them. He wore them again today. Top-Siders without socks. His shirttail stirred in the breeze, like a flag from the nation of the feckless and affluent. *There was a rush along the Fulham Road!*

Stamford was a vast, flat expanse below I-95, below the train station. The public-housing projects, a number of circular buildings over to the left there, languished disconsolately on the skyline. Beyond them rose Stamford's lone office tower. It was a gleaming rocket, sort of like the Fantastic Four's pogo plane in its sleek design. Or sort of like the Baxter Building. He could easily imagine them taking off from this impressive launchpad to battle Dr. Doom or Blaastar.

— Flame on, Paul said.

When the train arrived, he took up residence in one of the four-seaters, with his feet propped up across. There was the usual fracas when he realized again that he hadn't availed himself of the ticket window in Stamford. The conductor invoked a surcharge.

— Begging your pardon, Charles, Paul said.

The conductor stared blankly at him.

— The fault's all mine, sir. May I please purchase my ticket to Grand Central at the higher price?

Then he was thinking about school again. The Kittredge Cult — that was the name they had been given at St. Pete's.

He and his friends. They were Cultists. They had all opted to hide out in the dormitory of that name, one otherwise considered cheap, modern, and lifeless. For two years now, they had all lived there. What they had in common was that they were undistinguished. Paul could boast nonparticipation in any varsity sport. And he wasn't a rock-and-roll musician or yearbook photographer like some nonathletes. And he was unattractive. And he hadn't — unlike many of his fellow students — attended Greenwich Country Day or New Canaan Country Day or any of the other Country Days. The Cult was populated with just this sort of lost soul. The rest of the student body knew one another from summers on Nantucket or in Camden, or from tennis camp, or else they were related, or they were children of trustees or legacies or other prominent alumni. The Kittredge Cult was the remainder.

To them, adolescence was nearly fatal. Surprise. To survive a sober afternoon was heroic. Only a state of witless inebriation was really sensible. The best of life was intoxication. The promise of liberated sexuality, dangled before others of their age group, completely eluded Paul and his friends. They whacked off and got caught. They got stoned, and drank, and whacked off. They tortured freshmen, reinflicting their frustration on these new kids, javelining them with cross-country ski poles. Then they stole five minutes to jerk off a second time.

The Cult's precise origin was unknown. It included women, too. Not only Carla the Bear, but Christina Whitman and her roommate, Debby Vartagnan. Debby had these episodes in which she would permit guys from Kittredge, whom she usually loved only in a platonic fashion, to lie with her on a Saturday night, in violation of major school rules, and to touch her unnaturally large breasts.

Each victim would then be marked with a number of unmistakable welts on his neck. Paul hadn't yet had his turn, but he had seen Hal Frost, another Cultist, come back from one of these encounters at first elated — he was going to be the first one to stain her blankets! to shower with her! to meet her parents! — and then ashamed. In the days afterward, Debby Vartagnan wouldn't speak to Frost. Where was the free love in this? Where was the revolution?

The size of the Cult was shifting, as was its group identity. Francis Chamberlain Davenport IV, Paul's closest friend, was a founding member, as was Hal Frost. And there were Christina and Debby and Penny Belvedere and Johnny Wilde and Mike Russell and a host of secondary characters. Sometimes they all got along. Sometimes they could rest assured that the difficult moments of the day — the moment, for example, when each of them entered the dining hall unaccompanied and was subjected to its system of gazes and ratings — they had company. This company was worth the anxious apartness it also fostered in them. The Cult comforted, Paul Hood thought, as the train passed through Greenwich. The Cult was a tonic and a comfort.

But one thing the Kittredge Cult could not do was instruct about love. They were all orphans this way, from broken homes. They knew shit about love. Paul had *gone out,* in St. Pete's parlance, with Eileen Becker in fourth form, but late in the spring she began seeing, instead, his roommate, Stan Sinclair. A period followed in which Paul frequently disturbed them in his dorm room — the two of them pretending to be asleep, or Eileen clutching a rumpled frock around her. Hood struck back with a few crushes that didn't last more than a week. He struck back by being alone.

Then one night he persuaded Eileen into an empty reading room. In the sciences building. He had preyed upon her confused notions of fidelity. *I can't eat since you started up with Sinclair,* he said. *I'm all cut up inside.* Which was misleading, since basically he felt that way all the time. Paul knelt at her waist, her jeans and panties in a tangle around her sneakers — Tretorns with pink stripes — and held her vagina close to his face. She parted her legs, standing over him, lowered herself down until they touched this way. He got the tip of his tongue inside her. So briefly it was almost certainly a dream. And though this was as far as she would go, further than she wanted to, she had whispered one thing, shivered and whispered it, before going back to Stan Sinclair. *Paul Hood,* she had said, *I know what you're gonna be good at one day.*

The train roared through Pelham. Alongside, on the highway, cars were backed up in either direction. The headlights, the streetlights, were a forlorn effort in the sleet and snow.

Paul Hood had more ideas about the Wankel rotary engine than he did about love. But he was not dumb. Though Testors model glue in the bottom of a paper bag was his preferred companion, though he had once soaked his penis in milk in an effort to get his housemaster's cat to have congress with him — her tongue was like sandpaper — he knew the name of what he was missing. He had gotten his hand down the waist of Jeannie McFarlane's pants to feel the tuft of what she concealed there, and he had kissed a variety of girls for durations short and long, and he had read about blow jobs and sixty-nine, orgies, bisexuality, mutual masturbation, transvestism, ménage à trois, anal sex, fetishism, and even fist-fucking. He had perused Davenport's dog-eared copy of the *Kama Sutra;* he knew what love was. He was going to pursue this education. He didn't want to be as sad as his parents.

So he was on the train, on his way to meet Libbets Casey, a girl from school, who, unlike his friends from the Cult, unlike Carla Bear, say, was a fine conversationalist, who did charity work with the St. Pete's Missionary Society, and whose parents left her entirely unsupervised. Paul was infatuated. It had come over him suddenly. The Bear was just someone he liked; Debby Vartagnan was just someone he liked. He wanted Libbets, a girl who wore a mink coat with blue jeans. He thought about her day and night; he wrote her name into the stories he composed for English class; he dedicated songs to her on his radio show. This had gone on for days.

For two years now, he had spent virtually every afternoon with Davenport and Frost and Brendan Gilford. Out in the woods getting high. He breathed the same room freshener they breathed (Ozium); he had borrowed their records and loaned them his own. They all knew how to play the same Emerson, Lake and Palmer song on guitar. They knew the same jokes and disliked the same masters. They all volunteered for dish duty at the same time.

But he knew it was coming to an end, that the loose association that other people called the Cult was just something you had at one time in your life. In September, when Davenport had declared himself *King of the Cult* at his birthday party — he was on bounds at the time, unable to receive visitors in his room, for breaking curfew — the whole thing began to sour. And it had just been a joke anyway. A joke to make feeling like a loser tolerable. Soon everybody was giving themselves titles. It was just like the Fantastic Four. It was all relationships and politics and power.

The Conrail riders observed an unnatural calm. They were stretched out across the three-seaters with their luggage strewn carelessly around them. Paul always left things behind: watches, magazines, umbrellas. He borrowed articles and lost them. So he clutched *F.F.* #141, like it was a religious scroll or high-court decision, along with the November issue of *Creem.* And when the train rumbled down into the tunnel at 97th Street, and into the terminal, and when it disgorged its passengers with a sigh of hydraulic brakes, he was grateful to be a lone traveler, unencumbered with possessions or obligations.

Grand Central Terminal was deserted. The Kodak sign featured a happy, white family celebrating around a Christmas tree. As Paul had been instructed to do since he was a little boy, he found a spot against the wall and looked up at the stars on the ceiling. Sunk in dust and grime, the hulking simplicity of the constellations moved him. They were the imaginative work of another time. They were the superheroes of the past.

On the floor of the terminal, in the vast open spaces — bereft of the usual commuters — a platoon of men with blank faces and the cheapest spectacles sold books and records about meditation to the unsuspecting. Paul moved through them like a warrior.

Libbets Casey. Paul's destination. Deep in that stronghold of the silent majority, the Upper East Side. Her dad didn't have a job. He didn't need one. At an office in midtown, which he paid for himself, he occasionally wielded a gold letter opener and moved around lunch appointments and tennis dates with other professional board members and consultants. Libbets wouldn't have to work either. True idleness — ski-instructing, for example — was frowned upon in her family, but there was no need to hazard an office job. Generations of Caseys had pursued art collecting. They had donated a great number of cubist works, selected by Libbets's savvy grandmother, to the Museum of Modern Art. The Caseys had also established the reputations of some nineteenth-century American painters — Eakins, Childe Hassam. Collecting was a more than adequate vocation. As were any of the arts-related pastimes. Her mother was a docent at the Metropolitan Museum, and her various older sisters and brothers, all of them out in the world now, were art historians and gallery owners. As long as Libbets kept painting, she was in good shape.

The doormen at 930 Park let Paul up without buzzing. He suspected that they, too, had enjoyed her company for a joint or a beer. Libbets was everybody's friend. Her comportment was flawless. She knew the kids who hung out in the Central Park band shell; she knew Adam Purple, the guy who shoveled horse shit in the park for his garden downtown; she knew David Cassidy, whose father lived in the building. The doormen at 930 had long hair and shifty smiles, the smiles of men uncomfortable with the way their fetching-and-carrying jobs stretched out in front of them. These countercultural doormen knew the difference between their station and Libbets's, and they were ready for the first sign of condescension, just as they cherished the notion, like Libbets did, that the rich were just people, too. They could all share some dope. It was cool.

So one of the doormen asked Paul if there was a party.

Paul shook his head, mumbled.

He skidded out of that scrape and into the next one. The elevator opened right into the Caseys' foyer. They had the entire fourth floor of 930 Park. Paul set his blazer on a chair in the front hall. His heart raced with the recollection of Libbets's peasant dresses, with the smell of the skin lotion she used, with the lopsided way she smiled. Except for the dim stutter of the television down the hall, there was an austere stillness to the premises. The foyer was carpeted with antique Orientals and decorated with pre-Columbian urns and with small American impressionist paintings by artists recognizable from any day-camp art-appreciation course. The elevator slid shut behind him. Libbets called out cheerfully.

She came running out of the den. She slid, in stocking feet, across a bare strip of parquet.

— Excellent, she said. We were waiting!

We? We were waiting? The revelation of that horrible plural struck Paul like a blow in the solar plexus. *We?* And yet he followed his hostess. Sure enough, in the den, he found Francis Chamberlain Davenport IV, cleaning an ounce of dope on an open copy of *Six Crises* by Richard M. Nixon.

All hope drained from Paul.

— You oughta read this, Hood, Davenport said distractedly. All you need to know about the travails of life. Myself, I was just checking out about Alger Hiss and Checkers.

— You're gonna leave the seeds in there? Paul said. In the binding like that?

— All will be revealed, baby. When the student is ready, the master will appear.

Libbets circulated nervously around the living room. Paul wondered if the two of them, Libbets and Davenport, had already collaborated in some afternoon sexual experiment. Even Libbets, in her secure and privately educated skull must have known how Davenport fucked him up.

— Flame on, he said.

— Huh? Libbets said.

— Awesome sleet and rain, Paul said. Far out. Let's do some reef. Neither sleet nor rain will stay this courier. What's on the idiot box?

— *Lost in Space,* Libbets said. *Star Trek* at seven.

— Moisture, moisture, Davenport said from his station. Moooiiiistuuuuure.

It was from this episode, this *Lost in Space* episode.

— Yeah, yeah, Paul said. Or remember that one where there were the guys with glittering, plastic bowlers. Zachary Smith was . . .

Davenport rolled a joint as carefully as if it were bomb disposal.

— Howdy, there, he said. You, young knight. Can you check on the mead? Can you sally forth and secure us some more mead?

— In the pantry, Libbets said. She pointed.

Paul trudged disconsolately out into the foyer, past the living room where a portrait of the Caseys — Libbets was the youngest of the six, seated in her father's lap — occupied most of a wall. He stood in the dark.

— No, that way, Libbets said, leaning out into the hall, slumped against the doorjamb. Take a right, through there.

— Just looking, Paul said. Got my "just looking" button on.

The pantry was long, empty, spotless. The banality of this kind of housekeeping made Paul uncomfortable. The place begged for the release of cockroaches or lab rats. It begged for finger-painted floors, tie-dyed curtains, for graffiti and noise pollution.

Paul was a third term, an unwelcome geometrical element. Davenport hadn't even greeted him. And supernumerary was a feeling he knew as well as he knew that parched baby blue of Connecticut summer skies. Blundering in the kitchen, he felt sure that it would always be this way, this blunt little diorama of a life with its cessation of miracles would never change — except that it would get worse. Davenport wasn't satisfied with his own charm. He wanted to inhabit his friends, to neutralize them. He wanted Paul's socks and Paul's records and Paul's homework assignments and even Paul's nuclear family with its 2.2 children and its five basic food groups and its pristine genetics. They were the best of friends, Davenport and Paul. This was what friendship was like.

Paul formulated his plan. He removed the cold six-pack of Heinekens from the refrigerator. He trudged out of the kitchen.

— Frankie opens them with his teeth, Libbets giggled, back in the library. This wasn't news. It was part of Davenport's arsenal of entertainments. Paul had tried the same trick on a couple of occasions, with painful results. He had settled for opening beers with house keys, which involved no bodily harm. Davenport, after licking the second joint and setting it aside, used his rear molars on a Heineken.

— Hell on the fillings, Charles.

He opened the other two, passed them around, and then lit a joint.

— Everything's gonna freeze over, Davenport said. Big freeze.

— Yeah, Paulie, Libbets said, are you going to get home okay?

They explained about the predicted sudden drop in temperature, the predicted freezing of road surfaces, the devastation — you wouldn't be able to get a cab, the airports would close down, everything would have to be delivered. All the food. All the health and beauty aids. Then Libbets put on an Allman Brothers tape — 8-track, television on with the sound down — and they talked about Duane and the crash.

They drank. They smoked pot. Quickly. As though it were an obligation somehow.

No matter how many times the weather repeated its four symphonic movements, the specifics of rainfall and wind direction and velocity and barometric pressure seemed new to Paul. The false logic of marijuana was dawning in him. *Six Crises,* for example, absorbed his complete attention. He gulped for air: the enormity of this Nixonian schema! Urgently, Paul tried to make the various reversals of his life — his grandparents' deaths, his stolen bicycles, his father's drinking, his failure to make junior varsity soccer at St. Pete's, the time in first grade that his mother made him wear tights in the East School Xmas pageant — add up to six crises. In a flash of specious enlightenment, he saw that every life could fit into this ingenious brilliant systematization. Libbets's life. Davenport's life. Daisy Chain's life, even. Then Paul started thinking about Watergate, a *seventh crisis.*

— Holy shit, he said.

— How long have we been sitting here? Libbets said. I'm so stoned.

— Seven minutes, Davenport said. Who knows?

— How much beer is left? Paul said.

Davenport reached over to where Paul was sitting. He poked him in the chest.

— How the hell do we know? You're in charge of the kitchen, cowboy.

They all laughed. HA! HA! HA! HA! Paul went to fetch still more beers, and while he was there he tried to decide whether or not Davenport and Libbets were really trying to get rid of him. The evidence mounted. It was in their facial expressions. They were using some kind of facial code. Paul remembered that he'd had the same thought last time he was in the kitchen. His mind couldn't light on anything long enough to reason it out. His mind was a slippery, reptilian thing. How much time had passed?

The next beers went more quickly than the first. Paul was careful to permit Davenport to have more than his share. Libbets wasn't counting. She was just happy to be there.

Then Paul excused himself.

The plan was happening at some lower level of cognition. It was like collective unconscious or something. Next thing he knew: Mr. and Mrs. Casey had decorated their master bath in a style according to their age and means. Lavender shell soaps — they were everywhere, no home without them — occupied a china soap dish. Floral wallpaper, also flecked with lavender, adorned the walls. The soap and the wallpaper and the tissue paper and the hand towels matched. The medicine cabinet yielded precisely the kind of paydirt he had been hoping for. Besides some Preparation H and some perfumed douches, there were several prescriptions: phenobarbital, Valium, Seconal, and an old one, paregoric.

The Seconals interested him particularly.

Before he could effect the next stage of his plan, however, he unzippered his khakis and took himself in hand. An inevitable part of marijuana intoxication. When Paul felt irritable and forlorn, he noticed he was also especially prone to jerk that thing. He had elaborated a number of complicated masturbation scenarios. He always liked to begin, for example, when the second hand of his watch was precisely at twelve. (There was a small wind-up clock on the sink.) He liked to finish before the second hand made it around twice. He also like to whack off to pictures of girls he found by randomly flipping through his St. Pete's yearbook.

Once he had arrived at Libbets's picture through this procedure, and though these yearbook episodes were usually memorable, he found on this occasion that he wilted in his hand. He just couldn't bring himself to do it with a woman so adorable. He just couldn't bring himself to that point. He had tried a variety of lubricants. Skin lotions, lip balms, even Stan Sinclair's jar of QT tanning lotion. This failure turned out to be good luck. It proved that Libbets was appropriate for his worship. So appropriate that he got hard, this time, this day.

Shafts of light coursed through his penis. He could feel light in his scrotum, in every millimeter of that downy chicken skin. His ecstasy was religious. This orgasm would be compensation for Paul Hood's troubles here on earth. Yes, the best orgasms were characterized not by joy — he couldn't remember a joyful one anyway — but by earthly loss and the desire to fortify himself against it. With this in mind, he was about to tearfully leak a couple of teaspoons of disaffection in the sink. But a knock at the door interrupted him.

— Champ, Davenport called from the other side of the door. What the hell is going on in there? We are bored and desire your company. Come on out. Desist from choking that toad, champ. Desist.

Paul froze. Did Davenport really —

— Just gotta spill in the sink here first, Francis.

He giggled wretchedly at his floppy divining rod. — Then I'll bring out the heavy chemistry.

— Okay, but don't be long about it. If you're gonna

take your pleasures in there we want to know about it. We want to participate.

Paul caught his breath. Ran water through his hair. Took a deep breath. Back in the library. *Star Trek* with *American Beauty* soundtrack.

— What took so long? Libbets asked.

— Checking out the medicine cabinet, Paul said. Your parents have some excellent shit in there.

— What didst thou find? Davenport said.

— Wait a sec, guys, Libbets said anxiously. You aren't going to *take* prescription drugs from my parents' bathroom without permission?

— Never a thought in our minds, babe, Davenport said, holding in his lungs the last of another joint, so that his voice was husky and forced. But do you mean to suggest that you have never taken advantage of that most convenient supply? What are you, un-American?

— Lots of stuff, Paul said. Diverse items. Tranquilizers and sleeping pills.

He fell lengthways upon the couch.

— Elixirs, Davenport said, that have a promising effect, very promising, when combined in small dosage levels with alcoholic beverages.

— Let me go look, Libbets said. I'll go look.

Once she had gone, Davenport's demeanor changed. It was the strangest thing. Suddenly, he was friendly again. Suddenly. They were old friends after all. Davenport knew how Paul got encased in himself. They were old friends and they had been through a few things, but they could still have a good laugh about masturbation or at somebody else's expense. That Davenport's headband was stupid, that his beard was a little on the simian side — Paul could overlook this stuff. He could still like him.

So they talked about Thanksgiving. And since Davenport was adopted, as were his brothers and sisters, the notion of a collegial family get-together had its dark, obverse side. Davenport's younger sister actually aspired, he claimed, to a life of prostitution. She liked to hang around the bars in Times Square. And his younger brother was racked by psychosomatic illnesses. Lately, he had been hospitalized with phantom kidney pain. Which of these children could one day run the Davenport venture-capital organization? Which would entertain at their Sea Island summer home? Francis Chamberlain Davenport IV, the likely choice, wanted to be a Jungian psychoanalyst.

— What's to be thankful for at Thanksgiving? Davenport asked. Indian corn in plastic wrap for sale next to Velveeta? Butterball turkey with built-in thermometer? Rod McKuen? Helen Reddy doing "Delta Dawn"? Are you getting this all down, Charles?

They laughed. They sang. Half a line of "Delta Dawn." And of "Billy, Don't Be a Hero."

— Okay, okay. Libbets turned up again. There's plenty there. I don't see how they could miss them. What kind should we do?

— Seconal, definitely, Paul said.

— Hey, as long as it does the job, Davenport said. I am not picky.

— You don't think this is going to, you know, be a problem with the beers?

— Check the expiration date. Paul said. I thought they looked pretty cool.

The need behind teen oblivion overcame any reservations. Which was the way Paul figured it would go. Soon the three of them were crowded into the bathroom, around the medicine cabinet, looking at the little prescription containers. Libbets's hands were shaking as she handed around the reds. And Paul was moved by this. He put his hand lightly around her shoulder, her soft and fragrant shoulder. Did she notice? They were each embarked on a solitary narrative of intoxication. Repartee wasn't part of the whole thing.

Davenport looked the capsules over admiringly, like a collector of fine wines.

Paul let his settle under his tongue.

He felt a little bad about how easy it was, leading Davenport down this road, but in the long run, by late next week, they would forgive one another.

— Hey, maybe you should only take a half, old lady, Hood said to Libbets. Why don't you put half in a glass of orange juice or something? You don't weigh as much as we do.

— You guys aren't trying to rip me off or anything, are you? Libbets said. It was almost like she was going to cry for a second. Paul was shaking his head, he was trying to wave her off. She swallowed the whole thing.

— No way, Davenport said. You mean so we could have our way with your sleeping body?

Davenport laughed grimly. Libbets had breasts and hips — she was curvy in fact, she was all gentle curves — hidden under her baggy army fatigues and sweatshirt. Two against one, that was Davenport's idea. Her parents wouldn't be home for days. No, Paul would defend her against Davenport. Take me, but leave the girl alone. She was friendlier than she wanted to be, she smiled more than she wanted to smile. The fact that she'd permitted losers like Hood and Davenport into her manse proved it. Thank God these exceptions arose. Thank God for drinking a bottle of wine with Liza during first class Friday morning.

Thank God for snorting speed with Laura and Dave and going to the Tuck Shop to eat malted milk balls. Thank God for the confraternity of burnouts.

— Naw, Davenport said, we had a period in which we loved unconscious women, but we're over that now.

Time stretched out. The world was full of information, but it was all happening more slowly. Paul buried his capsule in a potted palm by the window. But he was succumbing to the pot and beer. Some labyrinthine and endless decision was being made about whether or not to go to a nightclub called Max's something or other. Would Sue Richards return to Reed Richards? Would Francis Ford Coppola make a sequel to *The Godfather*? Worlds real and imagined buzzed side by side, options and conclusions appeared and disappeared. When Davenport arranged himself on the couch, to watch *Sanford and Son* with the sound off, Paul saw how easy some things are, how you don't need to try so hard. Davenport wouldn't rise from that couch for twelve hours.

— I'm a hothead, Libbets, he said. I'm —

— Huh? Let's go into the living room. Let's let him sleep.

— He's just crashed. This doesn't last forever.

— Don't you think we ought to eat something?

But they couldn't just leave Davenport.

— I wonder how bad the weather is, Paul said.

— I was just telling you, said Libbets. Snow tonight. It's gonna be bad.

— The last train to Stamford leaves at. . . . I have to be on that last train or I'm fucked.

Paul switched on the lamp that illumined the Casey family portrait and they sat on the floor in its ostentatious glow. On Paul's radio program, on the ten-watt AM radio station at St. Pete's, he made hideously sentimental dedications to girls he'd never met. He wrote notes to them and left these notes in a drawer. He burned the names, or threw them out; he writhed in spoiled and cowardly silence. His outbursts of feeling were as unpredictable as sunspots. As he took Libbets's hand — she permitted it to be taken — he knew he was liable to say anything. His exacting standards vanished. He loved Cat Stevens. He wanted to fill a dictionary with flowers. He wanted to lie on golf greens with her. He wanted to spy on her through a hole in a newspaper. He wanted to make a better family than the one from which he came.

— Let's go back to your room.

— Excuse me? Libbets said.

— I want to show you my etchings, he said.

— Etchings?

— It's a joke, he said. C'mon. I just want to talk. I have stuff I want to tell you.

Libbets collapsed into indecision.

— Hey, Libbets, you didn't set me up or anything, did you? You didn't invite Davenport here because you were afraid to be alone with me, did you? You aren't afraid to have me here in your house, are you? Because I came a long way to see you. You wouldn't do that kind of thing, would you? Libbets?

II

THE BRIGHT HUES of the sixties had vanished from contemporary interior design. Let me interrupt again briefly here. Where the wives of southern Connecticut in the past might have embraced — carefully, hesitantly — gaudy neons and Day-Glos, they had by 1973 settled into milder pastels and earth tones. Subdued patterns figured prominently in upholstery fabrics and draperies, although you might also find in these items unusual marriages of color — puce and gray, or lavender and ocher. Vera Neumann, also known as Vera, winner of the 1972 National Home Fashion League Trailblazer Award, was the standard-bearer of these color harmonies. The decorator fabrics themselves were more durable than in the past. Synthetics and cotton/poly blends dominated. Plastics had also penetrated far into the home. Coffee tables, modular furniture, kitchenware, and electrical appliances — all could now be fashioned from plastic.

Shag rugs of rust and brown like fallen leaves and corroded automobiles or green and gray like cave algae or a thick beach-coating of seaweed — shag was the area rug of the area. Shorter piles with *startling* mandalas and floral prints were also possible because of new manufacturing technologies. Yet shag continued to exert its charm over the decorators of New Canaan. It was versatile — it could conceal crumbs, ancient pieces of chewing gum, spittle, disease-carrying fleas and ants and silverfish, shreds of paper, and other unrecovered items. And it helped the vacuum-cleaner business move units. The *seating unit* had come to replace the couch in the vanguard of living room accommodations. A minimalist vocabulary was evident in these ingenious designs, reflecting the influence of simple, primal iconography in sculpture and architecture. Single-color stylings decorated sleek, curvaceous, cornerless shapes. The modular pieces of these *seating units* could be easily moved and rearranged in a variety of amoebic configurations. The traditional couch — and with it the loveseat, the divan, and the chaise longue — was in eclipse.

The new seating units were often fashioned from polyurethane foam, a cheap, easy-to-manufacture, artificial filling. The Furniture Council of the Society of the Plastics Industry even presented a Poly Award for the groundbreaking adaptation of polymers. In 1973 it went to Donald A. Geddes, editor of *American Furniture Design*, who was named Polymer Man of the Year.

Benjamin Hood reflected on fashion only briefly upon taking his wife's hand — noticing in passing her ring and the raw, red crevices that surrounded it. She needed lotion. Passing across the Halfords' threshold, into the foyer with its large standing sculpture — a melted I-beam twisted into a sort of anguished helix — catching a glimpse of the clustering and valent neighbors arranged in the corridor, Hood realized the truth of the matter: his ascot was no longer in fashion.

In fact, *sweaters*, furry and dense and of Netherlandish origin, were numerous in the front hall at Dorothy and

Robert Halford's. There were a few old tweed jackets, but no ascots. Had Hood been in a mind to comfort himself, he might have approved of his ample shirt collar, spread wide on the wings of his lapels. But how had he managed to get out the door wearing the ascot? How had he let himself? Hood didn't wear three-inch cork heels or white loafers. And he didn't wear his hair long or wear double-breasted suits or pleated pants. His gesture toward what he saw as a more flamboyant presentation had been these ascots, fashioned of a silk he liked to feel against his neck, against spots irritated by his Wilkinson double-bonded razor. But these ascots were no longer appropriate. Only months before, Benjamin Hood had lived in the certainty that his dress was in accord with the prevailing climatic conditions. But now, just as quickly, he was solitary in his garb. He dressed poorly. He disgraced himself. His wife looked fine, in her slacks and Hush Puppies, but he disgraced her company.

Of women's fashion at the Halfords', Hood might have noticed ankle-length skirts, dignified and elegant, though there were also skirts at the knee and the midcalf. Here, too, sweaters were the accessory of choice, reflecting a polyphony of styles — sweaters of cashmere, mohair, and shetland. Sweaters, sweaters, sweaters. Sweaters, and pearls.

Dorothy Halford overtook them in the foyer. With a free hand, she waved a little celery canoe at them. It was loaded down with an aqua-colored dip. Dot wore a blue-and-gray crocheted sweater over a thin crepe de chine blouse, pants of gray flannel, black velvet beret. No makeup. She was petite; there was something Katharine Ross–cherubic, unthreatening, wholesome about her. She appeared both willing and unsullied in the brute arena of erotic love. She seemed to take no notice of how her guests, the Hoods, were turned out, and she couldn't have seen the traces of a recent disagreement in their eager hellos.

— Ben, Elena! Wonderful! wonderful. So wonderful to see you.

She swallowed the last of the celery canoe. With an adolescent sexual pout, Dot kissed the air near Ben's ear and crushed Elena in a manic hug. Then she seized the simple, white salad bowl that had been sitting on the table in the front hall. It was sinister in its simplicity. She thrust it at them.

— Would you care to play?

The enormity of the bowl took a moment to dawn on Ben. At first, he thought it was a joke, a joke with a visual gag — Did you hear the one about Spiro Agnew's accountant? HA! HA! HA! HA! What did Mary Jo Kopechne's mom say to Jack Ruby? HA! HA! HA! HA! — at which he might laugh agreeably without any comprehension of the punch line. But when he examined the contents of the bowl, he understood. Swimming there like uncataloged water bugs were a dozen or more sets of house keys. They chimed agreeably as Dorothy shifted herself from one pump to the other, and their sundry key rings — a yellow slab of plastic with the word MOM embossed on it in red, a Caucasian troll doll with magenta hair, a miniature can of Löwenbraü beer — caught the light like flea-market prizes. Dorothy examined Ben and Elena — Ben could feel this. She watched their faces set the way a dentist searches for the repressed shudder of discomfort.

— Strictly volunteer, of course. You can put your coats right in the library if you like.

— Oh, damn, Elena said, smiling herself. Oh, I've left the —

— You've —

— In the car, Elena said.

— Oh, yeah, Ben said. Yeah, we'll be right back. Dot.

Just as soon as the Hoods had arrived, they were gone. Cramped in the front seat of the Firebird, windshield fogged, defroster on high, in silence. Parked in the driveway. Surrounded by the wheels of the neighborhood — Cadillac Eldorados, BMW 2002s, and then an AMC Matador, a Plymouth Duster. Beetles, Beetles, and more Beetles, that design created with slave labor. Cars creeping into the Halfords' turnaround and then thinking better of it, thinking better of getting stuck in the bad weather to come, creeping out through the slush and onto Valley Road to park up on the embankment. The low chortle of expensive engines idling lazily.

A little history. The key party came into existence several years before, in a more freewheeling environment. This is one hypothesis. It came of age with hippie erotica and bohemian orgies in cramped apartments owned by poorly groomed professors. Or among the dangerously promiscuous, those who didn't distinguish between the sexes or who slipped into the tepid waters of dimly lit love grottoes and swamps. But like so many reasonable ideas that seem less bright in the harsh illumination of general distribution, it was soon exported to this land of tidy shrubs and the Junior League.

Maybe the key party first touched suburban ground on Long Island, on the bay side; it might have landed in New Jersey, in Bernardsville or Princeton; or it might have emerged in Westchester, or even as far north as the Boston suburbs. Or maybe even California, where lax-moraled filmmakers and artists lived contiguously with taxpayers and families. Whatever its true origin, or its distribution (its Poisson Distribution), west to east, south to north, it undeniably appeared in Fairfield County in the early seventies.

The rules were appallingly simple. The men tossed their house keys into a convenient container — or hung them on pegs or spread them like a buffet on the front table or on the master bed — and the women, at evening's end, selected a set at random. And then the party retired to taste novelty. Sometimes the men looked on as the women selected — leering, suggestive, hopeful, disappointed, or despairing; sometimes the women wore blindfolds fashioned from metaphorically rich garments, black silk stockings, for example; sometimes, the proceedings took place with a joyless resolve, as if the participants were merely plugged into a circuitry of compulsion.

In New Canaan, word had come of the key parties long before the first had been thrown. Local marriages awaited key parties the way a smart boy, already having pored over the dictionary definition of masturbation, awaits the day when he will understand it. The first one, thrown by some younger, unhappier residents over in the West School district, on Ponus Ridge, was viewed publicly with contempt but privately with much interest. And this contradictory posturing became the rule. At the Armitage party, held in the summer of 1972, partners at competing law firms bedded one another's wives, and women who were best of friends compared notes on the prowess and endowment of local men.

The ramifications of these first parties took some time to emerge. Love had woven its tapestry, and the Armitages, the Sawyers, the Steeles, the Boyles, the Gormans, the Jacobsens, the Hamiltons, the Gadds, the Earles, the Fullers, the Buckleys, the Regans, not to mention the Bolands, the

Conrads, the Millers, and others, had followed its complex thread. But the revelations of this inquiry weren't so surprising. No one returned with tales of dark new terrains — anal sex or urolagnia or masochism or coprophagy; in fact, the Armitage's couples coupled in the way they always had. But they walked with a new jauntiness. For a day or two. Their hearts twittered with novelty.

Then silence took hold of the participants. Whispers, that fall, at cocktail parties or on the paddle-tennis courts, spoke of unsubstantiated liaisons between those whose night of passion was intended to be singular, unique, unrepeatable. Annie Buckley told Maria Smith who told Maura O'Brien who told her husband, Phil O'Brien, the urologist, who told Steve Buckley in the very midst of percussing Buckley's enlarged prostate, who told his wife, Annie, who knew already. And as this information circulated — according to statistical order and disorder, according to summation, transition, and reciprocal induction — it became painful, injurious. It became compulsive. You couldn't avoid talking about it and yet you did nonetheless. Just as the key parties themselves persisted.

How could Benjamin and Elena have been so stupid? They ought to have known. Invitations usually didn't advertise a key party, but somehow the word usually got out. You had to be in the food chain to know, but then that was the premise of an invitation, right? The Hoods hadn't attended any of the key parties, but not because they had discussed it. No, they hadn't been to a key party because they hadn't been invited.

Anyway, Benjamin thought, Elena was no swinger.

Hood worried again about his ascot. In the half-defogged rearview mirror he unknotted the thing from his neck and breathed a sigh of relief.

— This just isn't the best moment for this, Elena said.

He did his best to avoid her distress. Trying to repair the situation would only be selfish. With his handkerchief he began to clean the window on the driver's side.

— It'll just streak, she said.

— I know. I know that, Hood said. Well, if we'd understood we could have fabricated an excuse. Plenty of movies to see. There's a little thing of tissues in there.

She opened the glove compartment.

— Well? she said.

He took in the cool glow of her pale, pale eyes. She had left her glasses at home. Sometime in the midst of that uncomfortable discussion back at the house she had left off her glasses. (For a time she had worn contact lenses, which clogged with pollution whenever she wore them, or which would pop out, pop like a fierce tear from her eye and drift to the floor, so that the two of them would fall into a prayerful attitude and comb the rugs and floors at parties.)

— I think we're here and we don't have to stay — we ought to simply put in an appearance and then we can head home.

He knew this wasn't her feeling.

— Darn it, Ben —

— I'm not staying at this party so that I can go home with someone else's wife, darling. Let's just talk about it. That's not why we're here. Right? We're simply being neighbors here, and I think we should do just that, and then we can go.

— You're going to —

— I'm *not.*

— You have some *marker*, that's what I think, if you want to know the truth. You have some marker and you're going to put it on the house keys so that Janey can find them and then when I get back to the house I'll find the two of you in there and Wendy'll be able to hear you and Paul will be back and he'll hear you and I'll catch you, that's what I think. She'll be moaning and swearing, banging against the wall and I'll catch you —

Elena smiled faintly when she was distressed — he attributed this to the way things went during her childhood — and she was smiling now. In a way, it was a diabolical smile, the smile of a conspirator or politician, just as she was rubbing her eyes. Her nose was red.

— Elena, he said.

And he offered to take her hands.

— It's not like you think, he said. It's not a big plot, honey. Honestly. Honestly. I don't know if you want to go over this now, but it's just something that comes over me. I don't feel good about myself. I don't feel good about it at all. I know that I've done what I didn't want to do, and I don't know why. So I'm not going to do it tonight, Elena. That's my solemn . . . that's my promise.

— Well, I'm really pleased to hear a confession, she said. I'm happy about that.

He said nothing. Switched the heat from defrost to ordinary heat. It roared from the vents in the dashboard.

— You imagine you're protecting me from some wicked ways of the world, but you're not protecting me, Elena said. I don't need your protection, you know. I don't.

— Oh, you're just getting wound up to get wound up.

— Thanks for the diagnosis, Ben. Living so close to the . . . to Silver Meadow, that's opened you up. You're very open tonight. You're at some magnanimous spot. I'm not an earnings model. And I'm not a subject for your casual sort of analysis. So let's go to this fiasco if that's what you want to do. Let's just go on in. I'd rather talk to anyone else but you.

And she threw open the door of the Firebird and gathered the Dubarry raincoat — $85 with liner, 65 percent dacron and 35 percent cotton — around her. She gave the door a good heave — with American cars it needed that — and left him there.

Hood reopened the glove compartment and fumbled around for the flask. With a brisk, purposeful negligence, he hoisted it in his wife's honor.

His capacity for drinking surprised even him, but it paled in the face of his capacity for self-deception. His denial was significant enough to suppress even any notion of denial. He concealed in himself all notions of motive. So as he lifted the pewter flask again — warm from its proximity to the heating vents on the dash — any questions about the key party or its farcical possibilities failed to occur to him. Where his motives were concerned Hood was like a blind man without a cane. He was night diving. He was flying without instruments. He was going to this party.

When he followed Elena in, minutes later, it was with the elation of stiff drink. Thus elated, he elbowed past the Sawyers — gabbing with Dot Halford in the doorway — and worked his way into the conversation. He wanted to get to the *bowl*.

— More than pleased to be part of the proceedings, he mumbled. And then he ceremoniously tossed his keys to Dot — a jaunty little toss — as though she were the parking flunky for the evening, and she, startled, angled under them with the bowl. For a moment she was frozen, with her carefully lipsticked mouth open wide, and then she made the catch. The keys were nestled among their brethren. The sound of keys seemed to follow. Dot frowned. The Sawyers said nothing.

This giddy feeling evaporated almost immediately. In the foyer, surrounded by couples he hadn't met, couples giggling nervously or ribaldly about the storm, the bowl, the party, their good luck, in the foyer, Hood ran into George Clair. From the office. Benjamin was on his way to the bar to get another drink, though he felt already that words were dissolving on his tongue, that the beginnings of WASP pronunciation were upon him — people always felt it was an ethnic thing. Then Clair appeared, in his bow tie and navy blue blazer. Elena was vanishing deep into the pantry of the Halfords' house and Benjamin could feel himself stretch out toward her, to apologize again, but Clair was in his way. A faint fecal odor perfumed George always.

The house of Shackley and Schwimmer had been at one time the most maverick and creative of the brokerage operations on the street. This was circa the Summer of Love. Though Hood hadn't sampled the psychedelic cafeteria of that time, he often felt that he had come close — as close as those subordinates who smoked joints and finger-painted at Trinity Church at lunchtimes, who knew the unemployed musicians who played there, who could read the hidden messages in rock-and-roll album sleeves. Even Shackley and Schwimmer themselves had been known to turn up at Trinity now and then. They also went to parties to benefit the Black Panther Defense Fund. They opposed the Vietnam conflict. They were fellow travelers.

Shackley and Schwimmer were Harvard-educated men who wore beards and studied like the Orthodox of their faith, though they were as secular as most of their Protestant counterparts. Sometimes they eschewed ties entirely or wore beat-up tweed jackets that must have been left over from their school days. Sometimes they ate at delicatessens and brought sandwiches back for the girls at the switchboard.

What did they have going for them? They were smarter then everyone else. Shackley and Schwimmer's reputation rested on this simple arrogance. Prior to S&S, the world of brokerage had been a world of congeniality and fraternity. Guys who had gone to the same boarding schools and who belonged to the same country clubs or squash clubs doing business with one another. This fraternity was no guarantee of business acumen. Shackley and Schwimmer confronted old-boy business with academic disdain and with statistics — debt, assets, amortization, dividends, quarterly earnings figures. A little analysis, a few hot tips. The old brokerage houses weren't prepared for it, and they didn't like it. About this time Shackley himself devised an advertising campaign, perfected by one of the expensive Madison Avenue advertising firms, in which individual members of the Shackley and Schwimmer team were introduced in full-page advertisements. A huge full-face photograph, retouched, with copy beneath.

Hood remembered his own, from 1969, with both pride and embarrassment. "Benjamin Paul Hood, Dartmouth College, '57. First Boston, '58–'65. Shackley and Schwimmer, '65–. Specialty: Media and Entertainment Businesses. Outlook: Bullish." And then the company's bold proclamation beneath. *Shackley and Schwimmer — The Conventional Wisdom Is Wrong.*

In the days following the advertisement, no one in the supermarket or at the country club mentioned it at all. It was as if the advertisement had fallen out of the paper altogether. As if its page had been excised or printed badly. No one mentioned it. Well, maybe the barber mentioned it, and the cleaning woman, but no one else. Hood wondered if it was the picture, of course. They had tried to whip his mottled, puffy features into an inoffensive and jolly paste. His beady eyes protruded from this pudding like some garnish, like unwanted raisins. They had clamped him into a tight shirt: he felt he would gag or asphyxiate during the photo session. And yet, his neck hung over that tightened collar, that tightened tie knot, like a precarious rock formation. Even Elena offered no encouragement about the advertisement.

With the picture began the problems at the office. George Clair arrived not long after, in 1969, at the age of twenty-four. Harvard B.A. and M.B.A. Though he arrived at the office unaware of the so-called Woodstock generation and the Summer of Love, Clair grew his hair when he arrived at Shackley and Schwimmer. He purchased a tweed jacket with patches already sewn on the elbows.

Clair gave new meaning to the idea of borrowed culture. He was full of clichés about Latin American debt and the ridiculousness of the Wage-Price Freeze, but he was more concerned with appropriating certain simplistic messages about film, music, and sports, and transporting them into the offices of his superiors. *Ya gotta believe!* Clair had remarked volubly throughout the autumn as the Mets scrambled for the pennant. *Ya gotta believe!* he would tell the secretary whose car had been towed. *Ya gotta believe!* he would say affably to Shackley about that weekend's yacht club race or to Schwimmer about Nixon's role in the conspiracy or the cover-up.

And there had been *Last Tango in Paris. Most erotic film ever made,* Clair had said to his secretary with that earnest and sheepish expression. *Most erotic film,* he said, while cleaning an ear with his pinkie. Then he would go down the hall to remind one of the institutional sales representatives. — Shachter, he would say, have you see *Last Tango?* What about that butter, huh? That crumbly butter? Most erotic film ever made! Shachter would look up from the phone, wave, and then shout it into the phone at the Fireman's Fund. — Clair says see *Last Tango.* Most erotic film ever.

Hood began to be isolated within Shackley and Schwimmer not long after Clair arrived. His assessments of things, of upcoming trends — suddenly they just didn't want to hear from him at sales meetings. The salesmen began to report late on his revisions of quarterly figures, or they would double-check behind his back. Or they would ask who his sources were. As if he had to be joking. This was a long, slow, incremental process of isolation. Soon Shackley himself took up the issue. Hood was called into his office to explain why he hadn't correctly identified the recent profit Gulf + Western was seeing, the profit as a result of *Billy Jack.*

— Isn't this a relevant earnings uptick? Shackley said. Isn't this altering their figures in a way we ought to be expecting?

Billy Jack? One tin soldier rides away? No one could have predicted the eminence of this Tom Laughlin, this established antiestablishment, middle-aged hippie in the Indian hat, who eliminated his antagonists with warmed-over martial arts. No one could have anticipated it. Except, as it turned out, George Clair.

The office problems became worse during Clair's romance with *Last Tango.* Of course, Hood didn't go around talking about Bank of America or First National — Clair's specialties. Out of the blue, though, Clair loved movies. Clair was first to discuss home videotaping and Super-8 as consumer electronics items that would soon transform the entertainment business. He was first to understand the importance of tabloid point-of-purchase magazines. At the weekly research meetings, Clair was constantly leaping in to help out with the media and entertainment securities. And it wasn't that he wanted to cover entertainment stocks: he just wanted the space Benjamin Hood took up, Hood's air and water and space and pension and office. Clair's photograph was a gleaming pinup. He was a Best and Brightest male model. A Harvard M.B.A. who could play touch football and get misty-eyed over a *Saturday Evening Post* cover. By the time of Clair's ad in the *Journal,* in 1971, Hood was beginning to see implications wherever he turned. Overlooked for an important lunch, not copied on an important memo, not tipped off on a hot stock. The hypocrisy and surveillance of office politics were closing in on him. There was a positive side to all this: Hood could read annual reports in peace; he could borrow them from the firm library for weeks. He could do the crossword puzzle and correspond with his accountant. The phone never stirred in his office. He knew the trouble that lay ahead. But he hadn't told his wife, hadn't sought the counsel of his friends, hadn't considered the future. He couldn't say it out loud. He knew what was coming.

While crosshatching his face each morning with the Wilkinson double-bonded, Hood swore that he would never live life like George Clair, at the expense of others, if he ever worked again — after that pink slip turned up in his In box. He would be a benevolent supervisor, a friend and confidante to working men and women, no matter how insignificant their positions. Then he would arrive late at the office and shout down his secretary, Madeleine, for failing to make his coffee light enough. *Get your ass down there and get another cup!* He was digging his own grave and holding it like a pearl inside of him.

— Clair, George Clair, he said, overfilling his glass, plucking a single ice cube from the silver ice bucket. What a surprise.

— Benjie!

Firmly they clasped one another's hands. Clair's expression was inoffensive and slyly confused. Smile lines skirted the planes of his face.

— What the hell has you here in New Canaan?

— Well, it's the funniest thing, Benjamin. I've been talking with some investors — a little outside venture, you understand, between you and me — about a scheme to manufacture a new Styrofoam packaging. It's little S-shaped Styrofoam pieces that can help keep an item free from trauma during shipping. Really miraculous. Really remarkable. Delicate stuff, stuff that can get tossed around by the shippers, still arrives intact. It's just going nationwide, the way I see it, nationwide. Anyway, it turns out one of the principal thinkers behind the whole project is your neighbor Jim Williams. How about that!

Clair hoisted his glass a couple of inches. Benjamin was almost certain: Clair drank club soda and pretended it was gin and tonic. The blood rose in Hood's face. That Clair and Jim Williams were bedfellows now augured some consolidation of bad energy in the universe. It was evidence of an order that chilled his bones. Either a paranoid assumption about the world was correct and it was filled with plots by human souls, occasionally selfish, occasionally generous human souls — plots that they pursued compulsively, recklessly, without regard for those they might harm — or else there was a force that ordered human society, ordered even the coexistence of plots and meaninglessness, that located oil under Arab countries and dust under Israel, that parched Bangladesh and froze the Baffin Bay, that raised up Richard Nixon from Checkers to dash him at the Watergate Hotel — while he realized the largest margin of victory in a presidential election in decades.

Either way, Hood detested George Clair. Detested him. He was the truest suburban phony: without culture, without native character, who was compelled here and there only by expedience. Hood would have liked to yank tight Clair's squeaky-clean bow tie and to watch him, in the process, swell and burst.

— Well, hey, Benjamin said, isn't that a one-in-a-million coincidence? A real dreamer, Jim Williams. And the sort of guy to turn those dreams into, well, bottom-line realities.

— Darned right about that. Look here, Benj, whaddya make of this film of *The Exorcist*, you know, William Peter Blatty's novel? You think it's gonna work?

— Don't see how, Hood said. The star's a little girl. Just devil-worship stuff. I mean, maybe if the little girl was possessed by an Indian spirit, angered by the white man's occupation of his native . . . ancestral lands or something. No, that's not it, George. Tell you what I like right now: disaster films. And air hockey.

Hood knew what came next — the competition to excuse yourself first. Clair didn't want to talk to him any more than he wanted to talk to Clair. What they would do now, in unison — Hey, well, *great to talk*, see you Monday — was make a run at the hors d'oeuvres. Or suddenly recognize a face across the room. Whoever got out first won. So Hood was already searching the room as he spoke, distractedly. And as he came to the end of the sentence, as he spoke the words *air hockey,* he saw his mistress, Janey Williams, wife of the S-shaped Styrofoam-packaging king, across a crowded room.

— Whoa, big fella, Hood mumbled, you gotta —

Only to find that Clair had already turned away. Clair was engaged with Maura O'Brien. Probably getting some inexpensive advice about a urological condition.

Janey was in black, silk pajamas, the top opened to just below her breasts. No bra. At her cleavage, turquoise beads swayed. As she leaned down to take up her drink, she stilled the shimmering pajama top with one hand. Her earth-colored lipstick and eye shadow matched her brown stiletto heels. Her frosted-blond hair was flawlessly arranged, like a fiberglass waterfall. Hood's first sensation was of reunion, of wholeness and conjunction, like he had the rollerskate and she had the key. But the feeling soured almost immediately, because he remembered the afternoon.

Janey pretended to be occupied with a vase of flowers beside the trapeze chair — chrome and steel with a pure rubber sling — in which the Halfords' cat was curled.

He made for her like any spurned lover.

— Oh, Jeez, Benjie, she said, fingering her beads. Well, here you are.

— Damn right, but where the hell were you?

— What are you talking about?

— Don't bullshit me around, Janey. Hood was whispering, but he was caught in some tidal or astrological imperative, some mood that would not be stopped, and the words poured from him as though their syntax was *using him* to express some mood. He felt, suddenly, that he might even cry.

— Jesus Christ, I waited around for more than a half hour, in the dark, in nothing but my boxer shorts, no wait, with the light on, so anybody could have come by and seen me in the window. What's that all about? What the hell happened?

Janey sipped. She set the drink down on the table, beside the vase.

— A prior engagement overcame me.

— What do you mean? What kind of stuff is this? I mean —

— Listen, Benjamin Hood, I have obligations that precede your . . . from before you showed up in my life. One or two, you know, good-natured encounters, that doesn't mean I'm . . . I'm not just some toy for you. When I remembered some chores I wanted to get done before the party, I just did them, that's all, because I wanted to do them before I saw Jimmy. I just did them. And that's how it's going to be.

The cat lolled on the chair in front of them. Hood's face was inches from Janey's. He mumbled.

— I don't know how to take this. And what do you mean, *Jimmy?* I thought you said —

— How you take it isn't all that interesting to me, Benjamin. I'm sorry —

— I just can't believe you would be so . . .

The talk stalled. The two of them fell to watching other molecules of conversation cleave and sunder. They circulated. Fragments of sense came and went in the room, evanescent fragments. Sobriety was dwindling. All over the room. The New York Mets and the oil crisis, Watergate and Rod Laver and Billie Jean King, and the unacceptable new rector at the Episcopalian church — all mixed up. No calamity would organize these fragments, no moment of high gossip. Ford had ended the production of the beloved convertible in July of this year. Modular furniture, flared trousers, plaids on plaids. Noise.

Janey lit a Virginia Slims and French-inhaled it.

— Things aren't going well for me, Hood said. You know, Elena is very unhappy and the office has become a really desperate situation. Really desperate. I wish you didn't have to make things hard, Janey. I don't understand why you have to. I guess I was dumb, but I was sort of counting on you.

— I'm not *making* it anything, she said. The situation just *is* difficult. And I'll tell you this, Benjamin, your domestic . . . your home life is no worse or better than anyone else's. In my house, we're living separate lives. Separate floors, separate lives, separate everything. And I don't go expecting a little afternoon something-or-other to alter that. A couple of hours with you isn't going to change that. I'm not going to threaten my family, my security, just so that I can listen to your problems at the office, you know?

— But why didn't you just say so? Why couldn't we talk —

— I —

— And why did you leave the lingerie out for me?

— What lingerie? I went to the store for God's sake, to Shopwell. I had to get some things before Jimmy came back. I just remembered. Okay? Are my answers good enough? What are you, a special prosecutor or something? And what do you mean about the lingerie?

— Never mind, Hood said.

— Hey, wait just a second —

— I thought when you didn't turn up that you were hiding somewhere. I thought maybe you —

— You what?

He began slowly, but then, as Hood re-created the details, he became a sort of erotic revenant. He gulped the last of his drink — his equilibrium was really beginning to fall away, like the first stage of an *Apollo* rocket. He reveled in the hot flashes, in the indignity of his predicament.

— I searched the house. I figured you were hiding, in a merry widow or something, in the closets, or else behind some piece of furniture. I figured you were there. I thought there was more to it than there was. So then I got to the bathroom and I saw the lingerie. I thought that it was part of a trail, a romantic trail or something, or it was a reminder of you. Something to be contemplated, you know, drunk in or something, you know? I was looking around, that's all.

— You need help, Benjamin. That was just out to dry. I was leaving things out to dry. *Delicates*. What did you *do* with my clothes?

He was flattered by the degradation of his adultery, and as he told the story he felt its shame and joy. He knew he wished to be caught, that it was always the cuckold or the betrayed who was honored by the adulterer. And he was a liar, too, an exaggerator. Hood's past lies swirled in this next moment of fiction, these past lies fluttered and squirmed in this liar's chrysalis. He was thinking about padded expense accounts and cheating on exams as he spoke:

— I took it, the garter belt, to your dresser and buried it with its compatriots, with the lacy underthings, with the slips and panties and bras and stockings.

— Jesus, you are a mess, Benjamin. You're a case history of hung-up behavior. Where's your wife?

— I don't know. She was a little upset about the, uh, bowl out front. She ran in ahead of me. Probably in the kitchen. Planning something, some covert activity in the kitchen.

He snickered desperately.

They moved over to the couch, a Stendig, designed by Ennio Chiggio and arranged in a semicircle with a big apostrophe at the end, where Hood now rested his weary feet. An earnest bunch of locals, dressed in plaid shirts and skirts and jackets, in double-knit trousers, in gray flannel, in velour and polyester, was conglomerated at the end of the couch, the system of islands. Dave Gorman, a fixture at the promiscuous events of New Canaan, was plundering the novels of Kurt Vonnegut, Jr. — the Dresden firebombing and Ice Nine — in an effort to impress a young and attractive woman beside him. *Welcome to the Monkey House,* he said, had been a seminal influence for him. No one on the end of the couch seemed to know what he was talking about. Gorman was in some kind of import/export business, which Hood figured meant drugs. And sure enough, as Gorman spoke he was lighting a flaccid little marijuana cigarette.

Hood had never tried the stuff though it turned up at the margins of New Canaan parties — to the consternation of the older generation, those who had been established in town for some time. But soon the joint came his way. Gorman leaned into Janey and Hood's sullen truce:

— Benjamin, give it a try, why don't you? This stuff will make some sense out of those larger questions. Promise you. Do yourself a favor.

Gorman grinned.

— Thanks for the advice, Dave, Hood said, waving the joint away affably. But then some carelessness overcame him, and he took up that tiny, aromatic cigarette and clamped it between his lips. He tugged on it, holding the smoke in his lungs, as he had seen it done on film and television.

— Good shit, he cackled, hacking and erupting with smoke as he passed it to Janey.

— Sure is good shit, Gorman said. It's opiated. I had it in my chamber for a while. I was smoking this other —

— It's what? Hood said.

— Don't fret, Benj, it's —

— Darn it, Dave.

Hood rose unsteadily, clapped his hand on the top of the modular sofa to steady himself, and stumbled, because it was nothing more than a piece of polyurethane mush, that sofa, steadied himself by grabbing hold of Janey, and then hastened to the bar, to preempt his new intoxication.

In the white noise of American conversation he picked up voices the way one discerns a particular orchestral instrument — the triangle, the viola d'amore — in the grand narrative sweep of a concerto or symphony. As he filled his drink, one name kept reappearing, like a leitmotiv. Milton Friedman. Across the room there was this extravagant praise for this economist who was violently opposed to the wage-and-price freezes of Nixon, who advocated such locally popular measures as the abolition of Social Security, the elimination of governmental aid to education, and the end of the minimum wage.

— Washington's solution to a problem is a problem, too, said a voice as Hood loaded his glass using the impressively ample ice tongs. Take the control of airfares. Friedman said this in an interview. This is how the whole thing works. If you didn't have this price fixing, airfares would be probably half of what they are now. Look at California. California has got its own airline within the state, and that's an airline that's not subject to the fare guidelines. None at all. Compare Sacramento to L.A. on Pacific Northwest with the price-fixed fares from L.A. to Reno — same distance more or less. Just look at the difference! The market prices are about *60 percent of the government's prices* —

Poor Madeline Gadd was stuck listening to this shit, and Hood was not surprised she was reapplying caramel-colored lipstick in a small compact mirror as she listened absently. Jack Moellering, the Friedman apologist, was, as he spoke, fixed raptly on the slit up the side of Madeline's harem pants.

— Supply and demand . . . less restriction, Moellering was saying. Less restriction.

The laissez-faire stuff was really traveling around the room. Several feet away, by the mantel, Bobby Haskell, normally a guy who concentrated on paddle tennis to the exclusion of all other forms of conversation, was proposing that unions were a kind of labor monopoly, just an antitrust problem in the arena of labor.

These Friedman arias swooped around one another like the diverging themes of a duet, until Hood began to experience the opera of economics as just that, an opera, an opera full of good stories: the chance of great or mean birth, the influx and egress of fortunes honest and swindled, the plunging and soaring of government statistics along the g- and f-clefs of official statistical graphs and indexes. Friedman's beloved money supply, new housing starts, durable goods, factory inventories, auto sales, and, of course, *Variety*'s top-grossing films of the week — each had its thrill of victory, its agony of defeat. Hood heard the long, bickering synopsis of lives in recitative, the surge of fine melody in an investment success, and the elaboration of a reversal in the sudden downturn in the market. The paisley and earth colors in the room swam before his intoxicated eyes, but the music of his business, the investment business, was music to his ears. America rose and fell on the melody of New Canaan's songs of the economy. Songs sung by a Jewish economist and mimicked by WASPs who would have thought twice before playing golf with the guy.

Hood was capable of formulating one last coherent thought: they were all scattered like seeds, flying outward from the primal fist of Europe long ago. Hood circled the room alone, and no companion — not Elena, not Janey Williams, not George Clair or Dave Gorman (now slumped by himself on the modular sofa) — would salve his isolation. He was as alone as Elena, who couldn't break a silence with a stranger, as alone as some fur trapper in the first light, in the wilderness of the new continent.

Janey was gone anyway, vanished. And so was George Clair. He didn't recognize any of these people. Outside, in the dim light of outdoor lamps, snow accumulated. In the corner of the room, for a split second, Hood thought he saw Buddy Hackett.

MORE ABOUT TELEVISION. From *Sunrise Semester* to *Love, American Style,* from *Banacek* to *The New Price Is Right,* television served as the structured time, the safe harbor for Wendy Hood. She gave the dial a spin, she let it land wherever it would, afternoons when she avoided extracurriculars — field hockey or Bible study or Super-8 Cinematography or the Quilting Club — mornings when her parents weren't up or had left early for church, evenings when, again, she was by herself.

She loved *Electric Company* and *Sesame Street* though she was too old for them, loved the hyperbole of puppets and the restless, kinetic pacing of these programs. The shape of advertisements ruled the world. Advertisements and comic books and teen fanzines. As she watched television, she gave herself back to her childhood, to some part of herself that had never passed beyond that demographic category. But she also loved reruns: *The Flying Nun, Petticoat Junction, Green Acres,* and *Family Affair.* She loved Gene Rayburn and Monty Hall. She respected enforcers of justice, such as Cannon, Kojak, and Toma — Tony Musante, so cute — and elegies to place, like *Streets of San Francisco* and *Hawaii Five-O;* she loved variety programs, *Sonny and Cher* and *Flip Wilson* and *Andy Williams* and

Ray Stevens, who had parlayed his hit "Everything Is Beautiful" into a summer replacement program that year; but she lived for the Saturday night horror films — *Chiller Theater* and *Creature Features.*

The *Chiller* theme's graphic was especially satisfying, a six-fingered hand emerging from some rank Paleolithic ooze. This was a gigantic hand — it dwarfed, just behind it, a tree plucked clean as a piece of driftwood, so that you could get a sense of the scale — a hand the size of a Mack truck. The fingers waved around a little bit, as though signaling to you not to abandon the show during the commercial. Meanwhile, a deep and ominous voice, a voice kind of like the one that announced the radio spots for local drag- and stock-car racing, intoned the word *chiller.* Long, low, and slow, this guy declaimed it, like it was a wind-borne message of evil sweeping across a steppe.

Mostly she watched television alone, since the days were gone when Paul snuggled with her through the horror flicks. She was alone that Friday night in the drafty library along the Silvermine River. She had a Duraflame log in the fireplace and a blanket wrapped around her, but the cold was relentless anyway. Snow fell, cascading, out in the driveway. Gales circled the house like the sound effects of low-budget movies. On the box, during the breaks, WPIX heralded tomorrow evening's dramatic television presentation — first ever — of the Shroud of Turin. Through these announcements Wendy had grown accustomed to this textile, to the faint traces of a likeness there, and in the midst of this dreamy evening of martyrdom and B-films, the scary weather outside seemed to be appropriate, like Old Testament vengeance.

She had played hooky during Sunday School and confirmation classes. Unitarian services: her mother had left the church of her birth and was on this Unitarian kick, though she still tried to keep Wendy interested in Episcopalianism. All the neighbors went. Wendy hated the discipline of waking early on Sunday — though she was up by then anyway — the donning of starchy and uncomfortable clothes, the confusing silence whenever she prayed, the confusing banter of church doctrine. Wendy felt the American Indians had the most reliable religion — with their peyote buttons and tricksters. When her mother scrunched up her face and dispensed morality, Wendy's ambition was to be as unlike her mother as possible in every way. In fact, this was almost always her ambition. Her mother's judgmental rap was her only real conversation. Sometimes Wendy felt her mom had turned deaf-mute or slipped into a coma; other times, the significance of Elena Hood's unhappiness, in the midst of plenty, in the midst of a town with forests, streams, and shopkeepers who remembered your name, a town of school crossing-guards who told you to dress warmly and policemen whose kids were the stars of the football team — the significance of her mother's unhappiness settled over the house and gathered all of the Hoods around it.

To avoid this trouble, Wendy got herself into trouble elsewhere. At a slumber party after her birthday, earlier in this very month, she had put her tongue in Debby Armitage's vagina. It happened suddenly, as if she hadn't been responsible for it somehow. She could recall the moment she yanked down her own pajamas and hiked up Debby's nightgown. In the corner, Sally Miller watched with an expression of excitement and horror both. Debby stood on the bed, her long, pubescent lower half uncovered except for heavy socks. Wendy parted Debby's legs gently, and in a posture that could only be described as religious, importunate, she craned upward to fit the tip of her tongue under the bed of Debby's soft, new, blond pubic hair. With one hand she cradled the perfect, divine curve of her friend's ass.

The taste was no taste at all. There was none of the rich marine life that she had read about in Paul's stash of sexually explicit materials. Debby Armitage was as clean as church clothes. No arousal disturbed the folds and recesses of Debby's vagina; no moisture, besides what moisture Wendy's tongue brought there. Still, the two of them went on with it. Sally Miller watched as Debby and Wendy positioned one another for mutual oral gratification — it was a position that dawned on them the way a small child stumbles upon the revelation of placing round pegs in round holes; Sally was watching in a state of frightened excitement, it seemed, and later in a state of arousal, though Debby and Wendy were no nearer a climax of any kind than if they had been outside raking leaves.

Sally, however, was able to take the story public at Saxe Junior High. She was still in the eighth grade. Because of her nonparticipation, she could go public. She could offer her opinions as observer and critic. She could stonewall on the subject of her own motives. Wendy had never wished, even in her idle algebra class fantasies, that she was a hummingbird darting between the legs of Debby Armitage. Not really. Though she hankered after some association with the people of her town, some sense of community that stuck deeper than the country club stuff. On the other hand, there was something compulsive about the way she got entangled, as though Wendy herself had picked the posture and activity that would most make her feel ashamed.

This strategy turned out to be pretty effective. Sally

Miller talked her up. Talked up her transgression, her instigation, her perversion. Her reputation as a slut spread quickly along the corridors of Saxe and across the street to the high school. She could sense at a distance of twenty or thirty lockers the snickering threesomes of popular girls. Now Sally Miller entombed herself in the Saxe library, that resource of the uncool, and even abandoned her Friday elective across the street at the high school, co-ed sports, in order to avoid Wendy Hood. At the same time, Debby Armitage was Wendy's friend for life, and actually Wendy didn't like her that much at all. Debby was a whiner.

So she changed the channel again, turned away from advertisements for the Shroud of Turin (Robert Conrad to host), to watch instead a *Movie of the Week* about a woman who was buried alive by avaricious kidnappers, buried alive and kept that way in a lighted, ventilated box (with one of those gerbil spouts in it, through which she could suck in water and nutrients). Ants swarmed over the woman.

In the midst of this drama, Wendy's brother called.

— Weather reports are bad, he said, like much snow and sleet and frozen highways and byways.

Wendy hadn't heard anything of the kind. But the snow was already falling.

— Well, you think I should come home now? Or should I wait until, you know, the absolutely last train out of Grand Central, which would be like maybe ten after eleven?

She told him *they* were out and that guessing from her dad's condition they weren't gonna wait up for Paul. *They* would fall into bed swiftly and permanently. Which meant no car service, no car service from the station. He could take a taxi. He could come back whenever he wanted.

— The thing is, Wendy said, you're not being watched. Take a cab.

— No one believes in the weather anymore, Paul said. He asked what she was doing and she described in detail the inside of the woman's buried-alive coffin and her strangled, desperate screams. Wendy even simulated a scream, a little yelp of confinement.

— But you know she's the mother from *Please Don't Eat the Daisies,* Wendy said, or one of those, *Ghost and Mrs. Muir,* so it's not like she's incredibly scary or anything.

— You mean to say you are just gonna hang around the house on a Friday night when *school's out?*

— I've got plans, Wendy said.

Abruptly, Paul called her *baby doll* and signed off. It happened all at once. There was a lonesome sound to his farewell, and it reminded her of the way her father would never say good-bye on the phone, the way he hastened to disconnect first.

Wendy wanted to tell Paul she missed him, that she had survived the long, painful stretches of junior high with tales of his good life away from home. Though she had sent him this letter one time, this letter explaining her feelings, she was never sure if it had been received. She thought Paul got all the breaks. He was the smarter one, the badly adapted one. There was no discussion of her being sent away, too. Wendy was a beauty, a pixie, a nymph, a sorceress, but she wasn't going to be any captain of industry. She could work the rooms of the P.T.A. Paul got sent away back at some moment when Valley Road was different, when family life was different, when there was movement between the generations, when there was exchange of sentiment and gifts and ideas and stories. Or that's how

Wendy thought sometimes. It was pretty obvious, actually, that no such time had ever existed.

In an interminable commercial break, Wendy gathered up the blanket and set out about the unheated and unlit portions of the house, looking for a sweater she'd left down here somewhere. She surveyed the exposed beams and warped floors, the masonry and wrought-iron latches of historic construction. The house was as cold as a tomb. The ghost of Mark Staples, repressive Episcopal minister and one-time owner of 129 Valley Road, tracked her movements. As Wendy imagined him, he was a *Chiller Theater* ghost, a flapping white sheet, with strings exposed and tennis shoes peaking from beneath. He was so like a Hood — so trapped in indecision, so glum, such a professional bumbler — that he was the perfect ghost for them, the perfect ancestor. She could feel his Halloween exoskeleton girding her. She was creeped out. Forget her sweater. It was lost. She didn't need it.

The decision to head back to the Williamses came soon after this tour. She foolishly settled in to watch first the grasping hand, and then the arm, of the buried woman from *Please Don't Eat the Daisies* struggling up from beneath the surface of her tomb. A team of policemen and paramedics were racing toward the spot where she was buried — they had been tipped off somehow. In the meantime, in the woman's back brain, in the most obscure recesses of cognition, she had effected an escape. Her hands, independent of the rest of her, pushed up through soft earth, grasping.

In a malevolent dusk, the buried woman stood now on a narrow spit of earth, shreds of some Beverly Hills evening gown barely concealing her transparent flesh. Shroud of Turin. What was left of her, as she reached out, covered with shit and pitch and dirt? The trauma had lodged in this woman, Wendy thought, the way a germ lodges in a dead body, to begin its fervent decomposition. The trauma might be wrestled into a repose, at a place like Silver Meadow, but it was never going to disappear.

Wendy had on her poncho and her skintight ski pants before the credits were even rolling. Her imagination had gotten the best of her. She needed a change. Her imagination wheeled around the house like an additional poltergeist. Wendy wanted to read *Nancy Drew* and have training wheels. She wanted deviled ham on white bread or sloppy joes or Twinkies. She wanted a mom who said that soup was good food and who reminded her to chew each bite thirty-two times. She wanted the basic food groups and a program of fitness. She wanted a childhood in which she was a kid.

The storm was in its second phase. Like wage-and-price controls. The methodical roar of the wind leveled out all unusual night sounds. The whole environment, the *ecosystem,* had become this one thing. Wendy felt she was at the center of it as she walked up the driveway, that she was the last girl on earth, that God had selected her and New Canaan as the center of His attention. The trees were doubled over, weary with wind and ice. The snow fell like jagged hunks of glass onto crusty, sheer surfaces. Wendy sank through the rippling, drifting expanses of crystallized stuff halfway to her knees. The crust scored her ankles and calves, drenched through the layers of her socks.

On the main roads, the state of emergency cranked itself up. The mechanized and hydraulic progress of plows and sanding and salting vehicles was somber and methodical. Their lights lingered in the air like the afterglow of bombardment. Wendy could walk in the narrow tracks of these vehicles without coming upon any other fearless traveler. Up the hill, she passed back over the path she had already marked out twice that day. Past Silver Meadow.

She called Mike's name at the Williamses' front door. Called it lustily and desperately. Called it as though she were pronouncing the exact whereabouts of her most secret longitudes. Called it as though if she were alone another minute she would have to be dragged down the road to the hospital and straitjacketed. She beseeched, she argued. No answer came. But the door was open and the front hall invitingly lit. She entered and crept around the house room by room. She was curious like any kid her age. She searched for Mike around the dining room table, in the living room, out on the patio — Mrs. Williams seemed to have given up halfway the process of moving her houseplants in for the winter. She looked for him in the kitchen, and stole a pair of Devil Dogs from the counter. Then she took a spin through the basement, searching in vain for Mike through the intricate architecture of Bazooka crates. The site of that afternoon's disgrace had a bracing and shameful effect.

Then she headed for the stairs.

Mike's trick buzzer greeted her as she reached for his doorknob. It broke the timeless quiet of the house. The hall light was on, but the place was empty. Wendy tried the door again, it buzzed again, and then she just pushed through the noise and opened the door six inches. Mike was turned away in his bed, curled over a pillow as if he had been humping it. Wendy flung back the door and without warning jumped the sleeping figure, flew like a banshee across the room haloed by her blond mane — only to find that it wasn't Mike at all, but some pajamas stuffed with dirty T-shirts and B.V.D.'s and sweat socks. What a joker.

He'd pulled that cartoon thing. He'd made a dummy of himself.

The house belonged to her. She held a worn T-shirt to her small, dainty nose and breathed deeply from it. She searched, knowing from Paul where such things were hidden, and found Mike's collection of pornography, in the closet. She even found a ladies' undergarment, still moist with some incriminating glue. At first the sticky lingerie shocked her and she dropped it gingerly to the floor. But then she felt some pity about the necessity of hiding those stolen bras or panties, about the shame and remorse attached to this prop. Choking the chicken, jerking the gherkin, polishing the nightstick, flogging the bishop, spindling your fist: the loneliness and anxiety that had Mike hiding himself away — she felt sad about it right then. Wendy decided to take the garment with her, and shoved it under her shirt, tucking it into the belt line of her powder blue ski pants. It was gross, but she liked it.

And then she went for a peek at the water bed. Mike had showed it to her once before. They had stood on the threshold of the master bedroom like it was one of those roped-off historic homes exhibits — like FDR's house, where they'd had to go on a field trip when she was nine — and watched the water bed. Mike hurried over to disturb its surface. She remembered it was a sunny day in early autumn, and she followed him to the side of the bed to sink her hand into its vinyl blubber. Then they hastily retreated to the doorway and watched it ripple and wave.

Mike was afraid of the master bedroom. The way she was afraid of her own parents' room. The idea of her father sleeping, vulnerable, maybe with one of those nocturnal boners, or in plain fetal position — it disgusted her. She preferred to think of him awake long hours, reading some tome on business or politics. She figured she could take comfort in the notion that her parents never made love. They didn't seem attracted to each other anyway.

But here in the Williamses' house, she was fearless. And since the door to the master bedroom was open, and since she could see that the water bed was unoccupied, she just settled right into it. She was engulfed in its amniotic comfort. It sloshed protoplasmically to one side and then shifted back into the center. She pulled the hand-sewn quilt at the foot of the bed over her — and then kicked it off again. She had smushed the Devil Dogs a little bit in all this activity, but now she opened them up anyway. They would be good whatever their shape.

And then she was interrupted.

— What are you doing?

Sandy Williams. He'd snuck up on her. Sneaking was his passion, so this wasn't a surprise. His tone wasn't outraged or even interested particularly. He just had to ask.

Wendy was startled up to the edge of the bed. She smoothed her poncho down over her lap. For a while she couldn't think how to answer. Then:

— What team is that on your jammies, little Sandy? Her mouth was jammed with Devil Dog. She stood on the hard surface of the floor again, the water stirring uneasily behind her.

— Oakland Raiders. But I don't follow football.

— Hand-me-downs?

Sandy said nothing. Just stood in the doorway. He was really short for his age. In his football pajamas and spectacles, with his cowlick and put-upon expression, he was an odd mixture of an infant and a middle-aged middle-manager. He didn't know where Mike was. His parents were at some party. The exchange of monosyllabic questions was short and unfriendly.

—So what are you doing in here?

—Just taking a look around, Wendy said. What are you doing here? I thought you were over at somebody's house for the night. Like anybody would have you over.

He turned and headed back down the hall. She wasn't thinking. She should have seen the light under his door. She should have known. Maybe there was no light, maybe he planned all his nefarious plans by penlight. Wendy followed, feeling leaden now, defeated, certain that her trespassing would be passed on to the Williamses. Suddenly she was afraid her father would tell them about her and Mike, too. She was caught between a bunch of bad examples of truancy. It was closing in on her. And she was only fourteen. —Sandy, she said, lemme see some of your models. C'mon, wait, what's going on?

He squinted at her from down the hall. His glasses were never strong enough. He wore a little clip-on sun-filter attachment on them these days, like a big-league outfielder. He padded around the banister and into his room without a reply. But he left the door open.

In the guest room, on the way by: rumpled bedding.

On his bed, beside him, Sandy had a G. I. Joe with Lifelike Hair, the newer model with the hippie grooming, the facial hair. There was a little scar on Joe's cheek, a vermilion, plastic scar. And he talked, too, when you pulled his dog tag. Sandy was quick to point out that his particular G. I. Joe, however, was malfunctioning. Joe had only one thing to say, no matter how many times you pulled the dog tag:

—Mayday! Mayday! Get this message back to base!

In his orange jumpsuit, Joe looked really comfortable, not at all like a P.O.W. or M.I.A. on the run. But Sandy had some grim plans for him. As Wendy looked on, Sandy was calmly tying a noose for his doll. He pulled the dog tag again.

— Back to base!

— Sometimes, Sandy said, he doesn't even make it all the way through.

— Mayday! Mayday! Joe said. Get this message back to base! Back to base! Back to base!

— Quit it, Sandy said, it's already driving me nuts.

Wendy cradled the helpless little man in her lap. She posed his limbs — so that he seemed to be giving some kind of Nazi salute, so that he waved, so that he was goose-stepping. Sandy attended to the noose, except when he was firing questions at her. Like about the weather.

— There's this crusty stuff, Wendy said. She had tracked the stuff in with her.

— You got that all over the water bed.

She probably had. Mud and sand and slush.

— Only a little.

— It's gonna get a lot colder tonight, Sandy said, I predict. Probably a blackout. Do you have candles in your house? I know where the candles are, and I have my own flashlight. Over there. Also, I know where every emergency exit is on this floor.

— So where's Mikey?

— I told you. How should I know?

Sandy looked up from his handiwork. He gave her a long once-over.

— But he's probably down at the hospital.

It would be a cool place to be. The way the grounds sloped down toward the Silvermine River. Tonight would be a good night to ride the refectory trays, as she and Paul had once done, down the hills. The trick was to bail out before you slid into the water. The tray shot out from under you, like some kind of low-flying bird, sailing out onto the Silvermine. They had to cross out into the river, on stepping stones, to recover the trays. Truly, though, the security guys had caught them, had run down the hill after them, slipping and skidding in their polished uniform shoes, to grab Paul by the shoulder and roughly commandeer his sled. She had a way with the Silver Meadow security cops. Paul never did.

— What's he doing down there?

— Looking for you, probably, Sandy said.

With that he stood, measuring by eye the distance from the top of the closet. He raised his makeshift lynching apparatus toward its anchor. Standing on a modern and insubstantial hammock-style desk chair, he tied the end of the rope around a nail he had already pounded into the top of the closet frame.

— This knot's called a bowline, he said.

He let the noose swing free now, and in the meager light of Sandy's swivel desk lamp its shadow swung with it, its ominous double.

— Mayday! Mayday!

— Not gonna give him a chance to share any last words, huh? Wendy said. She pulled the tags again.

— Get this message back to base! Back to base! To Base!

— Won't do any good, Sandy said. I've tried everything.

His tone was so woeful that Wendy was certain it was true. Disappointment about G. I. Joe with Lifelike Hair weighed heavily on Sandy Williams.

— Mayday! Mayday! Get this message back to base!

Sandy slid the chair back under the desk and stilled the noose, that awful pendulum.

— Okay, bring the prisoner here, he said.

— One more chance.

She couldn't let it go. Wendy climbed off the bed and carried G. I. Joe toward his executioner.

— Girls are always sticking up for the criminal. But I'm afraid, Sandy said thoughtfully, it's not gonna do any good.

Wendy yanked the dog tag one last time.

And behold:

— Major, incoming copter! Joe said.

— Far out!

— It's just chance, Sandy said. Maybe one time every fifty or so he says that, even though it's usually a different one. Something about a medic.

He folded his arms.

Together they stood over the prone body of G. I. Joe with Lifelike Hair, now supine on the folded comforter at the foot of Sandy's bed. Somehow the idea of trying him again, of going back to the well one more time, felt pointless to Wendy. She recognized a moment here in which she saw the machinations of chance in the universe, and she didn't want to ruin it. Sandy was adorable in this light. He couldn't wait. He wanted to dispatch Joe, because he had some dignity wrapped up in the notion of inferior goods and dumb culture and stupid America. He was one of those kids who spent hours in front of the television shouting *That would never happen*. Sandy Williams expected to be cheated. He was ready for it. And it came to pass almost every time, and in this way the world seemed good and true.

When he seized his doll, therefore, he pulled the elastic that connected the dog tag to its interior machinery as though he were going to strangle Joe with it. He seized it as though his certainty about being ripped off was the one thing he knew.

— We'll attack north at the next pass! Joe said.

Wendy noticed again how silent everything was, how silent the house was, now that the storm had settled in to do its worst for a while. Sandy was stunned by Joe's loquaciousness. Absently he scratched his testicles. He picked Joe up, shook him, held him up to his own ear.

— Let's hang him anyway.

— Sure, Wendy said.

So they did.

What's a noose but a slipknot? Joe fit snugly, and Sandy pulled the knot tight, and there he was, dangling. The whole gesture didn't satisfy, really. And it left Wendy and Sandy alone in the room. She asked if he could turn Joe's face to the wall and Sandy tried, but the rope was really wound up the wrong way. He kept spinning back around to face them.

And something strange was happening right then. Wendy noticed Sandy was sitting on the bed with his pillow across his lap. Some emotion was overtaking them. She knew what this meant. She knew that Sandy was emerging briefly from under the rock where he lived. Sandy had Wendy alone in his room, in this warm room, in the midst of a swirling winter storm when his brother wanted her, when his brother was looking for her maybe. The whole thing was a gigantic turn-on. Wendy wished she had a helium balloon and could inhale that stuff and whisper in her helium tongue in Sandy's ear. She wished he had booties on the ends of his pajama legs. She wanted to tickle him with a peacock feather. She wished he was standing naked under the swivel lamp wearing only hockey skates.

— Why've you been avoiding me? she said.

Sandy actually smiled.

— Not avoiding, he said. Then scowling again.

She slid up on the bed, and one by one with exaggerated slowness, she removed her snow boots, like they were stiletto heels. Fuck-me pumps. She knew what was under the pillow, she knew, like a little pinkie, like the stump of an amputated digit, Sandy's miniature, little penis. She slid up the bed beside him. She told him she wanted to be in his bed, between his sheets.

Sandy actually began to shake.

— We have to go to the guest room, he said. We can't stay in here. What if Mike . . . ? We should go in there and close the door. We can't stay here. My parents —

— Don't worry about them. They're at that party. They're getting drunk. Falling all over each other and making jokes about McGovern and stuff.

He looked like he was going to cry. Then he did. Wendy didn't feel exasperated, but she didn't feel sympathetic either. His tears were just embarrassing. He wasn't proud of them either. He tried to disguise their tracks; he was going to claim it was because he was tired, or because he had some special eye disorder, or because of his very strong glasses that even now he wore with a clip-on attachment. He didn't even know what the problem was. She asked him and he didn't know.

— It's just, it's just —

So Wendy took little Sandy Williams by the hand — his hands trembled and hers did, too — and led him around the corner into the guest room. She left the door just barely ajar, so that it would seem neither open nor closed on purpose, and together they settled themselves, as if they were going to be a photo portrait of young love, on the plaid comforter in the guest room.

— A drink? Wendy said.

Because the vodka was still there. It was right there on the table. Sandy was shocked by the request.

— You've never tasted this stuff? It's not like smoking pot, that's for sure. It's not as cool. But it'll do the trick, Charles.

A single glass remained from the afternoon. As she filled it, Wendy took a sort of pride in her work. She remembered the thrill of her own initiation, in which her brother had played an important part. The best thing about initiation was how it was sort of like destitution. It was destitution with trust. Sandy looked frail and willing and strong and old and vulnerable all at once. His glasses slid down his nose, on a glistening sheen, and stopped at the little bulb at the end of it. The vodka filled the bottom of the glass like liquid winter.

She held up the glass and Sandy held up the bottle and they clanked them together as they had seen adults do.

She tossed it back in one painful swallow. Sandy tried a tiny, little sip from the bottle, and when it had touched his palate he gagged. He coughed once and choked down the rest of the swallow. Wendy told him to try again. He wanted to do as well as Mikey, he was bound to move up in this matter of growing up, so Sandy filled the glass and threw back a whole shot. Drinking his first drink, Wendy thought, involved Sandy in a thousand trying decisions. All these components. But he got it down, and she figured he would get better at it. She had gotten better at it, on holidays when her parents let her, and on school days back behind Saxe with the delinquents, the junior high and freshmen delinquents, the adopted kids, the half-dozen working-class kids, the half-dozen blacks. And then there was the occasional afternoon when she just plain stole booze from her parents. Sure, there was always the worry that they were *marking the levels of the bottles with felt-tip laundry pens,* but she drank when she had to drink.

Sandy set her palm on the center of his chest:

— It feels warm.

— Your folks don't let you have any?

— Maybe a couple of times.

She knew they let Mikey taste.

— One more shot? she said.

She could feel the ease of it in her now; she could feel that the menace of the weather was a good thing, that the woman from *Please Don't Eat the Daisies* was doing fine. Any week now the woman would probably have a spot on *Love, American Style.* Wendy wasn't afraid of Sandy's naked body.

— Okay, he said.

And they drank again.

Outside, the weather trashed the landscaping.

When she wrapped her arms around him, she knew she could break him in half. She kissed Sandy; he consented to be kissed. Sandy had no taste. He was tasteless like tap water. She could feel his ideas all confused, his uncertainty. She opened the chest of his pajamas. This was how they wore them now on Noxzema commercials and in the movies, a couple buttons opened up at the neck, chest hair overgrowing. But Sandy was a downy little babe, not encumbered with a single dark hair. He leaned back so she could open the pajama top. Herself, she was doffing layer after layer, trying to keep the pace up — hard to do in winter — her sweater, her turtleneck, her T-shirt. And they rubbed their chests together, the tips of her breasts, just beginning to be breasts, and then they worked on the rest of their clothes. Wendy carefully pulled off ski pants and panties all at once — so that she could conceal the soiled garter belt, the one she had taken from Mike's room. Sandy was too preoccupied with his own nakedness to notice.

— Get 'em off, she said to him, laughing at the sound of haste. Laughing at her own forthrightness.

And pretty soon they were naked. His little soldier was at sharpest attention, like G. I. Joe with Lifelike Hair back when he was among the living.

— Under covers, Wendy said.

Sandy threw back the comforter and they slid under it. Sandy laughed again, and Wendy laughed, and the laughter was good. She took his hairless penis in her hand, and she cupped his hairless testicles, and she kissed his nipples, and they rolled around like that for a while.

— Have you had a nocturnal emission? she asked.

— Huh?

— That's the name for when you wake up and find this little pool of sticky stuff. Supposedly like after a sexy dream.

He shook his head.

— They didn't tell you this stuff yet? What planet do you live on?

Sandy didn't want to answer questions, though; he wanted to continue. When his knee pushed up between her legs, when his hip mashed against her, she shivered, but it didn't seem to be leading anywhere particularly. He didn't know what he was doing. She could kiss his little pig-in-a-blanket. But she realized pretty soon the futility of the whole thing. There weren't going to be any orgasms, simultaneous or even regular, old orgasms, in this guest room.

But maybe that was okay. She didn't know much about them anyway. Orgasm was a word she had looked up a dozen times, and still she didn't exactly know what it meant. Masturbation — excitation of the genitals, usually to orgasm, from the Latin *manus stuprare,* to defile by the hand. How many episodes, in the months before her first period, without anything but a nifty tingling. It was like the shock you got off a metal door handle after padding around in socks. Sodomy — any intercourse held to be abnormal, especially anal intercourse. Bestiality — sexual relations between a person and an animal. Huh? These things were impossible to imagine.

Orgasm was even harder to understand. Its only close relative in the word kingdom seemed to be something like *grace.* You could have grace explained to you a hundred times, but unless you got some, it was just air. One afternoon when Mikey had been busy humping away at her, suddenly part of his T-shirt right above his waist was soaked through, and then something overtook her, and she felt herself rushing up to a plateau. She pushed and shoved against Mikey, and then she just lost herself for a minute. She just slipped away entirely on some air mattress of breezes. It was like being spooked. It was an out-of-body experience, like grace.

She wasn't sure if that was one or not. But this was how she thought she understood that strange word, that word that seemed to come from some distant language-family, Tibeto-Burman or something very alien to the language of her own family. She didn't know if it had been an orgasm exactly, but she was chasing it anyway.

—I love you, Wendy, Sandy said.

—That's nice, Sandy, she said. I love *Chiller Theater* and *Nanny and the Professor.*

They lay there in just the light from the hall. This stillness seemed pretty close to contentment. Wendy knew she had done a powerful job of initiation.

—Another drink? she said.

—I guess so.

And she sat up and surveyed the carnage, the covers half-kicked off, the clothes scattered around the floor. Wendy liked the look of disorder. She filled the glass, spilling a little—on herself, on the sheets, down the sides of the glass—filled it all the way up.

—Are you drunk? she asked.

—I don't know, Sandy said. How do I know?

—I don't know either. You spin around. That's one way you know. You spin around when you try to lie down.

They enjoyed each other's warmth like refugees. Glad for the warmth, for the company. And then, because they weren't thinking very carefully about the night and its whirling array of parents and siblings, they fell tumultuously into sleep.

THE PARTY PEAKED around ten-thirty like a cheap acid trip.This party was going *through some changes.* Describing them, describing these changes — the personal growth, the group dynamics taking place at the Halfords' — would have taxed the keenest reader of *Psychology Today.* Thomas Harris, M.D., author of *I'm Okay — You're Okay,* put it this way: "Early in his work in the development of Transactional Analysis, Eric Berne observed that as you watch and listen to people you can see them change before your eyes. It is a total kind of change. There are simultaneous changes in facial expression, vocabulary, gestures, posture and body functions, which may cause the face to flush, the heart to pound, or the breathing to become rapid. We can observe these changes in everyone."

Elena didn't see how this transactional model was going to work for her. Though she was a reader of personal-growth books. She had read *Jonathan Livingston Seagull* and *The Teachings of Don Juan: A Yaqui Way of Knowledge* and *The Primal Scream* by Arthur Janov and *I'm Okay — You're Okay* and *Games People Play* by Eric Berne and *Notes to Myself* by Hugh Prather and *The Gestalt Approach and Eyewitness Therapy* by Fritz Perls and

Be Here Now by Ram Dass and *Soul on Ice* by Eldridge Cleaver and *I Never Promised You a Rose Garden* and *The Divided Self* and *Human Sexual Response* and *Island* by Aldous Huxley and *The Tibetan Book of the Dead* and *The Hobbit* and *The Lord of the Rings*. She read this stuff, but it didn't help her at parties.

And the party itself was of two minds, one mind in which the selection of house keys was a worthy and modern preoccupation, and one mind in which the whole game was a shame. Some people felt both ways, and some shifted back and forth between these two *belief systems*.

Uncomfortable as she was, how was Elena to account for the change that had overcome her? How was Elena to account for the joy that seized her not long after her arrival at the party? New Canaan society crept around trying to make decisions about the keys, about the repercussions of its participation. The conversations became vague, Elena noticed, as husbands and wives tried to avoid one another. They slunk from the bar to their conversations with eyes downcast, as Elena herself was avoiding Benjamin. Still, she found herself suddenly elated at the party; there was no other way to put it. She felt the loosening of the constraints that had bound her since she had come of age, and she realized she would play. She would select a key. She would clutch it to her, permit it to dangle around her neck, between her small, subdued breasts. She would play.

This decision was a function of her Parent, her Child, or her Adult. A function of one or more of the three. The Parent, of course, was a huge collection of recordings in the brain of "unquestioned or imposed external events perceived by a person in his or her early years," and the Child was the recorded responses to this first collection of "tapes." Adult data, in the meantime, accumulated "as a result of the child's ability to find out for himself what is different about life from the 'taught concept' of life in his Parent and the 'felt concept' in his Child."

The results of the battles that took place in these three *phenomenological realities* were the Four Life Positions: I'm Not Okay — You're Okay, I'm Not Okay — You're Not Okay, I'm Okay — You're Not Okay, and the paradisaical I'm Okay — You're Okay. One of these four had its hooks in Elena.

Any analysis of her mood would have to take into account the material that led up to this moment. She had spent the afternoon thinking about her family. She then confronted her husband about his infidelity and agreed to attend a party — as a good-faith promise — where her husband's mistress was likely to be present. Somewhere in this decision to attend — this good-faith decision that had simply come to her — lurked the seeds of this present instance of serenity. She had admitted to herself for a moment that her husband's infidelity was, in the end, his own business, however awful it made her feel. Or as they said in *est:* "You are at the cause of whatever ill you suffer, no matter what it is. It's time now to accept responsibility for it. That willingness to be responsible is the key." Elena created her world.

Thomas Harris, M.D.: "Three things led people to change. One was that they hurt sufficiently. Another thing that made people change was a slow type of despair called ennui, or boredom. And, finally, people changed because of the sudden discovery that they could." This was *the* Adventure in Contentment. To find in the circumstances around you the lemonade, the sustenance, the opportunity of the day. This is a gift indeed. As Hugh Prather said, Elena remembered: "open / and alert / empty / and available / human / and / alive waiting / (without purpose) / ready / (without wanting) / existing (without needing)."

Nonetheless, when Elena learned about the key party, she was stuck in Benjamin's own constrictive system of decision making. It was hard for her to open up, to *be* in her own needs, wants. She was stuck in the moment when Benjamin would somehow, through some prestidigitation, attach their house key, with its little equine key ring, to Janey Williams's hand. She was attached to the look on her son's face when Janey and Benjamin would slip out the front door, on some Saturday morning, to have breakfast in Darien or Norwalk, where no one would see them. No one but the other couples slipping out.

In this blue mood, she snuck in the door, past Dot and Rob Halford, past the Armitages, the Sawyers, the Steeles, the Boyles, the Gormans, the Jacobsens, the Hamiltons, the Gadds, the Earles, the Fullers, the Buckleys, the Regans, the Bolands, the Conrads, the Millers. Past the old families of New Canaan, the Benedicts, the Bootons, the Carters, the Newports, the Eels, the Finches, the Hanforts, the Hoytts, the Kellers, the Lockwells, the Prindels, the Seelys, the Slausons, the Talmadges, the Tarkingtons, the Tuttles, the Wellses. And past the new elite crop of divorced New Canaanites — Chuck Spofford, June Devereaux, Tommy Finletter, Nina Kellogg. She avoided the living room, where Janey Williams was already situated, heading instead for the kitchen and the library. Here she darted around conversations for an hour or more, never staying long enough to complete a thought or register an intimacy. She helped Dot, who disdained caterers, load up the hors d'oeuvre trays. Then she had a conversation with George Clair, a man her husband couldn't stand. Seemed nice enough. After this, her first stop was the bathroom, where she sat for a while crying and applying prudent amounts of the makeup before the medicine-cabinet mirror.

Right then, it didn't seem like much had changed or that much would change. But the fact is that most of us have mood changes as each part of our P-A-C (Parent-Adult-Child) makes its contribution to our behavior. "Sometimes the reasons for our mutability are elusive or do not seem to be related to any special signal in the present." While Elena was crying, though, Mark Boland entered the bathroom without knocking — it had no satisfactory latch — and found her — legs uncrossed and panties stretched between her kneecaps like a fancy wrapping paper — applying tan lipstick. Combs surrounded her, stuck up on all four walls. Dot Halford collected combs.

Boland blushed terribly, stammered an apology, and slammed the door. This was the real beginning of the evening's comedy.

When she emerged, she could sense the key party in the air like the grope games of elementary school. Spin the Bottle. Post Office. She was operating according to the promptings of chance now. She couldn't go any lower anyway. She would talk to whomever she talked to; she would let the conversation rise and fall like the wind battering the house with its arctic freight; she would dance to records by Antonio Carlos Jobim, the master of Bossa Nova, or to *Switched-On Bach* by Walter Carlos, or to the Carole King LP everyone seemed to have; she would accept any hors d'oeuvre offered; she would accept token offerings of drug or drink; she would go with whoever was suggested by the serving bowl in the front hall.

So when Elena emerged from the bathroom, it was as a butterfly sprung from the cocoon. Elena searched for the face of her seducer, wondering. Would he be hunched and remote? Would his posture be as perfect as freshly milled planking? And the first person this new Elena O'Malley Hood looked for was Mark Boland — the very man who had seen her in the bathroom. Mark, it turned out, was talking with Maria Conrad and her teenaged son, Neil. Both Boland and Maria were dressed in styles that had long since passed into attics and Goodwill bins. Mark's rep tie could have come from any postwar fall sale. Maria was arrayed in a simple, dependable plaid skirt.

Boland, who had lived for twenty years on Heather Drive, down near the Norwalk border, was an unofficial historian of the town in which he lived. As such, his dullness was legendary. He was a juggernaut of tedium. Even Elena, who on occasion sought out the bores of a party and built with them a fortress of social insignificance, had trouble with him. At the first sign of party discomfort, he sank into a long disquisition on the shoe factories that propped up the local economy in the nineteenth century — why, for two decades New Canaan was the second-largest shoe-manufacturing center in the country! — where the old factories had been situated (one on the site of the present firehouse) and how the industry weakened after 1850. *Did you know* they tried to build a railroad to attract business at that point, but no one was taking!

Hard to imagine that Boland was a regular fixture on the party circuit until you realized that behind the white hair and thick glasses lurked the true cheater's heart. He hated his wife. He had slapped a drink out of her hand in public once, when he was losing a game of backgammon at the country club; he had insulted her to her friends. It had gotten back to her. Still they were married. Still he talked. Sometimes you saw him trapping the same victim for forty-five minutes or more. The endless chatter about history or local elections or town meetings concealed some empty part of himself — the area where he buffered his own wounds, where he concealed the regret about his own miserable life. And since he no longer worked — Boland had invested in Xerox at the right moment — he had nowhere to take his misanthropy but to parties. But as the years went by, Elena noticed, his wife grew stronger. She grew more self-assured. She never appeared at parties with him. She seemed forever to be crossing Fairfield County on the Merritt Parkway in search of the arts, wherever they lurked. Betty Boland had become, in her dark green Mercedes-Benz, one of the informed of New Canaan. Elena imagined that the two of them slept in separate rooms now. Like so many of the older, Protestant couples, they were courteous, charming, and estranged.

So Mark Boland wanted a little of this key business. And that was why Elena was talking to him. She wanted to see it up close.

— Goodness, Elena, I'm sorry, he said.

— Not at all, she said. These things happen. Just have to get back on the horse, I guess. That's why you show up *chez* Halford. You never know how it's going to turn out.

Boland smiled. A little too long.

— Yes, that's right.

— Mark and I were just talking about the weather, Maria interrupted.

— The weather, Elena said.

— Yes, well, it's supposed to freeze up tonight. Quite dangerous by morning time, Maria said.

— Most dangerous storm in some time, Boland said. Have you and Benjamin made arrangements?

— Arrangements?

— Well, yes.

And when this aside had been exhausted, Boland launched back into his historical ramblings. Canaan Parish, separated by the Perambulation Line, he was saying, had at one time been composed of a Stamford section and a Norwalk section. Probably they had storms then, too, storms of this very type. The wall that marked the Peramublation Line had probably been rebuilt many times because of these storms. Did you know a small piece of it still stood behind the new high school? A tiny bit of spittle collected at the corners of Boland's mouth as he spoke, as though he were parched. It was an erotic froth, the milk of erotic starvation. On he went, about the differences between the New Haven Colony, which founded Norwalk in 1651, and the Connecticut Colony, which founded Stamford (or Stanford, because that's what it was called then) in 1650. In 1686, when the Perambulation Line was first erected, New Canaan was still entirely part of both Norwalk and Stamford. The first private purchase on the Norwalk side of the line was in 1699, for land at Silvermine Hill.

—Back then it was always two words, Boland said. *Silver Mine* Hill. Then. . . . Well, of course, the town was established as a church parish—I'm sure you know all this—Canaan Parish, so that the locals, the Stanford and Norwalk citizens, wouldn't have to travel so far to go to church . . .

It was a conversation designed to forbid. Finding a break in Boland's filibuster, Maria's son, Neil Conrad, moved in on Elena. He placed himself between her and Boland. Neil wore a tie-dyed turtleneck, patched jeans, and hiking boots. His hair was long. Elena wondered if he was going to play the game, the key party game, and if not, why Maria, who was here without her husband, had brought him. Elena considered his ectomorphic skeleton: what self-respecting adult would perch and grind against this *boy* in the act of love? Would Neil, only a year or two older than her own son, with his acne and his wavy, feminine hair, be someone with whom she could go home?

Absolutely not.

Young Neil mumbled in his confused way — under his halitotic breath — about how boring the party was and how boring this guy with the New Canaan stuff was — and then he began to fire questions at her. Elena had found herself the object of admiration from teenagers before. It was, she guessed, her nonjudgmental silences. They took this for listening. Anyway, as it turned out, Neil had just been through *the training*. That's right. His mind was a carefully brainwashed version of Werner Erhard's. He had spent weekends in an auditorium in which he could not leave to urinate, and now he had *got It*. He got that there was *nothing to get*. The effect of this had changed his life. Of the assembled in the party, he had chosen her to hear his message.

Neil mumbled that he was now interested in the spiritual basis of what Vonnegut was doing with Dwayne Hoover and Kilgore Trout. Drawings of assholes and everything. Also there was a record called *Dark Side of the Moon*. Getting into some pretty far-out shit. "Breathe in the air," Neil Conrad told Elena. "Don't be afraid to care." Jonathan Livingston Seagull was pretty hip to it, too. Each of us had an idea of the Great Gull within us.

— The movie sucks the big one, though. Neil Diamond music, forget it. Cracklin' Rosie.

— Well, I —

— And if you are into the ways the training can be used,

y'know, with what's going on in religion and like the. . . . Well, then there's this guy here you should talk to.

Suddenly, Neil was leading her into the next room — Boland and his mother waving at them — into the library, where the sound of Antonio Carlos Jobim, being played at 45 r.p.m., maybe by accident, was competing with the television set, which was rebroadcasting *Miracle on 34th Street*. Dentist-chair music, elevator music, and then that Macy's version of God, that Macy's version of miracles, that bearded fellow in the nuthouse. Or was it Gimbels. She was permitting herself to be led only because she knew that somewhere in the shifting associations of this party there was an individual who would transform this evening. And she suspected that she would be led to him by chance. A group was clustered around the hexagonal, glass coffee table (base of bronze and low-carbon steel, manufactured by Philip Daniel) — a couple of men and women shaking absently in time to the Bossa Nova — so Elena didn't see him at first. Outside, in the light of a patio lamp, the snow seemed to be falling up. It was almost eleven.

Then Neil introduced her to the man she had met in the coffee shop before, Wesley. Wesley Myers. She wasn't surprised to find him on the premises. Or her surprise quickly dissipated. She had recognized in that moment in the coffee shop with him a whole different narrative of her marriage, a whole sequence of intimacies and distances and textures and motels and wines and partings, and she had balked at it. It was hard to see that narrative here again, in front of her, but it was good, too. She liked the sense of possibility in sad things. Wesley was here because he was single, she guessed, but also because this kind of basic Ten Commandments violation, the kind of violation at the party, must have drawn out the undesirable element of New Canaan in just the way a pie left out overnight draws out the ants. And Myers was an undesirable. This she knew from their two or three mild encounters. He was a restless thinker, an irritable, curmudgeonly guy. On the other hand, maybe he didn't know anything about the key party. Maybe he had just appeared. Maybe he responded to pheromones in the air, to animal endocrinology.

Myers did look like one of those mugging characters, like Buddy Hackett or Don Knotts. He was squat, short, dissipated, like a de Sade version of Santa Claus. He gave off the aura of having masturbated too frequently and too far into middle age.

He smiled warmly.

— How nice to see you, how really nice.

The gin blossoms that traversed his nose wrinkled in his smile.

And then Neil got right into it. Because there was no delaying where spiritual issues were concerned. Because this was a time of great spiritual questing. The center of the conversation was again *est,* on which Myers had an inside track, as he seemed to have on a variety of nontraditional avenues of worship, including the Church of Scientology, Parhamansa Yogananda, the Peoples' Temple, Gestalt therapy, and transcendental meditation.

The main issue, the way Myers put it, was the *Fleece.* You had a right, as a struggling human machine, to the fleece, to get all the fleece in your daily life.

— But having a right, well, and I'm paraphrasing here, paraphasing Werner and one of his students, having a right is different from *being* right. Being right and being happy are on opposite ends of this dance that is the life of human machines. That's all that's going on here. Being right is the last refuge of scoundrels. Abdicate totally and completely. Right? Instead, as *est* accounts for it, you're going to have to search for your *flow* and negotiate . . . its currents and its white water. That's right. Once you have found the center-that-is-not-a-true-center, as a human machine you can partake of it at any time. Werner says pretty clearly that when you begin to communicate about your flow, it will take the shape of this globe, this world. That's the big secret that isn't really a secret. Once you've constructed this raft for this voyage along your flow, once you have copped to the twists and bends of this journey, you can think about becoming a spiritual adept yourself. That's the secret. That's about all there is to it.

— Now, good relationships in the dance, well, the problem there is simply adjustment to the other person's flow, Myers went on. You have to work toward an avenue of play and love that feeds on the dance. Your avenue of play and love becomes shelter for the object, the other human machine. These are your options. Your flow has tributaries, see, and these are called options, the way Werner talks about it. The field of tributaries just goes on and on. And the end point here is that everything in heaven . . . everything in heaven is fashioned from the mutability of these options constructed in your flow, whether with consciousness or unconsciousness. And that means that your feet rest in heaven. As Werner says, *you are* the higher power, the supreme being. You are.

Myers broke into an unashamed grin.

— Well, honestly, I'm glad somebody is, Elena said.

— I'll bet you are, Myers said, as cheerful as Buddy Hackett. Because that's getting it. That's getting It.

— Well, tell me, Elena said. How did you two meet?

— Well, he's my minister, Neil said.

And then it struck Elena. In fact, she was pretty stupid for having failed to put it together before. Myers was, of course, the new rector of the Episcopalian church, at St. Mark's. The church nobody liked. And though Myers was distasteful, though he looked like the sort of minister who might fondle a choirboy or -girl, or both, and though he had agreed to meet her on a couple of occasions for these furtive luncheons that were certainly testing-the-water types of things, and though he had never even — on these occasions — admitted that he was a minister, she felt bad for him. After each pronouncement of his search for grace in this community, she imagined, after each interpretation of the readings, after each admonition, the people of New Canaan rewarded him with silence, with that gloomy barometer of Episcopal failure: the empty coffee hour. In the weeks following he would reach further into his bag of incantations and prayers and critical exegeses to placate them, only to hear the same silence again.

— *Breakfast of Champions* is a failure. A flawed, questing work, not at all the work of the man who produced *Slaughterhouse-Five,* Myers was saying to Neil. Read those earlier books. The sustained period of creativity from *Mother Night* to *Slaughterhouse-Five* is. . . . Well, it's sustained.

Neil was smiling broadly at this display of hipness from Myers. There weren't too many New Canaanites who could talk to him in his own brutish tongue.

When Dot Halford came into the room a few minutes later — at twenty past eleven — the three of them, Elena, Neil Conrad, and Wesley Myers, had lapsed into an awkward party silence. The Wesley Myers Elena had met in the diner downtown, several months ago, was gone now. Myers seemed weary and preoccupied. Self-pitying, even.

When Dot turned off the television set, it became clear, in fact, that no one in the room was talking, that silence had settled on the room as a whole, one of those statistical silences. The key party was going into its next phase.

Elena noticed the modern art on the wall — a couple squiggles of red and yellow on a white canvas. And the rug pattern — reptiles on pebbles. Pebbles under water.

— Well, Dot said, slurring faintly, teetering on her pumps. Well, we have a little business to attend to now. So if you're going to stay, let's please gather in the living room now.

And she led the way.

The key party lacked a comprehensive system of manners. There were things still to be negotiated. No one knew quite what to do, how to follow. Most of those who had no intention of playing had already left. George Clair and his wife had left, most of the old families of New Canaan — the Benedicts, the Bootons, the Carters, et al. — had left. Yet from the rigid uncertainty that swept the room, Elena could tell that Dot's anxiety and her drunkenness extended to her remaining guests. Of the group gathered around the glass coffee table in the library, six or seven headed for the front hall immediately. For their coats. Those who remained also seemed to be getting ready to leave. They stretched and headed for the bathroom or finished off conversations, though all the while they were intent on that salad bowl in the front hall, that simple, white salad bowl with the keys nestling in it.

The range of uncertainties fascinated Elena. They were gathered there, just after eleven, like some convention of toastmasters. All putting a good face on it. Mark Boland, Maria Conrad, Neil Conrad, Sally and Steve Armitage, Alice and Pierce Sawyer, Ernest and Sari Steele, the Boyles, the Gormans, Janey and Jim Williams, the Gadds, Stephan Earle and his wife, Marie, the Fullers, the Buckleys, Chuck Spofford, June Devereaux, Tommy Finletter, Alicia Monroe. Dot and Rob Halford.

And the Hoods.

Because Elena was a forecaster of difficulties, a seer, she realized the crucial problem of the key party right away. The numbers were uneven. There was an extra guy.

And the pickings were pretty slim. Wesley Myers had slipped out suddenly, out some back door. Why had he been there in the first place? Elena couldn't imagine whom, of the assembled, she could stand.

Her husband was still there, though, and statistically she might well choose him. He was close by her now, holding her lightly by the shoulders, swaying from side to side.

— Ready to go? Benjamin whispered. I was. . . . You know, I was thinking I was. . . . Well, let's just go, honey. Let's get out of here. I want to go. I've had . . . enough. Enough of this shit.

A defeated look marred his features. In the lines and around the pouches of his face perspiration collected. He grimaced. He wanted help. But Elena didn't feel up to it. On other occasions, she had put him to bed. She had changed the sheets when, once or twice, he had actually, in the midst of some drunken episode, pissed in them. She had driven him to the station when he was too hung-over to drive. She had called his secretary at Shackley and Schwimmer to explain away his absences.

— We're not going anywhere, she said.

Benjamin groaned sullenly. It was an interrogative and preverbal drunken noise.

— That's right, Elena whispered.

She waved affably at Janey Williams, who was standing across the living room.

— Hi there, Janey.

Janey waved back. Without expression.

Dot had turned on some racy music to go with the event — theme music from the Tribal Love Rock Musical, *Hair*. Now she dimmed the living room lights. Those thirty-one betrayers gathered round, as though to stay warm. Elena and Benjamin were crowded in by the Armitages on one side and by Maria and her son, Neil, on the other. Certainly the kid would be the one leftover, right? The remainder? Would anyone in this town really spend the night with Maria Conrad's teenaged son, initiating him into the joy of sex?

— Well, what shall the order be? Dot Halford said with exaggerated calm. Alphabetical? In order of appearance?

— Golf handicap! bellowed Pierce Sawyer. Lowest handicap does the honors.

HA! HA! HA! HA! Nervous laughter.

— Golf handicap? Dot said. Ladies? Isn't it up to you?

— Oh, I'll go first, dammit, Maria Conrad said. Let's just line up and get it over with.

The bowl went around like the wine at Eucharist. The men stood behind hovering behind Dot's circle of women. A solemn pall overtook the room as Maria reached for that first set of keys. A dark, leather key chain dangled at the end of the prize she selected — an Alfa Romeo key chain. Stephan Earle. Elena realized how weak Stephan Earle must have felt as he came forward, how womanly and weak. He had had someone else in mind. On the other hand, who knew really? Maybe he felt real affection. Everyone applauded as Maria smilingly returned the keys to him and then, taking his arm, proceeded to the guest room, where the coats were piled. Just like that. Even Stephan's wife, Marie, wished them *good luck*. She watched her husband leave the way in the Middle Ages wives must have watched ships leave for the spice trade.

And what about Neil? Neil didn't even seem to notice his mother's grand exit. And still not a single adult had questioned his presence there. No one had told him to run along. Well, he was, what? Nineteen? Of majority, almost. Dot Halford was already on to the next couple. Her husband was standing off to one side rattling a drink with a sleepy smile on his face. They soldiered on, these pretenders to the Tribal Love Rock Event, like it was a civic duty.

Marie Earle herself went next and took up with Dan Fuller, whose wife then followed (a sort of order was elaborated in this way — the aggrieved party was next in line), taking up with the divorced Chuck Spofford, and this sent the narrative of adultery off on a digression, through the wilds of the divorced. After Chuck, June Devereaux picked Tommy Finletter, who thereafter tossed the baton to his neighbor of long standing, Elise Gorman, who took up with her husband's old golfing partner, Pierce Sawyer. And Sawyer's wife picked Tony Boyle, etc. One couple, the Gadds, managed to select each other, and rather than sporting the disappointment Elena might have suspected, they seemed greatly relieved.

The key party proceeded as flawlessly as a bank line. When Elena confronted again her own decision to participate, when she began to think of the practical issues — which house, how would she get a ride back, what if somebody's children found out — the room was no more crowded than a small dinner party. Mark Boland, Neil

Conrad, Janey and Jim Williams, Rob and Dot Halford, Sari Steele, and Benjamin.

Then, somehow, the order became confused. Because there were so many people there who had drunk too much. Because, in the end, it was not a game in which order had much place. So Janey Williams went next. For no good reason. She was simply ready to go and tired of waiting. Elena took note of Benjamin's agitation. Even in his dull, inebriated state he could see that he would certainly be the selection. He may have wanted to go, or to give the appearance of wanting to go, but now here he was believing in the fates, in chance. The numbers favored him. The record player had turned itself off and the fire in the fireplace had gone out. It was Benjamin's moment. Dot presented the bowl to Janey, whose delicate hands selected with all the care of a jeweler.

Janey knew their keys well enough. The Hoods' key ring with the horse on it. Janey had looked after the house on a couple of occasions. She could have found their keys with ease. But Janey selected *away* from Benjamin Hood. She found the keys and purposefully shoved them to one side, Elena imagined, because she wound up instead with . . . Neil Conrad.

The teenager! Jim Williams seemed to peruse an old copy of *National Geographic* as his wife publicly embraced Maria Conrad's underage son. Jim Williams, smiling mysteriously to himself. When had he arrived at the party, anyway? But the real drama of the moment was created by Elena's own husband. In that tight circle, he lumbered forth as if to separate Janey and Neil. For a moment, fisticuffs seemed likely. For a moment, Benjamin threatened the teenager with the flat of his hand. Elena felt shame rise in her like adrenaline. Shouts of *Hey, hey, Ben, hang on there a sec,* and Benjamin gathered himself up, realizing, even in his drunkenness, the enormity of his foolishness. He backed off.

And in backing off he tripped over the coffee table. Here at last was a story with beginning, middle, and end, a story that local scandalmongers could repeat with relish. Benjamin went down heavily, as if it were natural for him to be prone on the Halfords' shag rug. He settled there resolutely. Elena made no move to help him — she was chilled with dismay — and the Halfords didn't hurry either. Jim Williams looked up casually from his magazine. Benjamin Hood lay on the floor, muttering. An indistinguishable whisper of complaints about Shackley and Schwimmer, about his past, about New Canaan. Elena paid no more attention than anyone else. Or she tried.

But when Benjamin gulped back the first salvo of some intestinal disturbance, Elena felt she had to do something.

— C'mon, darling, she said, and she crouched over his back — because he was now kneeling wobbily by the edge of the modular seating unit. Come on, you've got to go to the bathroom. Let's go.

She could smell the vomit on his breath, and his eyes were like the bloody foam at the end of a bad shaving episode. She didn't have time to feel humiliated. His face was raw with sadness.

— Dot? she said. May I install him in your bathroom? Won't be a minute. I'm sorry, I really am.

— Not another word, Dot said. It wouldn't be a party without him.

With a lavender cocktail napkin, Dot Halford crouched to wipe up the last of an Irish coffee that Benjamin had taken with him on the way down. Only a small, gluey clump of rug tentacles was left to betray Benjamin Hood's fall.

Mark Boland helped Elena lift him to his feet, at which point Benjamin disdained — in incoherent, alcoholic grunts — any further help. He hurried himself to the bathroom coughing ominously. When Elena turned her attention back to the game, halfheartedly now, guiltily, but also angrily, Neil Conrad and Janey Williams were gone. In fact, Mark Boland seemed to be suddenly on his way out with Dot herself. They had managed to sanctify this bond quietly, on the margins of all the other activity. The game was accelerating, to accomplish its task without further mishap. People were pairing off without even consulting the bowl. Because there were only the four of them left now. Rob Halford and Sari Steele turned to Jim Williams and Elena, who found themselves alone standing together, and smiled.

— We didn't actually put our keys in at all, Rob said. But you won't spread it around?

He guffawed loudly.

— It's *my* party. And Dot isn't. . . . Hey, we're just going to slip upstairs for a little while. Would you guys like a cup of coffee or something before we go?

Jim looked at Elena. Elena was looking back.

They sized each other up. The decision, for Elena, was about like buying an expensive household item. A new hi-fi or a new dishwasher. She was valuing Jim strictly on the basis of design stylings.

— Rob, we'll fix it for ourselves, she said. You two go on and get acquainted. We'll let ourselves out the front door.

Then Elena and Jim Williams were alone in the Halfords' living room. Real holiday carnage marred the earthy and arty look of the premises. There were half-empty beer bottles everywhere, and these were filled with the ends of cigarettes, Virginia Slims, Kents, Larks, Winstons. Disposable plastic cups had been stuffed with the lavender cocktail napkins and scraps of hors d'oeuvres. Elena was stunned by the number of empty liquor bottles at the bar. The cushions from the polyurethane modular-seating unit had been scattered on the floor, near where Benjamin had stretched himself out, and there was a trail of slush and grime leading in from the front door. Wood smoke and cigarettes and pot had gotten into the curtains and upholstery. The room had an outdoorsy stench to it.

The last coals hissed and popped in the fireplace.

— Well, Jim Williams said, I have to say I don't have much faith that my keys are still in that bowl. Doesn't seem entirely safe, you know? Leaving your house keys around?

The salad bowl sat on the floor, next to one wall.

— Let me, Elena said.

Ceremoniously, she retrieved the bowl. As though the act had profound spiritual significance. She dipped her hand in. Two sets of keys remaining there. One set, of course, was her own. But she avoided these keys, just as Jim's wife had. At first it was a simple act of generosity — she was getting his keys for him — but somewhere on her way across the room she was playing the game, the key party game. Wistfully, she was playing. Resignedly, but by the time Elena handed him the dull, leather key chain, she was also hoping.

— Oh, I don't think so, Jim said. It's been a discouraging evening.

— You couldn't have hoped for much better when you came up the walk, Elena said. And that's the truth.

— Somehow it was different in my imagination when I

thought about it. Actually, I didn't think about it at all, really.

Williams was wearing plaid pants — kelly green field with red and yellow lines crisscrossing — and a striped shirt. Maroon stripes on white. A big collar wide open at the neck, spread out upon the wide lapels of his tweed jacket. Tan patent-leather loafers with heels. He had facial hair. Sideburns, and a large mustache that he stroked contemplatively as they spoke.

They sat. On the modular-seating unit.

— Do you want coffee or something? Williams said.

— If we can do it quick, she said. Maybe they have one of those filter jobs. . . . Did you come down from the city? Was the weather —

The weather was awful, and Jim Williams had heard gloomy forecasts about the effects of the sudden twenty-degree drop in the temperature that was expected. His conductor, on the train out, had grim prophecies.

— Well, if it's going to be so cold, Elena said, as they combed the kitchen looking for the coffee, the half-and-half, and the drip apparatus, you might as well —

— Look, Elena, he said, the fact that we're . . . neighbors, you know, close friends, well, it sort of makes this a little strange, don't you think?

Well, they didn't have to share their feelings on the subject of infidelity. They both had experience. A complex of feelings had passed through Elena since early evening. The tough job of naming feelings seemed overwhelming. It was a job for social workers, for the professionals at Silver Meadow. Her feelings, they would say, had a Reichian name. She could locate them in an orgone accumulator.

— My husband is passed out in the bathroom. I've been married to him for seventeen years and I don't have any intention of going in there to pick him up. This is one night I'm just not doing it. Come what may. . . . He's not my profession. . . . Do you know what I mean?

Jim Williams didn't say anything.

— So what I'm proposing is that since your wife has gone off with a boy, and since you are standing here alone, I'm proposing that you and I just do what makes sense. Stay warm. Pass some time. That's all. It's not elegant —

They were looking at their hands, looking at their coffee cups, looking at the lacerations in the very wood grain of the chopping board — celery ends stacked upon it; they were looking at the bowl of dip and the cellophane wrap crumpled next to it. They were looking around the room at refrigerator magnets and salt cellars and church keys and the stems of freshly cut flowers in the sink and bottle caps and a lone spice jar marked *marjoram.*

— I'm already married, you know, Elena said. I don't have any use for you in the long run. If that's what you're worried about. If you don't want to talk about it ever again, you don't have to. Now don't make me feel as though I'm being too forward, okay? Don't make me feel that trying to persuade is unbecoming. Because I can tell it's not the furthest thing from your mind.

A long, silent communion between the two of them.

— *What the hey,* Jim said. Let's go for a drive.

And then she hesitated.

— Okay. Okay. Should we clean up around here first? Elena said. Do you think it's all right —

— Nah, he said, that wasn't in the contract.

But they walked around the first floor turning off lights. Elena didn't pay any attention to the sound of running water in the bathroom there — where not so long ago Mark Boland had stared at the panties knotted around her bony legs — or to the light that still shone beneath the door there. They turned off the appliances in the kitchen, the lamps in the dining room, in the den, and back in the living room. They pushed the sculpture in the foyer back into the open space by the guest room, where Dot usually kept it. They helped each other into their coats.

Outside, everything had changed. Meteorologically, the phenomenon, which occurred rarely in that part of the Northeast, went like this: rain, sleet, and snow, propelled by subfreezing winds — warmer temperatures aloft and freezing temperatures at ground level — began to harden instantly on trees, rooftops, power lines, and other surfaces. The ice built up on every surface. (The worse such storm in thirty years, according to Mike Powers, spokesman for Connecticut Light and Power. *Stamford Advocate*, November 23, 1973, p. A1*ff*.) Moving up the East Coast, the low-pressure system spread from Virginia to Maine and from four hundred miles out on the Atlantic Ocean to Pennsylvania.

Elena and Jim Williams, therefore, like the rest of the carnal refugees from the Halfords' house, were traveling out into a storm that was no longer safe. Three or four inches of snow had accumulated now, around Jim's tires. The freezing rain was still pelting the Cadillac, and a thick glaze shellacked his windshield.

— We're going to have to defrost this thing for a while, Williams said.

Elena wondered if the car would even start. It started on the first try. This was a Cadillac, after all. She wondered if the other revelers had found, as she had, that their resolve failed them outside, in the elements. If you weren't into adultery for the erotic dementia, she thought, the amnesia it brought with it, why bother? But in the midst of the storm, infidelity felt almost ridiculous. She was about to tell Jim this when he leaned over to kiss her. The heating vents blew cool air on them; the exhaust bellowed clouds of obfuscation. — Do these seats go back? she said.

And that, suddenly, was the beginning of it. Elena had never made love in a car before. It was one of those rites of passage that she had read about in books. She hadn't known about rock and roll, she hadn't known about racial strife, and she hadn't known about heavy petting in cars. The logistics of it were demanding, she was finding out. Jim was unfastening her pants and getting right to business. She had trouble getting any purchase on him. She was pulling down her panties with one hand and settling herself across his lap. She whispered reassuringly about birth control pills. Then he was inside.

It was urgent and painless and soon it was over. Jim moaned plaintively. In less time than it takes to defrost a windshield.

Kinsey: "The quick performance of the typical male may be most unsatisfactory to a wife who is inhibited or natively low in response, as many wives are; and such disparities in the speed of male and female response are frequent sources of marital conflict, especially among upper social levels where the female is most restrained in her behavior."

Jim Williams was rubbing his neck.

— That was really awful, Jim Williams said, that was really awful. I'm so sorry, Elena.

They had trouble untangling themselves. Elena worried that she might have to open the door and slide out headfirst to regather herself. Eventually she slid down into the cavity by the glove compartment, and there she worked her trampled flannel pants around the right way.

—Things are rotten at home, Jim said. You wouldn't believe how rotten. Janey's sick. She's unstable. I guess. . . . It's not the right time to tell you . . . but that's it, Elena. That's it. She can't be happy. I don't know why. I can't make her happy, the boys can't make her happy. She just can't do it. It's like she thinks I lied to her or something. She treats me like I promised her something I have welched on. . . . She just doesn't want the life she used to think she wanted. It's not going to turn out well, I can tell you that much.

—Let's go, she said. I have to look in on the kids. Paul is supposed to be coming back from the city.

—Jesus, Jim said, refixing his belt. I want to make it up to you, Elena. I can do better than that, honestly. I mean it.

She sighed.

—Well, we can talk about it.

—That's fine. I wouldn't expect you to see it any other way.

—Maybe you just need. . . . We can talk any time, you know—

—I need that, too. I really do, Williams said.

He pointed at the seat belts.

He threw the car in drive, and that was when they noticed the skid marks on the driveway. Beneath the crust of snow was a much harder, more implacable layer of ice. An equalizing layer. It was like trying to drive a bumper car. The Cadillac had a mind of its own. As they circled around the gravel circle, Jim Williams turned wildly in either direction. Trying to catch the wheel.

They each fell into their own remorse. They were just neighbors again, if they had ever been anything else. Elena felt cheap and isolated. It had been as romantic as a pap smear or a home breast exam. She would rather wait in a gas-rationing line; she would rather watch war footage; she would rather — she was shocked to learn — clean up after the drunken Benjamin Hood. She let herself do certain things because of fashion, though she didn't think of herself as fashionable in any way, and fashion brought the unexpected along with it. So here she was driving home with the fraud next door, a man she had little respect for, after having fucked him in his car.

They went into the tailspin coming off Ferris Hill Road. Just as they saw the other cars abandoned at the bottom of the hill, Jim lost control of the Cadillac. It was more than one spin. They went all the way around twice, two three-sixties, and Elena could hear the scream coming from her, but it didn't seem like part of her. It was as alien, as elsewhere, as a radio signal during one of those emergency tests. Her frequency was pure and open. She was uninterrupted by decisions or responsibilities: there was time to think. She didn't notice or care that her screams originated in her own throat. In the second before she imagined death, she recalled many things to be done. The dog was pacing back and forth in front of his bowl. Paul needed a haircut. She wanted to see Wendy wear those lovely new shoes. They, she and Benjamin, were going to replace the curtains in the drafty living room. They were going to find out about energy alternatives for their drafty house. They were going to buy a smaller car.

The Cadillac landed nose down in a shallow ditch. The last revolution had been painfully slow, like a merry-go-round on the lowest kiddie speed. The front end of the car accordioned as though it were engineered to do so. The frame moaned slightly as the engine folded up within it.

Jim Williams cradled his head on the steering wheel. He asked if she was all right.

Elena nodded.

— Happy holidays, Jim said.

He untangled his legs from the engine parts that protruded up through the dash — he was miraculously uninjured — and helped her out. There were cars abandoned all around them. A *Who's Who* of Halford party attendees.

— Look, let's just put up at my place till morning, sweetie, Jim said. It's closer. It doesn't make any sense to be out walking. You can sleep in the guest room or something. If that's what you want. But this isn't a night to be going any further than you have to.

Elena thought it over.

— And your son. He isn't on that train, I'll bet you. He knows better than that. That is, if the trains are even running. And Wendy's in bed and will be until morning. So it just makes sense. Besides, I owe you one. I want to pay up. Let me do just that.

She thought about it.

And the next thing that happened, at exactly midnight, was that the streetlamp at the corner of Ferris Hill and Valley Road, the only one for miles, abruptly went out.

LIBBETS CASEY told Paul Hood that she loved him as a friend. Her reasoning was labored, her tongue was thick. The world outside vanished during this discussion. That class Paul hated, Origins of the West; Spiro Agnew's resignation; Gerald Ford's confirmation. All this stuff vanished. Paul told her she was his best friend in the world, the only person he felt comfortable with, some kinda exact opposite he had been circling around, but the way he said it, it felt desperate and exaggerated, even to him. He was trying to cudgel her with good vibes. And she knew it.

They sat on the edge of Libbets's bed. She said:

— But you don't even know me really.

— Sure I do, Paul Hood said. I know the aura you give off, Libbets. Sure. I know how you are in the cafeteria, where you sit, in the chapel, all over the place. It just seems right to me, you know? It just seems right.

— Well, I like you, too, Paul, but —

And she said it again: She loved him as a friend. Whatever that meant. They doodled in her blank book with colored pencils. Paul felt like some woeful responsibility of his was being held at bay, just while he was on that bed with her. As long as she let him sit there, whatever she said was just syllables flung at problems. She could still change her mind. These minutes were worth the hyperbole and the train ride and the Seconals. Paul penciled an approximation of the Human Torch on the page, and then filled him in with the yellow and orange. It was that sweeping-fireball Human Torch, from upper right to lower left. Laying waste at jet speed. That smoldering, adolescent Human Torch, who dropped out of college — as Paul expected he would, too — and who couldn't keep a girlfriend. In the balloon Paul scrawled a little dedication:

For Libbets, whichever way I fly.

She told him he was good at it, that he was as good as any comic-book penciller, but he just brushed it off.

Paul couldn't be certain he wasn't part of a dream, as he sat on the bed, watching her do a little cubist scribble across from the Torch. He couldn't be sure he wasn't the protagonist of a dream belonging, for example, to Francis Chamberlain Davenport IV, who slumbered peacefully on the couch in the library. A real wish-fulfillment dream, maybe, a mandala dream, or else an unpleasant dream that just happened to have a couple of nice moments. Moments that just set him up for the next long torture passage. One of those long, complicated narratives of missed planes or failed examinations or public nudity. As in a dream, the room was so still when Libbets told him haltingly that she loved him as a friend that he could marvel at the sheer beautiful predictability of it, the predictability of his loneliness. His whole life was someone else's dream and sometime soon that sleeper would wake. Or maybe his life was a weekly comedy series, and he would soon be canceled or replaced by a summer variety show starring Mac Davis.

— It's not that I don't care about you, Libbets was trying to say, because I do, or maybe I do, but I just don't think this is right. I feel more like you're a brother. I feel this love for you like a brother. You know what I mean? Because —

The pencils were spread out around the drawing book like a fan. What reply was there for a line like this? *You're wrong? You're going to regret it?* He didn't know what he wanted anyway, or how to persuade her. He only knew that he didn't want to move from this bed or from her side to return to the cage of his education. He thought maybe he wanted some sort of contact, some shocking and permanent contact. He wanted to be surgically attached to Libbets, stitched, cat-gutted to her, or he wanted one of those Looney Tunes kisses that were like electrocution. He wanted this moment on the bed to be in the absolute zero time of Marvel. She overlooked the magic in their predicament, the ramifications for the other characters in the strip. She didn't see how Paul single-handedly beat back the threat of growing up.

— Well, let's go to that bar, he said.

— I don't know. I'm so wasted . . .

— Don't you just want to. . . . Don't you want to get out of your head one time before going back to school? Don't you want to celebrate one night? Just one time? You'll be okay, right? I'll make sure you get home.

— Maybe, Libbets said. Maybe, if we take a cab.

This was about ten o'clock.

He called home first. He was supposed to keep his mom up on his movements, but the main thing was that he wanted to talk to his sister. He wanted to tell her how this wasn't going to work, how no girlfriend was ever going to work, and how he was always going to live in this windowless vault where no one ever touched his skin. His body, he wanted to tell her, was like the sweating wall of a wine cellar. He breathed the musty air of crypts. He couldn't sit still. But he didn't tell Wendy any of this. Whenever he told someone in his family this kind of thing, they always asked him if he could pass the dill spears or the apricot chutney. Would he mind taking out the trash? So he never did tell. He just got off the phone.

Libbets had an inexhaustible roll of bills her parents had given her. She handed the roll to Paul. She couldn't concentrate on the denominations. The snickering doormen had the cab waiting for them. Seventeenth Street and Park Avenue South. Paul tipped big.

The sign at Max's said *Big Star*. Two shows. From the street, he could hear their sweet harmonies. He held Libbets close, and they listened to the band for a while. From the street. Right out on the sidewalk in front of Max's. Because this was the closest they were going to get to that bar. All the way down there, and they couldn't get in. The bouncer frowned and pointed. *Out*. Paul Hood was sixteen years old and Libbets Casey was seventeen and they both looked like it. They weren't dressed in black jeans and black turtlenecks and they didn't dye their hair. They were a couple of preppies with fake identification cards — Citizen of the State of New York cards — who thought they could buy their way into any bar. They stood out in the cold, and taxicabs drove the slush and water out of the drainage depressions and up onto the curb. Pedestrians scattered.

They watched the parade into Max's Kansas City.

The rock and roll that was king in November of 1973 was Glitter. The New York band that was king was the New York Dolls, a collection of guys from the boroughs who wore makeup and fake furs. They had played recently at the Waldorf-Astoria, and at the State Theatre in New Brunswick. Their big hit was "Personality Crisis." Mott the

Hoople was also playing in New York that month. They had started out playing the usual Stones-imitation stuff, but by 1972, when *All the Young Dudes* was released, their costumes had become more creative. Lou Reed was playing at the Academy of Music, just down the street, in a couple of weeks. This was Glitter. These men all wore platform shoes and boas and blouses and leather jumpsuits. They were writing songs about transvestites — Holly Woodlawn, Candy Darling, Sugar Plum Fairy, Jackie Curtis.

In Paul Hood's November issue of *Creem,* one rock critic called 1973 "the year of the transsexual tramp. All of a sudden almost everyone in rock n' roll wanted to be — or at least suggest the possibility of being — a raging queen." Even Dick Clark had an opinion on the subject, in the same issue: "Bisexual . . . what's the other word, AC/DC? I think it's partially fad and partially goldfish swallowing, as protest was. A lot of kids got into protest because it was 'the thing.' That may be what's happening with the fag-drag crazy transsexual rock scene. I think that's a quickie. I think more importantly that's an indication of the desire to have show business return to music. That's why you have an Elton John, a Liberace, an Alice Cooper. That's show biz. We all know Alice is a put-on, a shuck. But what's funny is when you read the sociological commentators and how torn up the whole straight world is over this craziness. I can't attach any significance to that."

The Factory, on Union Square, wasn't far from Max's Kansas City. If Paul Hood had known, he might have been able to identify Andy Warhol. He might have seen that platinum blond eminence sweep by into the club. Warhol had been in Rome filming *Frankenstein* and *Dracula* in the summer of 1973, but by now he was back and hard at work revamping his magazine, *Interview,* which included the following item in the November 9 issue, concerning a dinner at Pearl's, a Chinese restaurant: "Bob Colacello in his emerald green corduroy suit by Polidori of Rome, Yves Saint Laurent silk shirt, Givenchy cologne; Vincent Fremont in his dark brown custom-tailored gabardine jacket, tan pants, white Brooks Brothers shirt; Jed Johnson in blue Yves Saint Laurent blazer, light blue Brooks Brothers shirt, striped tie from Tripler's, New Man pants; Andy Warhol in his chestnut DeNoyer velveteen jacket, Levi's, boots by Berlutti di Priigi, Brooks Brothers shirt, red and gray Brooks Brothers tie, brown wool V-neck Yves Saint Laurent pullover."

But because of the Valerie Solanas shooting, because he had scaled back his public appearances, Warhol didn't go to Max's on Friday night. Meanwhile, Glitter hadn't made it to the Stamford Local. Edie was a real tragedy — many in New Canaan and Greenwich and Darien knew her family personally, and they held Warhol responsible. There was no Glitter in New Canaan, and none in New Hampshire, where Libbets and Paul went to boarding school.

They were cold, standing there, trying to figure out what to do. And Libbets was feeling sick. This was what nightlife was like when you were sixteen or seventeen and you had enough money to go anywhere in New York City. Paul thought about going into Union Square Park, with its dense shrubbery and rich vein of drugs and crime. But he knew he would only end up with his usual fare — totally awesome oregano. They could go to another bar. One of those holes-in-the-wall on the Upper East Side where few questions were asked. But the fact that he was going to have to part from Libbets's side eventually was dawning on Paul. The necessitites of travel lurked in him. He needed his last ten dollars. To get home.

— Let's go back, he said. We shouldn't have come down here. It's my fault. I'm sorry. I'm really sorry. I'll take you back up to your place and then I'll go.

— I'll just . . . drop you, Libbets said.

— No, no, he said. I'll take you back. You're not feeling well.

Purest helplessness passed across Libbets's face. She shivered and frowned and bowed her head in a strange, almost grief-stricken way. And then she vomited on the street in front of Max's Kansas City. It was a thick, white soup and Libbets spewed it with the compressed fury of a fire hose. She doubled over. When it reached the slush and mud and water, those gloomy little ponds of Manhattan treachery that had overflowed corners and collected in gutters and potholes, it steamed like some radioactive substance. Some of the vomit splashed on Paul's Top-Siders, which were wet through and through now, and he jumped up, as though there were a way to escape it. As though it would be possible somehow to *ditch her* there. But he couldn't even wipe the stuff off. He couldn't do it until she was safe at home.

He was out with a woman who vomited in public.

— Sorry, Libbets moaned, oh, God, sorry —

He was propelled by this horror out onto Park Avenue South to hail a cab. He waved desperately at the traffic.

Libbets was crying as he helped her in. It was the day after Thanksgiving and her family had gone away and hadn't invited her. They had gone away on a ski trip. Paul saw her predicament, and his own. He wished he could have spirited her to safety like a Human Torch, like a roadrunner. Abandonment was in the parlors of America, in the clubs, in the weather. He wanted to abandon her, too, this vomiting girl. He loved her and he wanted to abandon her. It was 10:28.

— Sorry about your sneakers, Libbets said.

He didn't know what to say. He kissed her once on the lips, tasted the rank contents of her stomach. Kissed her just because he wanted to be unafraid of this simple biological event now and because he wanted to prove he could kiss her gently, like a decent guy.

He bore her up, out of the cab, held her up past the doormen, caressed her in the elevator, caressed the small of her back, and led her into her room. She went into the bathroom and vomited again, almost daintily this time. Paul gagged, too, as though he were going to spill his own guts in sympathy. He heard her shit after that, too, a torrent of insubstantial, watery stuff. He realized he couldn't remember ever having heard a woman shit before. Libbets was still crying. These were the sounds in the Casey household, Libbets's diarrhea, her choking sobs, and, in the next room, Davenport snoring in Libbets's sister's room. Davenport had moved. Sleepwalked, maybe. The sound of the snoring carried through the apartment like the country sound of a chain saw.

She was in her nightgown now, when she came out of the bathroom, and his eyes lit on her little woven anklet. And when she was backlit by the bedside lamp, her curvy shape shimmered in her transparent nightgown. She got under the covers.

— Are you feeling okay? he said.

— Much better, she mumbled. Gotta quit mixing things, I guess.

— Thanks for the night, Paul said. It was really a wonderful night.

— Mmm.

He went on:

— I never get to see much of New York City. I don't come in much. We used to come in with my dad at Christmastime. Once we came to see the circus. Three rings, couldn't tell where to look. Totally fried. But now I don't get into the city too much and you know, well, I don't have that many friends either so it's not too often —

It was like throwing a switch, the way she free-fell into unconsciousness. One moment she was there and the next, gone. She was a ghostly and beautiful sleeper, almost invisible, curled in the delicate question-mark shape Paul would have imagined for her.

He asked if he could just rest with her in the bed for a minute. Just for a minute, really, then he had to catch the train. Just to help her off to sleep and everything. When he got no reply, he removed his wet Top-Siders — speckled with puke and slush — and then his khakis. In his checkered boxer shorts — no self-respecting man of St. Pete's wore briefs — he climbed into bed with Libbets Casey.

He meant only to curl his arm around her and to feel for her the sentiment that parents feel for helpless little kids. He meant only to help, to feel that he could help. And when she rose and fell in the little drama of respiration, her breasts brushing up against his arm, when he brushed back her dirty-blond hair and touched his palm to her forehead, he knew that his life wasn't here to be squandered. This was the thing that anybody could do. He knew the comedy of the human body. He could share it. And it didn't matter for a moment that Libbets was unlikely to do the same for him. It didn't matter. This was where the storm worked its change on him. He was ready to do a little service.

But instead, his erection began to rub against Libbets's

voluptuous ass. He knew what he was doing, but he wasn't admitting it. He was feeling virtuous. His dick was making its own decisions, ones that involved chiefly sorrow and shame. His dick didn't give a shit about the community of lost teenagers. It only took a minute or so — he had hiked up her nightgown and was rubbing against her very flesh — before he was teetering on the brink of that fantastic and sorrowful ecstasy. What really gave masturbation its thrill was the possibility of getting caught at it at the moment of orgasm, when you knew that Jimmy Rodale, for example, was going to tell everyone in Manville that you used a nylon soccer jersey to accomplish the deed. Or getting caught by your mother. That cry of release was like no other — I wish I were in love! I'm never gonna be!

But Paul was gifted with a sudden moment of insight. He could see that the lovely cheeks of her ass, her coccyx, her knobby lower vertebrae, the breasts he held in his hand, would not bring him the good feeling he wanted. He could see what kind of creep he was. He would be no more *there* afterward than he was before. He was no sensuous man. And there was no colony on this planet where this kind of activity was rewarded. This insight was nothing more than a jab in the midst of the precipitous movement toward ejaculation.

He managed to roll over onto his side, though. To save himself a little heartbreak.

— Oh, Libbets, he groaned.

And he came. By himself. On himself. On his hand, and on Libbets's sheets.

Instantly, he was out of bed, checking the clock, his heart racing, looking for his clothes. Was he high? Was he a fool? Was he a deviant? He sprinted to the bathroom, where he gave his hands a good washing. He grabbed a flowered towel and rushed with it back to the bed. Libbets slept. He scrubbed at the puddle not a foot from her back. She rolled backward, from the commotion maybe, so that she was only inches away. He whispered apologies. He scorched the fitted sheet with scrubbing friction. It wasn't going to come out so easily. There were little clots of the stuff. It would just have to dry. He prayed that his semen would not make that journey of eight inches across the sheet and into Libbets's vagina. He prayed it would fade by morning. He prayed it would be transformed into the flaky and inoffensive crust he knew so well.

It was almost eleven. Had Davenport heard? The snoring had stopped. Paul's life was cheap. He dressed. He looked for his magazines. He was as alone in that apartment as he could be. A world of sleepers kept his secret. How could he sit across from Libbets in M. LeJeune's french class? How could he herald the birth of baby Jesus in a month's time? How could he ring in the fabulous year of 1974?

The best thing to do was to attempt to adhere to his normal daily schedule in all other areas of his life. To come and go according to his habits; the best thing to do was to catch the train as planned; to return to New Canaan as planned; to have breakfast with his parents as planned; to try to bask in the company of his parents, to try to learn the lessons of family; to catch the train back to Boston on Sunday, as planned, and from there catch the bus to Concord; to go to chapel on Monday morning as required; to attend Origins of the West, Geometry One; Chemistry One, English Five, and French Four as though nothing concerned him more than the usual battery of exams and the stress of selecting the correct St. Pete's bumper sticker for his parents' station wagon for Xmas. The slim rewards of habit would be his.

His clothes were straightened out (though he was dripping slightly into his pants), his tweed jacket was buttoned. His penis hurt. He leaned over Libbets's shoulder to grace the clean, broad plane of her cheekbone. She slipped halfway out of delirium.

— Mmmnn, Libbets said.

And then she sank again. He muttered another apology, as if words were going to do the trick.

Paul Hood begged his cab driver to make it to Grand Central Terminal by 11:00. This required haste. The grand avenue they hurtled down couldn't impress him now. Nor could the snow and sleet drifting in the streetlamps like ash from an incinerator. He was unaware. He had plunged himself into the netherworld of troubled adolescents. He wasn't a man at all. He was a boy. A privileged kid. His parents could get him out of what he had done. He would go to Silver Meadow. His dad had money. His dad could pay for psychiatric treatment. His dad would turn up during visiting hours with fresh socks. His dad would ferry him home to Silver Meadow after he got thrown out of St. Pete's. His dad would ferry him into that subspace of forgotten perverts.

He was at the ticket window by ten minutes past, and he slipped between the doors on the train just before they closed. A dozen other burnouts, including some older guys he thought he remembered from public school — bar drinkers and lonely souls — were strewn around the empty car. When the train began to roll, Paul Hood laid himself out lengthways on the three-seater like a corpse on the marble mortuary slab.

And in that first moment of repose, he remembered

issue #141 of *The Fantastic Four*. Like a desert oasis to him. Deviants and losers and mutants and the loveless, these, Paul Hood's people, were the proper readers of Marvel comics.

To recap: In issue #140, Annihilus was busy trying to take control of the world. Natch. This was all happening in the Negative Zone, that universe beside our own, where the laws of nature were subtly altered. Annihilus was a sort of insect — a late-model Gregor Samsa — who had been transformed through the agency of some extinct Negative Zone creatures, called Hereroes, into a winged, metallic fighting machine in pursuit of immortality. The control of the universe was his goal. The means to this end, in Annihilus's view, was none other than the F.F. In particular, he intended to sap the powers of young Franklin Richards, who was being held in the country by his mother, Sue — away from Reed, her husband, who never gave enough time to his child, who was no kind of father or husband.

Agnes Harkness, Sue's former governess, had been hypnotized by Annihilus into leading Sue and Franklin to the Negative Zone. Reed, Johnny, Ben, and Medusa — who had assumed Sue's spot on the team way back in issue #112 — and Johnny's old college roommate, Wyatt Wingfoot, followed.

Most of the issue, though, was just a setup. Annihilus narrated at length his origins to Wyatt Wingfoot. This was the kind of issue that had no purpose but to insure that Paul Hood would purchase the next. Which brought Paul to #141.

Reed was set to rescue his estranged wife and son. He was half-crazy with paternal and marital loyalty. Paul had never seen him so frenzied, so . . . irrational. Yet as the issue opened, Annihilus had immobilized Reed and the rest of the team in some kind of antigravity paralysis. "You brought us here for a reason, Annihilus," Reed cried out to the insect. "Revenge was part of it — but so is my son. What is it you *want* with him?"

Meanwhile, Alicia Masters, the blind girl who loved Benjamin Grimm was traveling to Latveria, to try to find a cure for her blindness.

The F.F. escaped from their suspended animation — they *just did* — and were soon walking the surface of Annihilus's desolate planet. They fought off and befriended the telepathic aliens who lived there. And they tunneled through the rock under their foe's fortress. Soon they had managed to penetrate the laboratory chamber where Sue, Agnes Harkness, and Franklin Reed were being held in an enormous test tube.

These last eight pages were enough to life Paul Hood from the murky bog of self-recrimination. As the cover promised, little Franklin was indeed glowing like an ATOMIC BOMB! It began with this light in his eyes, this internal and eternal cosmic power raging in him. Galaxies, endless expanses of primordial creation, *were spread before him like mere toys.* Medusa, Johnny, and Ben launched Annihilus into a tomb of corroded machinery. It was that simple. The stage was set for the final act of this grave domestic tragedy.

Reed wanted to get them all back to N.Y.C., where he could use his untested antimatter device to try to stabilize Franklin. Using a bogus spell in bogus dimeter, Agnes Harkness transported them back to the city. Reed rushed off to find his invention. "Wait, Medusa," Sue suddenly cried, "what is he doing? That looks like some sort of *gun!* No — Reed, no!"

When Paul reached the panels on the bottom half of

page thirty-one, it was as if the entire day, the entire vacation even, were leading up to a single moment. He felt certain then that Stan Lee was in some direct communication with the universe — in the way, say, that The Watcher, that most mysterious Marvel character, was content like some Gnostic entity merely *to know* of the machinations of creation — and that through Lee's spiritually advanced vision, Paul's own destiny was entrapped in the monthly serializations of these kitschy superheroes. He seemed both influenced and influencer in the world of Marvel.

So Reed blasted his son. In his haste and confusion, he used an untested weapon with all the ionizing force of antimatter particles on his own son. The alien glow in Franklin's eyes dimmed, ending the danger of the moment, dimming in him the ancient soup of the Big Bang. But with it went the life in Franklin's eyes, the twinkle of his joyous and questing cognition. To be replaced by darkness.

"What have you done, Reed? You've turned your own son into a vegetable. Your own son! . . . "

The last panel showed them all — Sue, with Franklin in her arms like some lifeless marionette, Wyatt Wingfoot, Johnny Storm, Medusa, and Ben — turned away from Reed. Reed, devastated, wordless at the enormity of his slaughter. The end of the Fantastic Four. The end. Until next month.

Then the lights on the train dimmed, sputtered, and fell dark. The engine rolled casually to a stop. Paul knew, having logged a number of hours on the New Haven line, that this was just part of electrical train travel. But after ten minutes in emergency lighting he wasn't as sure. Soon these lights, too, began to dim. Ominous darkness. A conductor hurried past Paul's seat, carrying a flashlight, and the other sleepers in his car stirred, turning restlessly, as though, in their dreams, they were being roasted on spits. Out the window, Paul could see the lights along I-95, where the slush was piled far into the lanes. The train was disabled somewhere between Port Chester and Greenwich. The snow fell, a relentless piece of bad news, and the cars crawled along, skidding and spinning. This wasn't a simple delay. When the conductor appeared at the end of the car and gave them the news — *'Fraid we got a downed power line, hope to have it fixed shortly* — mumbling because he no more believed the news than did the restless sleepers in that car, Paul knew he was here to stay.

So he dredged the awful bottom of his loneliness, because the train was as void and still as a sensory-deprivation tank. There was nothing else to do.

He had been on every platform on the Connecticut section of the ride. He had carved his initials in the men's room in Greenwich; he had sat on the fenders of the station cars parked in Darien; he had snuck into the bars in Cos Cob, urinated on the bushes by the station in Westport, flirted with the little girls in Rowayton and Old Greenwich. And he had traversed the southwestern part of the state by car on I-95. It was a noxious artery, more like an intestine, really, a bearer of wastes and bacteria. He knew the hotel between Darien and Stamford that had a Nixon banner on it all through the election; he knew the exact location of each and every HoJo's between here and New Haven; he knew Norwalk Harbor and Five Mile River and Cos Cob Harbor, and the bridges there; he knew the way I-95 came down a hill into Norwalk, the way it divided in New Haven, he knew its view of the Baxter Building as the train pulled into downtown Stamford.

He knew all this, but it didn't change his situation. His short, privileged life on the golden corridor of Fairfield

County made no difference to the storm outside. It was different when you were being driven through these towns, or when you were just idling in the train stations for an hour or two. Now he was stranded. He was a stranded kid, a kid on the verge of not being a kid anymore. A kid who would be getting his license soon. A loser from a family of losers. And he was near Port Chester, the only stop on the New Haven line that had a lot of Afro-American residents.

Paul Hood had met a few of them, black people. Though there were none in his elementary school — East School — there were five in Saxe Junior High when he was there. They all came from the middle of town, from the rented rooms above Fat Tuesday's or Pic-a-Pants. Three of them were girls, and they kept pretty much to themselves. When he looked back in his yearbook, in fact, he could never really remember seeing them at all. Except maybe eating cafeteria pizza in a little lunchroom clump. Probably they were so scared they skipped school. The guys, on the other hand, the two black guys were unavoidable. Brian Harris ruled Saxe Junior High. He wore his hair long, in a Black Panther Afro, and this spooked everybody. And he was a superior athlete, but maybe only because every white kid in New Canaan had been brought up to believe that Afro-Americans were superior athletes. This was something Paul's dad had actually told him. In basketball, Brian Harris had developed this double-pump reverse lay-up thing that some white guys were trying hard to copy. All he had to do was walk to the basket — they just let him through. Harris was a walking god in Saxe Junior High. A superhero. They worshiped him.

The other black guy was Logan Krieg and he had a reading problem or something. He had constantly looked over Paul's shoulder in English class. Krieg panicked visibly in class. When he began coming into school drunk or wasted, only the teachers were surprised. Krieg turned all the letters around in his assignments. He wrote baby writing. And then he pleaded with guys he didn't even know, with white students, to cover up for him. Because he was trying to stay out of the special-ed class. He didn't want to be in class with the retards. They all knew he was lying in class, lying about having done the homework, lying about having been sick, lying all the time, caught in this thick web of deceits, until he was immobilized by it. And then he was gone. Dropped out, shipped off somewhere, who knew? He wasn't *friends* with anybody, really.

That was Paul's experience with black kids. There were a few at St. Pete's and they all stuck together, too. They were brilliant and militant. For the rest of his information, Paul had to rely on reports from the idiot box. *The Rookies* had a black actor on it, and there was *Sanford and Son*. And in the dimly lit mausoleum that was his 11:10 Stamford Local, he remembered watching the news one night with his father, the night Angela Davis was acquitted. From the Naugahyde reclining chair that was his dad's chief consolation, Benjamin called out listessly, drunkenly, at the screen: *Fucking communist dyke cunt—*

Port Chester—where he was stranded—was something else altogether. Had Paul been able to leave the train then, to walk beneath its glittering electromagnetic force field, he would have trod streets without a white face on them. He had heard about places like this. These streets were the reason, probably, that his mother had repeatedly told him, when he was a kid, about a friend of hers who had set about crossing the railroad tracks. He had climbed up over an electric train, this boy, shortcutting from one side of the town to the other, and, on top of the train he had *stood.* To get a better view, maybe, or to feel the aggrandizement of standing on a train. But he had died in the process, of course. This story was where Paul had learned about electromagnetism. Because when the guy stood up he hit the voltage lines. The lines running over the train.

After forty-five minutes, the conductor reappeared to tell Hood and the other sleepers the news.

—Ladies and gentlemen, afraid we still don't know when the train will be moving. Best thing is to just stay put here in the car and we'll advise you as soon as we hear anything.

Down to the other end to repeat the announcement.

The next hours, in the deep part of the night, were as slow and ominous as the hours in a hospital waiting room. The emergency lighting dwindled and the sleepers in Paul's car turned uneasily, cursing under their breaths. He wanted that oblivion of sleep but he couldn't manage it. He was beginning to shake a little bit from the cold. He could see his own breath. And he was scared.

Then, sometime in the early morning, a large, hulking shape moved down the corridor. Paul was jumpy, he was expecting the kinetic bad guys of comic books. But it was just an older guy from the next car, a grizzled, gin-soaked–looking guy. In the blue glow of the fading emergency lights, the guy looked a little bit like Stan Lee, creator of the F.F. He was part C.I.A. operative, part elementary school teacher. He was fat, sinister, and jovial, and he fell into the seat across the aisle from Paul.

Paul didn't know what to expect. He figured he was

going to be attacked now, or raped, and that he deserved it. After Libbets.

— Seen the john anywhere, young man? the C.I.A. dude said.

— Excelsior, Paul said. Dunno, next car maybe.

The man had a good laugh over something. He hacked up some gunk from deep in himself.

— Hell of a train ride, huh?

Paul nodded. Not wanting to say anything, not wanting to encourage the rapist. But then he did anyway.

— Wish I had a flashlight. Or maybe some lantern, some kinda camping lantern. And some freeze-dried stuff. And a battery-powered record player, a Close-and-Play, and a bunch of forty-fives or something. And comic books.

The man leaned over the aisle.

— And a girl, he said. A little company.

— I wish I was home, Paul said. That's the truth.

The man nodded. The highway was empty, out the window. Sanding trucks inched along.

— You're going to New Canaan, I think, he said. I have a feeling about that. I think I have met your parents once or twice. I think I knew you since you were yea-high. Huh? Like they always say? Yep. That's right.

He told Paul his name. William something.

— Nope, Paul said, I'm . . . from Stamford. Citizen of Stamford.

Paul was wondering when the conductor might be coming back.

— That so? My mistake. Not Ben's son then, huh? My mistake. Well, I was going to offer to give you a ride when we get there. If we get there. But if you're only going right into town, I won't be much help. Unless you want to share a taxi or —

— No, Paul interrupted him emphatically, my parents will be waiting for me.

— Waiting for you after all this?

— Well, that's what I'm hoping.

— I see.

The older man heaved himself up into the aisle then, and suddenly Paul could see his baggy eyes, his thick neck, his gray, metallic flesh. Up close. The man loomed over him. He clapped a hand on Paul's shoulder. Breath like formaldehyde. This guy was an emissary from Dr. Doom. Only way to explain it.

— I'm guessing you don't want a serious conversation, Paul. That's my guess. And that's fine by me. Have to visit the head in any case. But you have a safe journey.

— Hey, I —

— If you want a ride or something when we arrive, you just look me up. Back a car.

— I'll do that, Paul said.

As the door slammed shut behind the man, Paul gathered himself up and ran back, as far in the opposite direction as he could, past the sleepers and their uncomfortable dreams, waking some as he hurried. *Rapist,* Paul thought, *murderer*. He settled two cars back. He buried his head under his tweed jacket. The things that went through his mind were the things he would have tried to put down, the thoughts he would have purged on a better day. He was thinking about the fellowship of modern sex criminals, guys who got off on the sound of women's screams, elderly men sucking the cocks of little, fat boys, guys who beat up fags and got erections while they did so. Then he was thinking not of Logan Krieg, but of another guy who used to copy from his papers in class, a guy who used to threaten him at Saxe Junior High. Skip Maundy. Maundy used to stop Paul on the way to the cafeteria to demand his lunch money. Since Paul had led his parents to believe that school lunches cost a dollar, though the actual cost was only seventy-five cents, Paul gave Maundy the profit. In order to avoid being beaten up. So Maundy waited for him every day, making jokes like *Hey, Paulie, we've got to stop meeting like this!* HA! HA! HA! HA!

Then Maundy moved into the academic arena with Paul. Coming down the long hallway that ran along the gym, he would break free from his platoon of handlers and harass Hood over by the water fountain. *Pass your test over to me during math. Just do it.* Maundy always smiled during these demands, as though he were engaged in an act of philanthropy.

Paul wished, as in after-school specials, that he had lived to see Maundy brought low, or that he would learn of some terrible tragedy in the Maundy family — his father's cancer, his mother's alcoholism — that would explain their son, the thug. But Paul never told anyone about the situation. He never turned Maundy in. He just took it.

Wendy also lived with the responsibility of isolation in public school. He had seen public school kids turn away rather than talk to her; he had heard her called *whore* and *freak* by the children of judges and social workers. In the dark, under his tweed jacket, Paul got stuck, all over again, on his parents and their chemistry. What kinds of genes gave him a life like this?

And the truth was that the story of Skip Maundy did have a conclusion. Later on, at New Canaan High, Maundy apparently dallied with a retarded girl in one of the lavatories. It was that girl Sarah Joe Holmes. Here's what they said: that Maundy had *pissed on her,* held her down and pissed on her. That was the alleged crime. Held her down, exposed himself, pissed on her, and then smoked a cigarette. Maybe it was just a story someone concocted to explain a horrible situation. But maybe, on the other hand, the miracle of inheritance had produced a guy who felt comfortable in this crime. Paul went over the story again and again.

How did Sarah Joe account for that moment, that moment when the urine splashed across her face and smock, puddling around her? Was Skip sad about it, afterward, the way Paul was sad about Libbets? Paul didn't know.

It was a story that didn't lead anywhere. Just something that happened. Just something to think about in the locked vault of familial regrets.

III

OKAY, the time has come in this account for a characterization of the mind of God. Just briefly, for thematic reasons. Happily there's no need to concern ourselves with this mind as it has expressed itself directly—because it hasn't, really. Therefore this story can be content with indirect examples, with metaphor and with evidence from nature. For example: Benjamin Hood, who was on Saturday morning asleep on the floor of the Halfords' bathroom, had a dream—an uncomfortable dream in the midst of a grueling hangover. Dreams retold are a burden, so this will be brief. In Hood's dream, a special tax had been levied against him because of fruit-bearing trees growing in his yard on Valley Road. He learned of this tax while taking a drive with Jim Williams (in a station wagon with simulated wood paneling, though Williams actually drove a Cadillac). Hood was trying to explain the presence of government inspectors in his yard, those inspectors in white, lead-lined suits, measuring the size and yield of his plum trees and then blowtorching them.

—The thing I can't figure out, he told Jim Williams, is whether this is happening in 1973 or in 1991.

—Well, pal, Williams said, the past and the future happen in the present moment. *That's just how it is.*

That's it. That's the dream. And the amazing thing about this dream is that Benjamin's son would dream it, too. Years later. Really. In Hoboken, New Jersey. Paul Hood. With his father as the main character and everything. Benjamin, however, as he lay on the floor of the bathroom dreaming uncomfortably, couldn't know — would never know — that his son would dream this very dream, that his son would wake and retell it and in the retelling become his father's imaginer as well as his father's son. His father's narrator.

This congruency — between Paul and his dad — is sort of like the congruency between me, the narrator of this story, the imaginer of all these consciousnesses of the past, and God. All these coincidences and lapses of coincidence were set in motion long before Benjamin or Paul was conceived, the way the topography and history of New Canaan — the shifting course of its rivers, the rise and fall of its tax revenues, its past, its future — preceded Benjamin and Paul, preceded all of us.

That's metaphor. I mentioned an example from nature, too. It follows. Though metaphors of the mind of God are characterized by coincidence and repetition, examples from nature aren't as tidy. Nature is senseless and violent. So this part of the story is violent, and because it's senseless, too, it's not from the point of view of any of the protagonists. It features a minor character. Mike Williams.

The ice had built up on every surface, on roofs and shrubs and avenues and cars and waterways. It formed a glittering and immense cocoon on tree limbs and power lines, a cocoon of impossible mass. The sound of tree limbs giving out under this weight was like the crackling of gunfire. Mike Williams, who was wandering around in the earliest part of dawn, heard these explosions in the stillness and laughed giddily at them. He was up really late. The threat of heavy weather impelled him out into the elements. To watch.

Danny Spofford's had been his first destination, up on Mill Road; Mike walked up Silvermine. When the occasional vehicle skidded past, he hid. The Conrads' AMC Gremlin went by. Somebody in a Corvette. It took a while to get to the Spoffords' on foot. When he got there, though, he and Danny stayed up watching television — *Don Kirshner's Rock Concert* — until the electricity went off. Then they became inventive, resourceful and inventive, as though the storm could in some way end all conversation, all teenaged fraternity. As though they only had a little time left. They began to counsel one another on what sexual intercourse would really be like. Fucking. At one point, Danny went into the kitchen and fetched a jar of strawberry jam out of the dormant refrigerator, Shopwell brand jam, into which he slid his middle finger. In an effort to simulate the velvet interior of a woman's reproductive apparatus. Standing in the middle of the kitchen, licking the jam from his *fuck finger,* Danny Spofford said that if it was going to be like that he wanted to do it right away.

— Pop the cherry, Charles.

Mike, of course, had experienced more of this than he was letting on. He was a Casanova. But since Danny Spofford was homely, since he was a kid with a big beak and a sloping forehead, ears that stuck out too far, Mike didn't want to insult him with too much experience. Not right away. But then as the night got deeper and colder and they wrapped themselves tighter in the blankets and quilts that Danny's dad had piled up on the old couch in the basement, Mike started to tell Danny about Wendy Hood.

— That slut? Danny Spofford said.

—Hey, you don't know her. Don't say that.

—A harlot, Charles. She's a *lesbee.* You're not gonna tell me—

—You don't get it, Spud. Let me finish.

But Mike was powerless to render the intricacies of unconsummated teen lust, the way it flattened out differences and made everyone compatible and everything tolerable. He couldn't explain how Wendy's dad had caught them with their pants down, because it was too embarrassing, and how this entrapment (kind of like that other arrest, in which Frank Wills stumbled upon Egil Krogh's men: James McCord, Bernard L. Barker, Virgilio Gonzalez, Eugenio Martinez, and Frank Sturgis) had only deepened his feelings for her. In the flickering candlelight, in the riot of competing flashlight beams, he couldn't say why he was always thinking about her, how he doodled her name and her initials in his ring binder, how he concealed it in english assignments, how he searched out songs in which her name appeared in the title or lyrics, how even words like *wind* and *when* had become pleasant because they were phonetically near to her name. Mike couldn't think of a way to tell Danny about any of this without sounding like a *sap,* a *moe,* a *fag,* a *homo,* a *feeb.* And anyway, he wasn't too good with words. What he liked to do was wander around.

—Forget it, he said. I'm gonna walk down to Silver Meadow. Wanna come?

—Nah. Let's toast some weenies. On these candles. Weenies, awesome.

Mike knew Danny wouldn't come with him. Danny's dad would probably show up from the party soon and would probably have some woman with him, and before he went upstairs with her, he would come down into the basement to see Danny. Maybe even the woman would come down and plant a single, moist kiss on Danny's forehead. Danny told Mike all this. His dad would check to make sure he had enough candles, that the batteries in the flashlights were fresh. His dad would tuck in an errant corner of his blanket and smooth back his cowlick. Because his dad had sued for custody and won. It was a rare thing and Danny wanted all the benefits of it, Mike figured. He was a kid blessed with a dad.

Mike's dad was okay, too, really — when he was home. But here Mike was: out in the cold. One of the unsupervised kids of New Canaan. The Spoffords' front door locked behind him. The creaking of the trees was like the sound track of some haunting. He thought about the blackout at Silver Meadow, about how the orderlies would be trying to keep all the loonies in line, in the dark, with the gunfire of trees snapping all around them. The loonies would be breaking out of the padded cells, breaking out onto the shuffleboard courts to conduct silent competitions with one another, they would be breaking into the medicine cabinets looking for opiates and tranquilizers, huddling with one another to give loony reassurances; they would be going out for booze, raiding adjacent homes for scotch and rye and gin and vodka and bourbon or Lavoris or Skin Bracer or Old Spice or Hai Karate.

It was the perfect time to sneak in.

So he did. He passed the Hoods' house, without so much as a look — he was denying himself — and then he snuck onto the grounds. It was a cinch, as usual. It was so easy that when he came to the Silver Meadow bowling alley, Mike tested the door. Impulsively. It opened! These guys were ridiculously casual! In the glow of emergency lighting he surveyed the two lanes. Since they were automated, the reset button obviously wasn't gonna work. And there were no balls to be found. Mike violated the first rule of bowling — proper foot attire — as he paced up and down the lanes. He had always wanted to walk right down to the pins. With a deft kick he tipped them over. And then set them up again. Knocked them over, set them up. It was too easy. Then he heard voices, the voices of authority, and took off.

He slipped back out onto the grounds. This went on for a long while, this trespassing. He imagined himself and Wendy in a wood-paneled station wagon with two children in the way back, puking from motion sickness. He walked from building to building, was chased off by a security guard — waving an impressive flashlight — and returned to trespass some more. Everywhere New Canaan was sheathed in this ice, in this coating that seemed to render the stuff of his everyday life beautiful again — magic, dangerous, and new. He recognized trees in a way he never had, recognized the vast, arterial movement of roads in his neighborhood, recognized the gallant and stalward quality of telephone poles, recognized even the warm support, in the occasional candlelit window, of community. Man against the elements, man. Everything was repackaged, sealed into a cellophane wrap that assured singularity and quality control. Mike was happy.

And then he saw his first live wire. It was in the middle of the night, the very center of night, in the darkest part before dawn. The sound of a maple coming down was familiar enough now. Mike laughed as the branch tumbled to earth and with it the telephone pole, the wires, a couple of shrubs. These things fell across Valley Road in a considerable impasse. He roared with laughter, coyote of the suburbs. The severed wire was anything but still. It hissed, of course, and there was the gold-dusting of electrical sparks. And it danced. The jig of the dervish, of delirious and religious mad persons, of hyperactive children and their weary parents. The dance of the charmed snake. The electrical line hopped and skipped and nothing could stop it that Mike knew of. It was just one of the hazards of life now. Cool!

Look, he was not a brilliant kid. He had not scored well on standardized tests or on any other tests. He was a little lazy, in fact. Mostly he tried to sit next to Mona Henderson and copy answers. But he knew about live wires, about the lore of live wires. So he made a wide berth several hundred feet around the moiling electrical field and then back onto that thoroughfare, Valley Road, back onto his trail. He wasn't lonely now. He was full of life. He wished Wendy Hood were here to see all this. As he climbed carefully over the cable guardrail, he checked the icy sheen on the incline there, where Valley Road started down toward Silvermine. He checked the surface and found it to his liking. It could be burnished into a fine sliding surface. He cleared away any chunky, crusty stuff on a good twelve or fourteen feet of the roadway. With his sneakers he brushed this surface clean, as carefully and lovingly as if he were going to sign his name to it. And then he positioned himself ten feet or so from the beginning of this runway to get up speed.

Oh, the solitude of that moment! Mike could hear his breath as he chugged up to the ice, and then the sharp intake as he held in the chilly air and careened down the hill. It was good. Cool. He cleared a few more feet. No one was up, but he thought he could make out the glimmerings of dawn in the east. There were stars and moonlight and the intimation of dawn, and these occasionally illumined his solitary competition. No cars would be coming, because the road was sealed off now by the splendid devastation of the elements. Mike was like the hockey stars so prized by New Canaan high schoolers. He was like Ken "The Snake" Stabler, quarterback for his favorite football team, the unforgiving Oakland Raiders. He was like the intrepid skiers at the beginning of *The Wide World of Sports*. He was like Dave Wottle or Mark Spitz or Tug McGraw or O. J. Simpson. He was a citizen of the physical world.

He trudged to the top of his giant slalom again, and again he navigated it flawlessly, coming to the bottom of the slope on his feet. The Russian judges scored him well. The noise of some imagined crowd buoyed him up. He would take the gold and then save the Israeli athletes from their fate. Even the live wire, hissing and spitting, applauded his efforts. Again he executed this stunning turn, this wild communion with air and snow and silence.

When he set up for his fourth frisky plunge, he was aware that he was tired all of a sudden, that the wind was blowing harder, that the live wire was wobbling grandiosely in the wind. He wanted to go home, to be supine in his own bed. But he had a boner, an actual erection, for all this, for toys and dramas and the unknown of sexuality and athletic accomplishment and the future with its distant fuzzy glimpses of business and responsibility. So he couldn't sleep yet. First one more passage along his little corridor of ice.

Mike got up a real bit of speed this time, his arms waving wildly as he listed first this direction and then the other, but when he hit the landing area, he stumbled and fell. Ice was all in his jacket now and in his sneakers, down his socks, down the neck of his ski jacket. His hands were raw and red as he held them up to his face. Fucking shit. Fucking A. He held them under his arms to try and still the pain. He moaned quietly. It was another quarter-mile uphill to his house. And he was just going to get yelled at. If not now, later.

So he decided to sit on the guardrail for a second. To relax.

This is the kind of guardrail they had on the secondary roads of New Canaan: a steel cable stapled onto, at predetermined intervals, substantial wood posts that were then cemented into the embankments on the side of the road. The idea was that if a car struck the cable, the guardrail would give a little bit with the impact, instead of destroying the vehicle and its inhabitants immediately. The problem with this kind of guardrail, though, was that unlike a totally steel construction, which is grounded directly into the earth, this steel cable was essentially freestanding. And therefore conductive. And the live wire hopping gaily beside Valley Road was also touching the guardrail at the moment at which Mike Williams sat upon it. His sneakers, immersed in the snow beneath him, acted as a ground, and what power was not lost — very little — in the movement of electricity along three wooden posts, along seventy-five feet of cable, and through three heavy staples — this electricity passed into Mike.

First his face grew terribly red and he began to foam at his mouth. His teeth chattered and his hair began to cook. Then his heart stopped. This happened almost immediately. His heart seized up, arrested. It was a strong, young heart, untroubled by erratic beating, or by any sort of buildup in the arteries, but it gave out anyway. He was magnetized, because that's one thing electricity can do, magnetized to the cable, but after he died, after the electricity in him that was his own, that was the accumulation of his fears and affections, traveled out into the ether, his body, his remains, slumped over backward, smoking a little bit. His hands were scorched black from where they held the cable. He smoked from the ears and bled from the nose and mouth. He slumped over backward, fell off the guardrail — because gravity was stronger in this instance, and because the capricious live wire was now dancing in another direction — and he rolled backward down the hill a little bit, down under a shrub on the furthest edge of the property belonging to Silver Meadow. A corner of his orange ski jacket was visible from the road, but you needed to be looking to see it.

This moment passed twice. Once, in the simple narrative of that night, the narrative belonging to the town of New Canaan, and once in the last instant of Mike's consciousness. And so this second account is appended here. Suddenly, Mike's weariness and remorse, his regret about having left the house to wander the streets without ever being caught, without ever being searched for, overcame him. His hands were raw and aching. He was chastened. He longed for the consolations of some imagined and perfect family. He sat because he was tired, just plunked himself down ass first, and then steadied himself by grabbing the cable. No preliminary warning troubled him. Maybe there ought to have been a noise or a shock when the downed electrical lines touched the guardrail, but the shock of that night was so routine he wouldn't have noticed if there had been. The sound of hissing, the ominous sound of modern technology loose in nature — Mike was used to all that. That was his language.

His last thought, a simple, adolescent *oh, no,* was all he had time for; in fact it was exactly simultaneous with his electrocution, because through some strange celestial circuitry, he knew at the moment of his death that it was his death. A jumble of images appeared at once to him, a jumble of dreams and recollections, condensed and displaced. And then Mike said, *oh, no,* subvocalized it. And then his consciousness split from this plane:

Benjamin Hood knew nothing of Mike Williams when he awoke on the floor of the bathroom at the Halfords' place. Sometime before dawn. Throat parched, throat napalmed, Agent Oranged. Mouth full of canker sores. The sinister combs, of all shapes and stripes, plastic and onyx, contemporary and antique, the combs that decorated Dot's half-bath, pressed in against him. He guzzled water from the spigot, his lips curled unsanitarily around it. He was unshaven. His ascot had disappeared somewhere. He wondered if his overcoat was still in the guest room by the front door, and if his wallet was in it.

The modern domestic tale always features the ordeal and dismemberment of a father. This was the dim certainty to which Hood awoke. His consciousness had closed down, had narrowed down to a dot, like the old monochrome television sets when you shut them off. Sometime in the midst of the party his consciousness had closed down. He wasn't sure how he had arrived in the bathroom, how he had spilled these flecks of upchuck on himself.

Gray, isolated moments of conversation returned. He had a vivid recollection of being inches from his wife's face and, in the midst of some debate, losing control of his own saliva, so that a tusk of the stuff protruded from his cavernous and angry mouth. Later, he remembered trying to speak to Rob Halford, trying to apologize for something and finding himself suddenly, inappropriately alone. Halford had just walked out of the conversation, had simply walked away without excuse or apology. Hood had been in the middle of a sentence, in the middle of a heartfelt confession, and Rob had simply given up on him. Benjamin was treated with contempt at these parties, it became obvious to him now. He was treated like a common bum. And like a bum he remembered finishing his conversation out loud, to himself. In isolation. Alone.

Now he wandered the spotless first floor of the Halfords' house as though its emptiness was his responsibility. None of the lights worked. The clocks were stopped. Hood's coat remained on the bed in the guest room where he had left it. It was like a disconsolate body spread there. In the front hall, his keys lay in the salad bowl, unchosen from the night before.

So Benjamin Hood left the way he had come, trying to undo what faulty recollections he had of the evening's mindless pleasures. He'd felt worse, but not that he could remember. Outdoors he came face-to-face with the crippling elements. The ice was like some polystyrene coating that separated him from the world, some wax curtain that pronounced his guilt — guilty of drunkenness, of boorishness, of adultery, of forging a bad relationship with chance. Guilty of presuming upon chance. Guilty of weakening and diluting what bonds of family remained in his family. Guilty of following bad impulses to their bad conclusions. He was quarantined and he deserved it.

At least the Firebird remained in the driveway. But the driver's-side lock was frozen. This was just the next embarrassment. He didn't even curse. He undertook that procedure well known in more northerly climates. It was time-consuming but he had time. Back into the house. Boil water. Bring water (in a teacup) and a key and towel out to car. Immerse key. Dry vigorously, quickly. Insert warm, dry key into lock. And this proved effective. The next hurdle was the ice frozen onto the windshield. In these small contretemps, it was surprising and rewarding to Hood that the larger questions of that morning — where his wife might be, what his children were going to think — were lost. He involved himself in scraping the windshield with one of those ineffective plastic scrapers — this one had the name of a dry cleaner on it — and this involvement seemed to take all morning. It was good.

The whole world was white and gray as he inched down Ferris Hill. He passed the cars parked along the road, or stalled in the ditch. The conifers, weighed down with ice and snow, were shrouded mourners. His heart lurched when he saw Jim Williams's Cadillac folded up on a fallen tree. Hood left the Firebird running, coughing, and popping, as he skidded and trotted out to be sure there was no one inside the wreck. There were no faint footprints around the car. And there was no one inside.

This drive home. Holy Center Approaching. He would put it all behind him. Towing vehicles, emergency vehicles, these chasers of calamity had proven ineffectual. But Benjamin Hood's protectorate, the gale that had buffeted him from one situation to another, was at last blowing in a good direction. That was clear. (The Williamses' house looked as abandoned as the Halfords'.)

And then he reached the fallen tree and telephone pole, the roadblock just down the hill.

He sat in the car for some minutes. There was a live wire, up there, a goddam live wire. Where were these utility guys when you needed them? Were tires an effective ground? If the wire somehow snaked up the street and zapped his Firebird would he be safe? How long had this situation been this way? He didn't know whether to get out or to await further instructions. At last, Benjamin Hood, scaly and unlovable, decided to act. He would telephone from Silver Meadow. He shut the car off — with emergency lights flickering — stepped carefully out of the car, and then sprinted twenty feet back up the road, stumbling on the ice. His girth heaved, his chest exploded, the frigid air daggered his lungs. His migrainous headache blossomed. But he was still alive. He stepped over the guardrail and down the embankment, intending to give the live wire a wide berth, and that was when he chanced upon Mike Williams.

It was a piece of orange fabric lodged under a tree. No, it was someone asleep under the tree, some errant boozer, some other boozer like him. No. Hood knew. It wasn't someone sleeping. Oh, please. Hood fell to his knees. No. He froze. He whispered religious oaths. In the ice and snow. He held his face in his hands.

Then he decided to run. He was already running. Back toward the car. He slipped. He was up running again. He fell again. Hood was no troubleshooter. He was not resourceful. He had to get out of there before someone saw him, saw the car. He would just leave.

But then fate smiled on Benjamin Hood. It was this simple. Just as he was putting a leg over the guardrail — where Mike himself had fatally sat — Hood found himself flushed with calm. The morning was still. He felt grief, sure, but he felt he could contribute something, too. Grace flickered in him. There was nowhere to run to, particularly. No safe port in this storm. What was he going to do? So he traced his steps back down toward the body.

He held Mike Williams's blue head in his hands. He fumbled at the boy's ski jacket, pulled open the shirt beneath, pressed his ear against a Yale T-shirt. No. An emptiness in there like the sound in one of those plastic conch shells. Hood pressed his lips against the lips of the dead boy, the boy he had never liked much, and sang into his mouth. He punched on Mike Williams's chest the way he had seen people punch the chests of the dead on medical programs. No. He didn't think it would work, and it didn't.

The revelation of death was that Mike Williams would be dead as long as Benjamin knelt by him. None of Hood's remedies would work and none of his wishes, his fervent wishes now, would either. Mike would be dead all afternoon and into the next. This was the miracle. Death was terribly durable. It was the sturdiest idea around. A body was dead, and before long it wasn't even a body anymore, it was just elements. But it was still dead. Hood was embracing Mike now, caring for him in death as meticulously as he had disliked him in life. He heaved him into a sitting position. Mike was getting rigid now, like any winter thing, even though soft, pliable memories still circled around him. Memories and seraphim.

The ineffectual sun had risen just above the treetops. The temperature would inch beyond zero centigrade. It was two or three hundred yards across the front of Silver Meadow, past its shrubs and walkways and parking lot and security gate, to his house, to Hood's house, and perhaps three-quarters of a mile uphill to the Williamses'. Hood decided to carry the boy to his house. The decision, made quickly, if with foggy, hung-over reason and with a hundred-and-ten-pound frozen corpse in his arms, was one that would stay with Benjamin Hood for good. Suddenly it seemed, truly suddenly, that this body, this abbreviated life, this disaster, was *his*.

Of course he intended to give the body back. To Janey Williams, whom he loved, and her husband, to whom he was now bound in a much different way, but he would take care of the situation first. He would exercise an almost parental control over this tragedy. He left his car behind and bore this body up grimly. Its gloved hands brushed across his face. It slid out of his arms and he had to lean it against the bench on the walkway at Silver Meadow, his own matted hair and his glasses brushing against Mike's, cheek to cheek with the frosty, dead skin of Mike Williams. He needed rest. Each step, with its meager vocabulary of progress — only ten more feet until that blacktop there — seemed interminable.

The security guys rushed down the road toward him, when he got Mike heaved up over his shoulder again. They were sprinting, and, though they looked familiar, there was no way Benjamin could have known that they were the same guys who knew his daughter by name, who had chased his son from the same hillside where this catastrophe had taken place, who had chased Mike out of the bowling lanes the night before. Out of breath, their mottled, black uniform shoes covered in snow, they called out to Hood.

— Is that your boy? What happened?

They stood in a circle around Mike and somehow Benjamin found himself telling them the story. They tried to comfort Hood, who was shaken now and having trouble putting sentences together; at least they tried to comfort him to the degree that one male — in New Canaan — can comfort another. It was Hood's first dead body. They didn't pat him on the back, or hug him, or tell him it would be all right. They stood aside, each of them as far as possible from the other. Their heads bowed.

— You better try to get a hold of yourself, one said.

— Are the . . . ? Can you tell me if the phones are working? Hood said.

— We've got radio, said the other.

— Well, you ought to call an ambulance then, Hood said. Or the police . . . or the paramedics. Whoever can get through on the roads. I think this boy — his name is Mike Williams and he lives just up the road . . . I think he must have been burned somehow. He's all . . . he's burned.

— Whyntcha let us —

Hood pointed at his house, down below the main buildings of the hospital.

— I'm over there. That's where we'll be. 129 Valley Road. That's . . . I'm going to put him in the other car. . . . I'll wait —

And the security men stood by, hands in pockets. When they realized there was no persuading to be done, they sprang into action, jogging toward the little booth with the little two-way radio in it, where reports of college football games and new developments in the unraveling tenure of the President were overwhelmed by the machine-gun blasts of two-way radio static.

Hood's odyssey across the front lawn of Silver Meadow and into his own driveway, down that meandering path and into the house was as heroic as anything from the epics of the past. He wasn't quite as execrable as he thought. The magic involved was not visible to the naked eye. There were no swords or orcs or dragons or elves or rings in this adventure, but it was magic anyway. Hood had been transformed on Saturday morning from a self-pitying and disliked and hung-over securities analyst into, however briefly, an agent of sympathy. On the other hand, which life wasn't heroic? Just living was heroic. Just talking to your family in the morning, before coffee, was heroic.

His home, meanwhile, had been ravaged by the elements. As Hood came up the driveway he called out his wife's name, and the sound of that name, its elongated vowels, was dispersed across the frozen wastes to echo and reverberate upon the Silvermine River. No answer. He called again. He called Wendy's name. He carried Mike to the garage, had to drag him part of the way, because Benjamin was starting to feel weak, to where the station wagon was parked. He left the body outside while he started the car.

Except that it wouldn't start. It coughed feebly and then lapsed into silence. He dragged the body back to the house. Because he couldn't open the door without setting down his burden. *Oh, please open the goddam door.* Hood wasn't at all prepared to find the house empty. Where the hell was everybody?

When he had laid Mike lengthways in the front hall, Daisy Chain trotted out from under some table someplace, his tail wagging wildly, violently. Benjamin swallowed hard on what he now perceived as the outrageous treatment of this dog.

— Poor pooch, poor, old pooch.

He let the body slump to the ground. Daisy Chain, skittering desperately at the door, would not stop.

— Need to go out, pooch? Okay, okay. Even you don't want to be stuck in here, huh?

The dog jumped at the door. And maneuvering around Mike Williams, Ben released his hound, like the rest of his family, into winter. He slammed the door shut.

Then he found out about the pipes. Water was trickling down the walls in the living room. The house had turned into some Revolutionary War fountain, the Reverend Mark Staples's fountain. Water was trickling, no, *streaming* down the walls in Hood's house. The enormity of it took a moment to sink in — as the water itself was sinking into the antique planks and walls of his home. From the ceiling the water came in sheets, and beneath it a large, brownish stain, more than eighteen inches wide, with the curvilinear shape, say, of a Smiley Face, perhaps, or the flame of some Yuletide candle. Rorschach stain. For a second Hood was reminded, in the midst of the crises around him, of the burning of the Yule log, that video loop that played on WPIX for five or six hours on Christmas Day. The water stain was inching outward along the linen-colored paint job. And on the floor of the living room, there was a large puddle of standing water. While the cascades from the ceiling ran down, the puddle trickled through the floorboards into the basement.

Maybe Hood was not thinking clearly, but he followed the water where it led. He left Mike to look after the flood. On the other side of this wall, too, in the front hall closet, more falls fell. The stream ran down onto the floor and in a winding, indirect creek down toward the kitchen. Away from Mike. In the closet, Elena's furs, some leather items, and a bunch of tennis and paddle-tennis rackets — everything had been touched by the curse of this flood.

Hood ran past Mike and up the front stairs to the second floor. He was guessing that the leak originated in the master bathroom, and, although the wall there had indeed partly caved in, although this water closet was directly above the worst manifestations of the flood, he could find no direct evidence of a burst pipe. He could see in past the Sheetrock, though, into that strange netherworld of wiring and struts and joists that resembled nothing so much as the inside of a human body. He felt he could reach into the thundering heart of his home, and thus into the heart of his family. He felt almost certain that the heart he would find there would be stilled. The frozen part of the plumbing must have emanated from that point. The water flowed out into the hall, down toward Wendy's bedroom and then disappeared, miraculously. It meant to travel, this water. It was *flow*. Its motion was no respecter of dignity. It simply moved. And there wasn't much Hood could do about it. He tried to call the plumber, got right on the phone in his blue-gray bedroom, a deep red rotary phone with a pleasant shape and heft. Then he remembered that the line was dead. He tried the tap and the shower. A sigh, like a last breath, issued forth from each of them.

The house was frigid, wet, and dark. In his perturbation, Hood recalled a lecture he had received from his own father about burst pipes. Like any paternal lecture this one was probably full of half-truths, digressions, polemics, and nostalgic anecdotes from the past. Still, one point stood out. *Sometimes a leak skips a whole floor. Sometimes the leak is on the whole other side of the house from where the problem originates.* And pipes, he remembered, usually split lengthways.

He didn't know what to do next, whether to try to find his children, whether to presume they had been spirited away by his wife, who had reached the end of her tolerance, whether to try to shut off the water somehow, whether to further inspect the damage, or whether to do something about Mike, the son of his former mistress.

Each time he passed through the front hall, Mike seemed to have moved.

A strangulated yelp punctuated the silence at the front hall. The dog was back. Scratching at the door.

— Jesus, Hood said to Daisy Chain, letting him in. I have a lot on my plate here. Could you look after yourself for a little while?

Hood fished out a pair of galoshes from the hall closet. He descended into the basement, where the washer and dryer were located. The water in the basement grazed his kneecaps. It seemed to flow out one end of the basement into the Silvermine River, as if Hood's house had now become a part of the river itself, part of that topographical movement from the Appalachian foothills to the Long Island Sound. The river had reached out to incorporate the Hoods and their residence into itself.

A sort of gushing also issued forth — there in the basement — from a particularly damaged line against one wall. Hood stepped down into that river just the same. It was only because of its motion, Hood thought, that the water wasn't yet frozen. He shuddered as he waded across to where the washer and dryer protruded — craggy water hazards in that dank loch. He stepped on a pair of roller skates and fell, yelping, against the banister. Drenched to the waist. No theory of the flood, of its origin, would satisfy him now. He wasn't going to think reasonably any longer. He would abandon all thinking about causes. He decided instead just to take the sheet he saw on top of the dryer up to cover Mikey. The sheet — a blue, floral print that usually covered Wendy's bed — was drenched. But what were his options? Hood waded through the oily water and up into the front hall again. It was the least he could do.

When he reached the top of the stairs he found that the dog was now preoccupied with Mike. Vigorously, Daisy Chain circulated around the body, sniffing and licking, tail oscillating. The dog seized Mike's sleeve in its mouth and began to wrestle with it.

Hood clapped his hands feverishly, sheet clamped under one arm.

— Hey! Fuck, Daisy, get the hell away from there. Come on, oh, fuck.

The dog paused to lick Mike's palm one more time before dancing just out of reach of Hood and into the living room.

He covered poor Mike.

— What, am I going to have to chain you up outside or something? You're going to eat the neighbors now? Jesus Christ.

He followed the dog into the living room and grabbed it by the collar. — C'mon with me. He locked Daisy Chain in the kitchen. And then, with a Duraflame log from the pile in the living room, he headed for the library. He thought: Naugahyde recliner. He was exhausted and he needed a minute to think. He had learned to build a fire well, in New England. With these instincts guiding him, he relaxed, but he also accelerated the pace of his home's destruction. The pipes would melt faster.

He was awakened by the ambulance a little later. The ambulance from the police department. Janey and Jim Williams had drifted in and out of his sleep, looking like the parents in a Claymation Sunday-morning television show his kids used to watch. Religious programming. Their worried expressions and wooden movements, their beseechments and entreaties stretched a shadow across his uneasy nap. The police pulled up in the driveway without a siren, and rapped on the door knocker — the doorbell was electric — as though there were no emergency at all. Hood rose after a while. The banging had become a strange, percussive factor in his dreams. The dog was barking, too, in the kitchen.

— Got a call about some burns, the driver said.

Behind him stood two other men, sleepless and overburdened. One scratching under his ski cap. Fully certified Emergency Medical Technicians. The body occupied most of the foyer there. They couldn't miss it.

— That's him, Hood said, eyes falling back on Mike.

— He's —

— That's right.

The ambulance driver strode past Hood to the draped Williams boy. The other two men retreated to the ambulance to construct one of their foldout stretchers.

— Cold enough for you? the driver said grimly, as he peeled back the edge of the sheet and pressed his hand against Mike's neck. What do you mean burn? No trace of a burn. Why's this sheet wet, anyway?

— Well, he's —

— You weren't trying to treat him, I hope.

— No, I —

— Where'd you find him? Are you related to him?

Hood condensed the story.

— What's the condition of the roads up there? the driver asked.

— Well, there are some downed lines, Benjamin said. My car is —

— Electrical or telephone? How far was he from those lines? What time did you find him? Why didn't you leave him at the, uh, at the psychiatric hospital?

The technician had Mike's jacket and shirt open now

and was looking for markings of any kind. But this expert knew the answer, Benjamin could tell, and he knew, too. When the other two volunteers had hoisted the stretcher up onto the front step, the driver pronounced Mike's fate, as though breaking a spell. He turned over one of the boy's palms.

— Electrocution, you guys. Electrocution.

— You wanna wire up the —

— No point, the driver said. He's been this way for a couple of hours, I'll bet. Radio it in?

They flung Mike's shroud on the floor by the stairs and covered him with a fresh, dry one. Then they strapped him onto the gurney and rolled it back toward the ambulance.

— Listen, Hood said. You're going to Norwalk Hospital? Before you go we really ought to tell his family. Or at least drop me there. It's just up there. The phones are down and my car is. . . . Do you think you could?

The driver said nothing.

— They're my neighbors. This boy is my neighbors' son. My kids have played with him. My daughter was going steady with this boy. This boy right here.

Hood had become firm. His demeanor had changed. He was acquainted with this bad luck. He knew what he was saying.

— Imagine if it was your son, he said.

The driver sucked on his lower lip. He had a prizefighter's dull glare. Said nothing. But he led Hood out into the driveway, and he held open the back of the ambulance for Hood. Benjamin was going to sit in the back, with the corpse. He was out in the cold air again, in just galoshes and the jacket from last night. He was aware that his hair was mussed, that he needed a shower. They wheeled the stretcher up to the ambulance and hoisted it in. The radio in the ambulance was clear on one point — the temperature would plunge again, in the afternoon. Yes, radio. In that swift moment, when the door was closed behind him, Hood was put back in touch with the all-news format, with its blessed and conflicting voices — Britain slashes budget, Brendan Byrne opposes Jersey Turnpike extension, United Nations peacekeeping force patrols heavily mined areas between Egyptian and Israeli armies, Hall Bartlett's new film, *Jonathan Livingston Seagull,* opens to mixed reviews, move in Congress to impeach. The Concord, California, murder case: two popular locals, Walter and Joanne Parkin, their children, their baby-sitter, the baby-sitter's boyfriend and her parents all murdered by drifter from the Bronx, Dennis Guzman, and his accomplice, Archie Stealing, also of Concord. Elsewhere in California: an Oakland school superintendent executed with cyanide bullets by unknown terrorist organization, the Symbionese Liberation Army, which objected to the superintendent's "fascist" policies.

— Which roads are clear? the driver called back.

Hood didn't know. The two volunteers in the back of the ambulance with Hood stared down at the floor.

They proceeded by guesswork. Here is how Benjamin Hood reached the Williamses' house. The long way, because of the power lines. Power lines down everywhere. The ambulance, with sirens cutting through the still day, through the subtle tinkling of melting ice, drove back to Silvermine Road and up to Canoe Hill, which was impassable because of multiple fallen trees, down Ridge Road to Rose Brook (past the wildlife sanctuary), back on Canoe Hill, where they went into a slide, which the driver quickly righted, down Route 123 to North Wilton, back down Laurel Road all the way to Turner Hill and then onto

Valley Road. They passed the hulks of abandoned BMWs and Volvos and Volkswagens, they passed destruction in every forest and yard. The longer the drive took, the more Hood's insides knotted. His bowels were full, his life had changed, and he had a lot of talking to do.

THOUGH THE SORTS of love songs Wendy sang in her semi-sleep were all mixed up, though they mixed the Eros and the Agape, gift-love and need-love, pseudo-love and the art of love, courtly or secular love (that conceit of twelfth-century poetry) and the love of God, the love of nature with the fetishism of objects, the love of parents with profane premarital love, she knew as the sunlight streamed into the guest room at the Williamses' that the house of love was the house she inhabited. Its many windows, dormers, gables, ingresses, and egresses were hers. Its sagging gutters and leaky roof, its unusual additions and secret staircases. Love was a sweet, soft thing and a force that could batter communities. Too late to turn back now, she believed she was falling in love. She was dirty-sweet and she was his girl. *Sandy, I'm a fine girl, what a good wife I will be.* Precious and few were the moments they two would share. *Call out my name, baby, just call it out.* I'll be there, on that midnight train, I'll be there. Gimme the beat boys, free my soul . . .

Wait a second. Guest room? Wendy opened her eyes again. She could see her breath, it hovered before her. Sandy's slow respiration, too, like winter exhaust. She was in the Williamses' house? Still? She lurched from the bed.

The floors were like ice. She danced. But soon her implacable mood returned. The electricity was off: no heat. She was already here. It was morning. She couldn't leave the room without running into Sandy's parents, without running into Mike, and that was just the way it would be now. Anyway, she loved Sandy. Anyway, she wanted to write Sandy's name on her breasts in indelible marker and to wear his band of gold. Anyway, she wanted to have his baby, to introduce him to marijuana, to watch him grow his first mustache.

She woke him roughly, just to see his expression. She called his name. His eyes opened immediately into regret and panic. Still sleepy, rubbing and scratching, he threw himself into a sitting position. His feet dangled over the edge of the bed.

— Oh, boy. . . . Oh. What are we gonna do?

Wendy laughed.

She was gathering up her clothes and, including the soiled garter belt from Mike's closet, carefully concealing it from Sandy, pushing it down into her ski pants, as she drew her turtleneck over her head again.

— We have to get back into my room, he said. You have to get out somehow.

— Huh?

— Don't talk so loud, Sandy whispered.

— I'm not, and besides, you're being a prude, you know? Who cares?

Sandy was out of the bed now, looking for evidence of something on the sheets, though there were no stains, looking anyway, the way an alcoholic will go through a metal detector convinced that he probably picked up a handgun somehow. Sandy looked for the abject beginnings of his own sexuality drip-drying there, or for the popped cherry which, according to school-yard sex studies, must have accompanied Wendy's night in his bed. Then he folded back the blankets, organized the bedspread. Everyone's bed-making style was their own, Wendy knew, as personal as their fingerprints or their heartbeat. Sandy wasn't doing anything more than forestalling his moment of coming clean. His neat but imperfect hospital corners would never fool his mom.

The way Wendy saw it, in this enclosed space, in this first flush of morning, they were secure — young lovers like avid readers gazing at the frontispiece of a dusty, inherited volume — refracting the movements of the outside world, of Canaan Parish and beyond. Eventually the door would swing wide. But for now they could just ride the love train.

So Wendy stopped, and removed her turtleneck again, cradling it in the pile of outer garments she held at her waist. She felt the frigid air on her nipples, those small, pink announcements of her sex, and she headed for the door.

— Clock's stopped, Sandy was saying behind her.

She was ravished, and what difference did it make? She was changed. What was the loudest noise a girl could make? What did buildings look like when they collapsed? Did the Pentagon actually levitate? She opened the door and loped without regret across the threshold of the guest room and into Sandy's room, where G. I. Joe's execution was still being played out. She began to lift her voice in song, to mumble lyrics from the Led Zeppelin songbook and other head music. Hawkwind. The ringwraiths rode in black!

Her mother's appearance at this point was swift, stunning, and unpredictable. Wendy cried out, in fact, at the sight of her mother, disarranged, wearing last night's clothes. Standing in the hall. It was as if her mother had learned the techniques of the sorceress — had learned actual invisibility — and through one of her spells had been observing her daughter's movements. Her Valkyrie mom. Later this moment replayed itself again and again in Wendy's consciousness, as if things would have turned out differently if she just hadn't gone out of that guest room.

— Put your shirt on right now, dammit, her mother said. Put your clothes on.

Beside them, between herself and her mom, Wendy could see the door to the guest room swing back — less than an inch. She could feel the worry that collected on the other side of it. In the meantime, though, she got hold of herself. She padded into Sandy's room. She was ready to deal with what was going down. She was sullen and erotically slothful. She scattered her turtleneck and her sweater and her poncho on Sandy's bed as though she were laying out a bounteous harvest. She took her time. She had goose bumps. She hugged herself with crossed arms. Her mother followed her into the bedroom.

— What are you doing here? Wendy asked.

— What business is it of yours? Elena Hood said. I might ask you the same question, young lady. It's my business to ask the questions. Did you spend the whole night here? And who gave you permission to do so? And where exactly did you spend the night? Where in this house?

Her mother's attention darted around the room as Wendy dressed, lit upon the doll swinging from the noose above Sandy's closet, didn't take it in. Then, peering out into the hall, Elena saw the guest room and understood. She called out Jim Williams's name, called down the hall,

Jim!, and seized the doorknob — behind which Sandy stood in the dark, clutching his pajamas right at the crotch — ambushing the youngest Williams boy, with his dad not far behind her.

— What have you two been doing in here? Oh, dammit. Jim. Oh, *shoot.*

And so forth. With the imposing, yellow flashlight he bore — as long as his own forearm — Jim Williams and Wendy's mother examined the room, as though this entrapment didn't tell the story itself. They peeled back the bedding that Sandy had so laboriously organized; they turned over the pillows like archaeologists sifting through the dust. Finally they pulled the covers and the fitted sheet off the bed and searched the mattress itself, where there was an old dried menstrual stain. The pad on that bed — it was like some bloody shroud. Then, Elena Hood began to focus her attention upon the empty vodka bottle. Wendy and Sandy lingered guiltily behind their parents. The time for punishment was upon them.

— You drank this, bub? Williams said to his son, as Elena brandished the bottle. You realize the trouble this can get you into? Do you know anything about alcohol poisoning? Do you know what to do if someone suffers from alcohol poisoning? Have you ever heard of people choking on their own insides? From this stuff right here? Can you imagine what that's like, son?

Elena dragged Wendy out into the corridor to give her the same dressing-down. A long, familiar disquisition. She had watched so many people in her family destroyed by this and she couldn't watch it again. It was just too painful. Because of the way it ran in families, she or Paul could easily. . . . If you could have seen your grandmother. . . .

Your uncle and his sadness and failures and all that suffering. . . . And don't forget about your dad . . . and mental illness, and death. Young lady. Death.

— Are you listening to me?

— All ears, Mom.

The next act of parental justice, the meting out of corporal punishment, arose swiftly from the lecturing, like a flash flood or act of God. Wendy had a sense that the scale of punishment that morning was a little out of whack, but she didn't know why at first. There was some adult thing going on that she didn't yet understand. Where was Sandy's mom, for example? Where was her dad? Then it began to register. She permitted herself to be led down the stairs as though to an execution. She permitted herself to be swallowed. Into the continuity of police logic. Pigs.

And there was a history to corporal punishment among the Hoods. There was a locus for punishment. It started with Paul. Paul was often a sickly child, out most of his kindergarten year at East School, with various infections and ailments — a case of strep throat and double ear infection, measles, whooping cough. Paul howled in the earliest morning hours, calling into question his own short life, in shrill, desperate shrieks that kept his parents awake, cries that in their desolation seemed to reach into his mother's heart and wrestle with her competence as a parent. This much was family lore. Elena had developed the habit, during this period, of taking Paul's temperature anally — because of his throat problems. It was one of those lovely, glass thermometers that was immersed in a glass case full of alcohol, the sort that seemed to foretell good by its very seriousness and simplicity. This practice persisted, until Paul came to see his mother's approach — the mysterious darkness into which she plunged her medical instrument — as the cure itself, bringing with it a legitimation of his distress.

This practice carried over to Wendy Hood, who also came to appreciate these ministrations given in silence, given with the dispassionate, preoccupied air of a jeweler or orthodontist. In silence, wreathed in isopropyl incense, the thermometer would tickle her hidden pink aperture, and she would be cured.

This, however, was not the only attention visited upon her ass in the Hood household. For the ass-spanking was a regular thing there. These occasions were grandly stylized, full of careful and loving ritual. Wendy's first spanking was the great organizing event of her early memory, though the crime that precipitated it was long forgotten. Her father carried her into her parents' bedroom. Her mother stood by, wordlessly. She refused to take down her pants. Her father humiliated her with language until she did so — called her a *slut* and a *hooker* and a *princess*. It wasn't difficult to degrade her with language — she was four. She took down her pants of her own free will. He then set her across his lap, and her mother presented the hairbrush — in the lore of the family, the bristle side was occasionally used — and, after pausing to contemplate the blank innocence of her hindquarters, her father drove the blunt side of the brush down upon her ass. What was her mother doing? Her nails?

Wendy recognized these diverse attentions on her ass, and they had become in some way indistinguishable, one from the other. They had become the Gestalt of her body. Which came first — the good-natured nursing of her mother, or the stern, but thoughtful, beatings of her father — was now unclear. It was all wound up together. What she ate, how she dressed, whether she ventured into the crass world of facial makeup, these seemed unimportant compared to how she attended to that site of medicinal and patriarchal attentions. She was mom and dad's little piece of ass.

So the trip down into the Williamses' living room had one purpose only. She could hear Sandy crying upstairs now and she could hear Mr. Williams's escalating monologue. These words had a mumbled, cabalistic sound. Hindu sutras. T.M. Elena Hood gripped her daughter's wrist tightly. The stark and pristine order of the Williamses' house surrounded them. In the living room, Elena commanded her to take down her pants. Wendy would have suffered this abuse — it seemed inevitable, almost natural — even though she was fourteen years old, because she had other things on her mind, because it had been a long twenty-four hours. But then she remembered that Mike's soiled garter belt was still tucked down there, tucked into her ski pants, and this was the one secret she wasn't going to part with. She refused.

— I said take down your pants, please, Elena Hood said.

— I'm too old. What are you going to do, Mom, spank me at the prom? Come find me in college so you can spank me?

— There's not going to be a negotiation here.

— Why, Mom, what are you going to do, *fuck me?*

This ended the conversation. Her mother restrained Wendy in a choke hold. The room turned sideways, and suddenly Wendy was screaming, crying, and being dragged along the front hall. The details she could make out in the midst of this grim procession were strangely satisfying: the Oriental rug in the front hall bunched up under her heels; the morning sun reflected on the brass frame of a mirror in the front hall; her mother's face, distorted in the frame. Water was dripping somewhere. Her mother's strength was all out of proportion with her tiny, retiring body. In the bathroom — by the entrance to the basement — her mother held Wendy's mouth shut, clamped her palm there, and ran the tap with one hand. She immersed a handy little soap ball under the tap, until it had a good head of lather, and then she forced her daughter's mouth open — Wendy was begging for her not to do it, but these cries were wordless, strangled — and forced the wet, soapy ball into her mouth. Elena held Wendy's mouth shut again.

Wendy might have, ought to have, struck her mother back. She felt in her rage that she ought to have struck her mother, knocked out her straight, white, capped teeth, watched the blood flow across them (those faintly lipsticked teeth, even now faintly lipsticked), stepped over her mother's body stretched out on the floor — but she didn't. In an isolated chamber in her heart she complied with this torture. Maybe she had a feeling about what was coming next. She accepted it, accepted her humiliation, and the burning taste in her mouth and throat. Her limbs were weak. At last, her mother released her and she gagged and spit the little, blue soap on the crocheted rug on the floor. She wept.

— Let's have some breakfast, her mother said. Her voice was chilly and strange.

Wendy collapsed into a heap on the floor.

— Get up now, her mother said. Get up off the floor.

But Wendy wouldn't move.

— Pick that up and get up off the floor.

She lay there.

This time when her mother moved Wendy's body, when she lifted that frail doll's body from the bathroom floor,

Wendy knew she was barely capable. Her mother's superhuman strength, the force field of care that surrounded her, these had all failed. Wendy would win in the end, just because she would live longer. This was how family was a bluff, a series of futile power grabs. Love was water torture, and sex was the physical abuse part of love, so sex was the torturous part of torture. Except that family was the worst torture of all.

They repaired to the kitchen, then, as though it was the last-chance kitchen, the last place where they might share a notion about women being together. It came over them all at once, how they could make breakfast for the men, the men upstairs. It was for the men, but it was for themselves, too. Wendy and her mom might, through the alchemy of breakfast, repair the situation before going home. Wendy moved in the kitchen like a wraith. Not talking to her mom. Eyes red. Swollen. Since the Williamses' stove was gas, Elena Hood was able to put on the kettle. She searched around the kitchen for a drip coffeemaker. She motioned wordlessly for Wendy to set the breakfast table. They rummaged through Janey Williams's drawers. Then, in the next room, the den: Wendy mushed up the old issues of the *Stamford Advocate* and the *New York Times* and made a small pyramid of kindling on the grate over these rumpled sheets. The sounds of her mother's modest domestic activities comforted her. She reached for the Ohio Blue Tip matches (strikes on any surface). She struck a match on her zipper, as Mike had once taught her to do.

And when Mr. Williams and Sandy ventured into the kitchen, Mike was on their minds. The fire wasn't going very well, and the two men squatted down beside her to advise on the subject. It was their job, right? To advise?

Mr. Williams used the fire iron to nudge Wendy's Duraflame log around a little bit. Sandy manned the bellows.

— Wendy, Mr. Williams said calmly, as he poked the fire, you didn't see Mike last night, did you?

She told him how she had been at home watching the film about the buried woman. By the time she got over to their house, Mike was already gone. The words hurt, coming out of her mouth. All words hurt. They tasted corrosive.

— Sandy said he was at Silver Meadow, she said, but then maybe I might have seen him there on the way by. Or maybe not. I might have seen him if he was out on the hill sledding or just running around or something.

— But he also said he might go down to see Danny Spofford, Sandy said.

Jim Williams placed one hand on his son's head, and one on Wendy's. He stood.

— Keep your hands off each other while I make this phone call, okay? You two monsters —

And he was smiling as he picked up the phone by the upright piano — sheet music on the stand for *Moon River*. But when he realized that the phone lines were down, too, his countenance changed. Out in the kitchen, suddenly, Wendy could hear him talking it over with her mother.

— You don't think that Janey picked him up somewhere, do you?

— He's probably fine, Elena said. He's probably down at our house having sausages with Ben.

— The phone's dead.

— I don't think you should overdo this.

The house was still for a moment. The fire consumed its fodder.

Then Mr. Williams said:

— Okay, you two, c'mon in here, because the time has come for a little discussion.

Wendy and Sandy were warm in one another's company. In front of the fire. Not talking, not feeling comfortable even, just there. Not knowing what had happened with the vodka the night before, unsure of how it got them here. Silenced by the power of the vodka to take events and reshape them somehow, to make them wild. Wendy didn't feel like she knew Sandy exactly, but there was something she shared with him now. He offered her the bellows and she squirted a tentative stream of air on the artificial log in the fireplace. Sandy picked up the fire iron and stabbed the log savagely. A shower of blue, green, and red sparks exploded from it. Wendy choked, trying to swallow again. The lye was in her now. Traveling in her bloodstream, clogging her liver.

The two of them padded into the kitchen, where Elena Hood arranged strips of bacon on a large skillet, broke eggs into a mixing bowl, searched for her miracle ingredient, paprika. These culinary efforts belied her shock, the blank, numb look she had, a look Wendy understood clearly, but that was lost on the Williamses. Still, Elena had reached some sort of an agreement with Jim Williams, somewhere along the line — this was obvious, in the way they gingerly circled around each other in the kitchen, in circles along the linoleum, not lovingly, exactly, but respectfully. Honoring each other just a little. Some kind of impermanent appreciation, which didn't admit all the ups and downs but was heady for a brief moment. The result of this appreciation was going to be a joint lecture. Mr. Williams pointed to the the breakfast table. Sandy and Wendy sat.

— Okay. Uh, everybody comfortable? Williams stood, right at the edge of the parquet in the alcove, with his arms folded. All right. Now, this isn't an easy thing we have to talk about this morning but I think we have to talk about it anyway, and that's why it is that your mother, Wendy, stayed here last night and not at your house. . . . She stayed here with me last night. That's, uh, the first thing we have to tell you. And although the reason she stayed was primarily the electricity and the fact that we had to, uh, abandon the car in a ditch up on Ferris Hill Road, it would be dishonest if I didn't tell you that we did spend the night together . . . in the . . . on the water bed. I have to be clear about this, kids. Now, sometimes as a marriage gets familiar it starts to age a little bit — this happens sometimes. It just happens that the people who are married — like your mother and I, Sandy, or Benjamin and Elena — get to a point where they want a little something in their marriage. They get to a point when they find themselves, uh, straying away. Look, it's not that complicated. It's sort of the way you might want A.1. sauce on your burger one week and mustard the next. It's that simple. Or the way you might want to go to a McDonald's one Saturday and to the Darien Pizza Restaurant the next time. Marriage contracts, yeah, that's right. It gets smaller. It's hard to get back to that place of just liking each other, or else you love one another, your love is strong, but you just don't care for one another in the way you did. And society teaches us right now that this isn't necessarily a bad thing to want — to want some spice. It's an okay thing. It's a little far out, it shakes some people up, but it's okay. Your mother and I and probably Mrs. and Mr. Hood, too, well, we grew up at a time when, no matter what kinds of desires you were experiencing in your marriage, it was considered wrong to violate these vows that you took at the altar. What happened because of this was that our parents and their parents were angry . . . angry and ticked off at each other for just wanting a little variety. They were yelling at each other and sleeping in separate bedrooms and ignoring their kids — ignoring us, because we were the kids then! — while they were battling against each other — *battling* — for the right to have these desires. These weird little infatuations. That's right.

Elena's eggs, their aroma, filled the kitchen now, and lent it concord and harmony it didn't exactly have. Mr. Williams was getting nervous as he traveled down the rich, salesmanlike path of his reasoning. Wendy's poisonous mouth stung. She hung her head.

— So now we can do this if we want. We can bend these bonds a little bit; we can borrow somebody else for a night and not have it . . . without endangering our families or anything. Borrow out of affection, right? Not callously, but the way you would call on a friend to share something. That's it, just sharing. And that's what I want to say to you kids. You can wake up one morning like this, when everything outside is so pretty, and you can wake up to something confusing like finding your mother away from home and someone else — your friend's mother, say — in her place. The car's missing, you figure out it's totaled someplace. But I want you to understand, bub (and Williams was sitting at the table now and leaning out over his designer place mats to look his son right in the eyes), that this doesn't have any effect on our family. I'm here in this house. I will always be here in this house. And your mother and I may have our patches of white water, but we're still together. We're in this house together, electricity or no electricity. And we want to be together, to help you kids and to help each other.

— Now, your mother, Williams went on, your mother . . . left the party with someone else. I want to be honest about this. I have to be straight with you. Okay? And so we can figure out what kind of situation she's in. She has taken advantage of this opportunity that same way we have. She might be happy about it, she might not. We don't know. But she can't call now, because the phone lines don't work and probably there are trees down along the roads. The electricity is out, and the roads are dangerous. And that's why she's not back yet. But when she gets back and when Mike gets back we will all sit down, Sandy, and probably Wendy you can count on sitting down in your house, too, with your dad, and have a long conversation about what's happened.

Elena sat at the table next to Wendy. She passed around the plates. To Wendy, the eggs tasted bland and cold. They tasted like blue soap. Sandy was shoving eggs into his mouth without passion or joy.

— There's one last thing we have to go into here, Jim Williams added, and that's the matter of you kids staying together last night. Now, I guess I don't have to give you two a brushing-up on the birds and the bees. (Here Williams laughed a deep and hearty belly laugh that nonetheless sounded phony.) I mean, I guess I don't have to explain to you about sexual intercourse. I will say, though, that this is a very serious business. I'm not sure in your case, bub, that you're quite ready to handle it — I mean, when you've got a few dark hairs on your upper lip we can get down to some real conversation on the subject. Then I'll teach you how to take this matter into your own hands, but until then, firstly, you guys aren't ready and so you should confine yourselves to less, uh, invasive kinds of investigation, and secondly, if something miraculous were going to happen . . . say you were suddenly able to conceive — you would be in a very difficult place. Right? This is serious. Imagine, Sandy, if Wendy were to get pregnant right now, when you are thirteen and she is — what? Thirteen, too? Imagine what Wendy would have to go through over at the high school in her maternity gowns, trying to cover up the fact. And then how would you two take care of the baby once you had it? Who's going to take care of it while you are at school? Who's going to pay for the obstetrical care or the delivery of the child? Do you expect us to carry the expenses you two incur through stupidity? Hell, no! And who's going to teach this kid the morals it needs to have? Its morality is already a little sloppy based on the job you're doing now. Get it? You two aren't even done learning morals yourselves and already you want the responsibility of taking on a kid? And add to this the fact that you don't know how you feel about each other, because there are other . . . extenuating relationships going on around here. You don't even know what you think exactly. . . . Well, obviously, there's some kind of contagious quality to behavior like this. You guys didn't get an idea this far out just by yourselves, that's what I think. So you must have gotten it somewhere. That's something to think about, whether you were reading one of our books and you found references to behavior like this, or what. We'd be happy to discuss this with you, rather than leave you to get all your information from books. Just bring the book down here with you, Sandy, bring the book to me, *The Godfather*, page whatever, that one Mike likes to read. We can go over the hard words. Look, making choices is an important thing for young people. So that's what I'd like to offer you guys . . . choices. Until you have all the facts, until you know, when you're getting into bed, how the other half lives, it's just not a good idea. That's what I'm saying to you, and if it's not a good idea, you should put it off. Put it off, okay? Get it, kids?

Wendy had been staring at her plate, watching the eggs sink into a lukewarm and clotted state, stirring up the arrangement of toast and jam and eggs. It was safe to look up again.

— Elena, do you have anything to add?

Elena shook her head drastically.

— No, no. Wendy and I will take this up on the way back to the house.

So that was the end of it. Whatever stray impulse had led Wendy's mother into the Williamses' house — and it had been passed along to Wendy in full, just as the volatility of the O'Malleys had been passed along to her — whatever the impulse was that had led her mother from the party onto the water bed, where she had swam in Jim Williams's arms, whatever revolution had taken place in her mother, it had been succeeded by a harsh return to her old constitution. That was the way of things with adults — they trailed after ecstasy and then denied it, rationalized it, dressed it all up in talk. Her mother regretted being there, in that kitchen, regretted having cooked the breakfast, regretted even having hurt Benjamin, however justified this hurt might have been. Her mother regretted everything now. Wendy could see this regret playing across her face.

— Hey, bub, Jim Williams said, your shortwave radio have any batteries in it? Think we can get news radio or something on there?

Sandy nodded halfheartedly.

And the two of them rose together and in synchronous, almost choreographed movements, they wiped their mouths with the cloth napkins Elena had set on the table, set these napkins across their plates, and left the plates behind.

And then Wendy thought about the complications of the whole night. What if there was a sort of swap with the neighbors and it exceeded everybody's expectation? Just to start with, Wendy was going to be sealed into a town where everyone knew her mother slept with the man up the street. This knowledge would circulate like her own dalliance with Debby Armitage. Then, take it a little further, go a little further down that road, she might be stepsister with the boy she loved, and stepsister, also, with his rival, whom she had also once loved. She would commit incest with a stepsibling. She would permit each of her stepbrothers to touch her. She would dry hump them together, maybe. Then her stepbrothers would fight to the death for the right to seed in her a two-headed baby who spoke Greek at birth and knew the date of Jesus' next appearance. Her father and stepfather would not speak to one another. Her mother and stepmother would not speak to one another. She would be enjoined, when in the company of her father and Mrs. Williams, against speaking about her mother and Mr. Williams. Or: she would never see Mikey and Sandy, because they would have opposite weekends of visitation. Or: they would split up visitation, one week with Sandy, one week with Mikey, and she would swap them, as her parents had swapped one another. Or: she would return home with the Hoods and this whole weekend would remain a horrible episode no one ever talked about, which left in its wake the moral carnage of a whole town full of kids.

— We should get going, her mother said. Let's finish

this up and you can get your things. I'll borrow some boots. . . .

— We have to walk?

— The Williamses' car is back up on Ferris Hill and your father has the Firebird.

The silence between Wendy and Elena was long and durable. Almost unbreachable.

— You don't love Dad anymore, Wendy said.

Elena gave this statement a respectful space. Then she said:

— That's right.

Wendy would think about this moment a lot, later, and she would conclude that Elton John's drummer, Nigel Olson, meant more to her than her parents' marriage, and that her own heart had shrunk down, like the heart of the Grinch in *How the Grinch Stole Christmas*. Because she didn't feel that much right then. She had learned well the parsimony her family had taught her.

— But you're not gonna divorce him, are you?

— I don't know the answer to that yet.

— Aw, Mom, you . . .

Lurching through this conversation, they rinsed dirty plates under cold water. This was the last of what they could share. Then Wendy left her mother to find her stuff — her poncho, her boots — up on Sandy's bed. At the top of the stairs, she could hear Sandy and Mr. Williams. In the bathroom.

They were sitting on the bath mat, with an array of tools spread out before them, as though this were an operating amphitheater. Before them, through the tiles in the bathroom, a steady leak had developed. It wasn't much more than a drip really, a drip that was collecting in the bathtub, but it spooked the Williams men nonetheless. It wasn't coming from the showerhead, or from the tap. It was coming from the wall.

Sandy handed the tools to his father one by one. Wrench. Pliers. They were turning off the water at valves, behind the toilet. This had no effect on the leak. Beside them the radio chirped away about the storm and its swath of destruction. Then the announcers moved on to the subject of that 18½-minute silence.

— We're going to go, Wendy said.

The men of the Williams family didn't look up.

— Come again, Jim Williams said. Always happy to see you, dear.

Wendy slipped out of the bathroom and gathered up her things, bundled herself up. Sandy's bed was as carefully made up as if it had been the guest room, as if he weren't a permanent resident in his own room. G. I. Joe hung listlessly above the closet.

And then, downstairs, just as she and her mother were buttoning their last buttons in the kitchen, there was a knock at the front door.

— Let me in, Janey Williams called. I don't have my keys.

Another louder pounding. The sound was muffled.

Then Jim Williams on the staircase: worried, preoccupied, caught between a number of different reactions. Sandy stood right behind him, stalled on the eighth or ninth step, gripping the banister, his chin pressed down upon the tops of his hands. On the doorstep, Janey Williams was unraveled, disarranged, unhinged even. Wendy could tell. And this was *before* Mrs. Williams saw Wendy's mom.

— Top of the morning, Janey said, as Wendy pulled

back the door. Is the lady of the house at home? She placed a hand absently on Wendy's head.

— We have a problem. Jim waved her in.

— What happened to the car, dammit? she said. And then she saw: Oh, so happy to see you, Elena, and so well put together. What's going on? Why so many long faces?

— How did you get back? Jim Williams said, as he came down a couple of steps. His tone was detached. It was the tone that preceded a long, difficult conversation.

— Maria drove me up and around and down Ferris Hill. I passed the car. My car. What the hell did you do to it?

Jim Williams gripped his wrench as though he were making a point with it. Sandy looked down at the fuzz on the carpet and Wendy looked at her mother, who seemed to be staring vacantly at some empty region out in the yard. Upstairs there was the sound of a drip in the bathroom.

— Your car seems to be stuck on the road, too, your Firebird, Janey said to Elena. I hope Benjamin didn't, you know, encounter . . . the legal authorities on his way down the hill.

— We wrecked the car, Elena whispered stupidly. Wendy watched her mother fumbling to deal with the situation. And she could guess now the way the map of the evening went, even if she couldn't see all of it right in front of her. Some of it got put together by her, some by others. But the feeling of those stories was on her now. Those stories circulated around her. Maria Conrad returning home to find her son, Neil, getting his first blow job from Janey Williams, Janey actually crying while she was doing it, her salty bitterness falling on his pale pink erection —

Neil too stupid in contentment to know the effect he had, or didn't have, on her; Maria returning from Stephan Earle's house, where Stephan had ejaculated prematurely and promptly fallen asleep after having called Maria by the wrong name — not her own, not even his wife's name; Stephan Earle's wife, Marie, stuck at breakfast with Dan Fuller when Chuck Spofford appeared, with his son in tow, to accuse Fuller of stealing his mistress; the logistics, the geometry of accommodation at the Gorman residence, the Sawyer residence, the Boyles'. All these cars trying to get around town behind all these other cars. Each with its freight of betrayal and lost opportunity. On top of everything else the storm. Wendy didn't want to think about it. She wasn't old enough to think about it.

— Did you two have fun? Janey said.

— Oh, be quiet, Elena said. If you want to discuss this at least let's do it in private. We don't have to drag all this out in front of the kids. They already know enough as it is anyway.

— We've told them, sweetheart, Jim Williams said.

— You what? Janey said.

— Look, this isn't all that important now. We have a couple of real problems, Jim Williams said. There's a leak in the bathroom somewhere. I'm a little concerned about the . . . that the pipes may have burst. That's big trouble. And —

— You'll figure it out, Janey said.

Like Wendy, Sandy was paralyzed. Halted by the snowballing of points of view, by the partition and division of points of view. As Janey Williams swept by him and his dad on the stairs, in her wrinkled silk pajamas (draping her wool coat on the banister), she leaned to kiss Sandy on the forehead. She began to sob, choking, heaving sobs. Some women in New Canaan were beautiful when they cried: all sorrow was bound inside them like the bound feet of Asian women. Their tears cut delicate tracks in their pristine cheeks. Not so with Janey Williams. She coughed and gasped and hawked up more of what she was keeping down. Her nose was red and raw — Wendy could see — like her dad's gin-blossomed nose. Janey tried to shout some invective as she cried but the flash flood was too heavy now, and the best she could do was struggle away from her family, struggle away from all that promise and kindness. On the way to her bedroom she paused — at Mike's door.

She reached for the knob.

The trick buzzer sounded.

Janey swore. And then she turned the knob and found the bed empty.

— Where's Mike? she called.

— That's what I . . . Down with Ben, Jim said. We think.

— Why would he be down there? she called, hysteria creeping into the mix of her temper. Ben hates Mike. Don't be stupid. Don't tell me you didn't even —

— Calm down, why don't you.

Jim was turning the wrench over in his palm. But he didn't move.

Janey was at the top of the stairs, frozen in latitudes of regret. They were all isolated in that foyer, all of them.

Then the ambulance pulled up in front of the house.

AN AMBULANCE of quaint, nostalgic design. An old American station wagon, in bright red, with a revolving yellow light on top. The light, rotating slowly, coming to a stop. Sunlight picking up the reflectors in the lamp and elsewhere on the ambulance. The sun reflecting on the limitless array of reflecting surfaces. The sun, the reflections of the sun, the fallen limbs of trees. A vast sweetshop of sugar-coated treats, some kid's fantasy of a Christmas world of candies. Sweetmeats.

Ice everywhere, and icicles, brittle, crunchy snow and ice, through which Benjamin Hood trudged now, falling into ice, rescuing himself, jogging from the ambulance to the exterior of the Williamses' house. Hood's face was swollen and pink-orange with embarrassment and anxiety. His progress up what would once have been a flagstone path — he was actually veering across a flower bed now — couldn't really be called progress. He hustled, he urged his flaccid thighs and calves on, and yet he wasn't getting anywhere. He was stalled on that walkway, on that flower bed, stretching out his fat, puffy palm toward the front door. No closer.

The sound of radio static coming from the ambulance. Wind rollicking in sugar-coated trees. Reflections. The sound of icicles giving up their form, returning to rivers. The restless movement of water. Wood smoke drifted on the wind and scorched a sad spot in Hood's heart. Even on this mission, he couldn't ignore it. The past was so past it hurt — afternoons in duck blinds with his father, northern New England and its bittersweet citizenry. He missed the past and he could have been kinder. He was only ten steps from the front door now; his movements frozen to a crawl.

The front of the house: white, orderly, colonial. A flagpole (unflagged), an array of carefully tended shrubs garlanded in ice. Two-car garage. Imitation gaslight beside the front step. Columns. Behind, the hill. Below, the Silvermine River.

At last, when it seemed a whole day would come and go before Hood reached the Williamses' door, when it seemed inside to Elena Hood and to the Williamses and to Wendy Hood that the ambulance had pulled into the driveway for a coffee break, or for a morning bird-watching excursion, when it seemed to Janey Williams that she had opened and closed the door a dozen times and each time had found a different day, a different tragedy — a day in which the ambulance drivers were simply asking directions, on their way to some coronary event; a day in which it was just a red station wagon with a flat tire, not an ambulance; a day in which the loss belonged instead to the Hoods and Ben was simply looking for Elena and Wendy — after all these alternatives, the knock came at the door. The door opening, and then the knock. It was all backward.

— Janey. Uh. You and Jim had better come out here for a moment. I'm afraid there's something. . . . You'd better come on out here. I . . . you need to talk to these men. Listen, I —

Then the splash page. The procession was like pipers,

like some medieval crew schooled in gymnastic — Janey and Jim Williams launched themselves desperately out into the snow, dressed only in what clothes they wore in the house; followed by little Sandy Williams, who carefully jumped into each of the foot holes his parents depressed in the walkway in front of him, balancing, nearly falling over; followed by Elena, arms folded, shoulders hunched, lips pursed, not knowing why she followed exactly; and then Wendy, snow-blinded by the reflection of light and the sound of water running everywhere; followed by Benjamin Hood himself, now relieved of his responsibility but anguished, knowing. Hood in his galoshes.

The ambulance driver waited for them, slouched against the car. At the same moment, a police car slowed and parked on Valley Road. Two officers emerged and listlessly ambled toward the column of observers.

— Your neighbor here found the body of a young boy over by the hospital, the ambulance driver was saying, mostly to Jim Williams. Says he has reason to believe that the boy is your son. I'm afraid . . . well, we have attempted to *revive* the boy and we have failed to do so. To revive him. But we really ought —

Janey Williams's face — featureless, bland, and then twisted. Tragedy mask, comedy mask, tragedy mask. She smiled, she trembled. She knew, she didn't know. The year had sprung a leak. Loss surged and waned according to its own itinerary. Janey's hands were red and importunate, as if she was conducing the scene somehow, waving through its downbeats. She danced and wept and conducted and spoke in tongues.

The ambulance driver let the news sink in, looked down at tracks in the snow — he was an accomplished messenger of ill — and then he went over to seek consel from the police.

— You think it's okay to let them identify the body? This was all done in asides.

— I'll take care of it, if you want, the officer said. He moved toward the circle around the ambulance.

— These guys got to move along to the hospital. To make it official. And we're going to have to get a full report, but first I'll need to know your names. You know, the usual stuff. And you say your boy has been missing how long?

Distractedly, Jim Williams parted with the information. His answers were blunt, contradictory, imprecise. Ben Hood stepped into the circle and told his story again. The policeman — unconcerned with the usual logistics of Hood's account — pointed to the ambulance, to the treasure housed there.

— Somebody probably ought to identify, he said. We could do it and get it out of the way. To Jim Williams: You want to come here and have a look?

No, absolutely not. Williams didn't want to look, to taste that scene. He found himself looking around, ready to suggest almost anybody else. They all watched him swiveling, each of them ready to volunteer. Maybe Sandy ought to have done it, or Janey, though she was far away, back in the past, jousting with all the hurts that were now called up alongside this one. Jim didn't want to look at his dead son. Fathers shouldn't have to. It should not have been a configuration of any paternal fate. It was instead the sad responsibility of sons — identifying the dead — a responsibility Jim had already fulfilled in his life. Sons should bid farewell to fathers.

Then Jim Williams, trembling, resigned himself to the duty. He climbed into the back of the ambulance. His cry emerged, long and hoarse and elastic and then muted, choked off. And they could also hear the ambulance driver venturing the probable cause. And they could hear the other two men inside — there was routine conversation. Football scores. Jim climbed unsteadily from the ambulance, a husk.

Williams tried to get out a sentence, an explanation for his family, but each time he was interrupted by the threat of his own speech, now weak, growing fainter. Then no words came forth. He simmered. Elena and Janey took hold of him, one on each arm, and in that way they shivered while the machinations of the state went on around them. Mike was being entered onto statistical rolls.

The driver climbed out again — the driver's-side door swung shut behind him.

— Okay, we're gonna have to take, uh, the deceased down to Norwalk. Would one of you like to go along? Don't need all of you. In fact, it'll be best if it's . . . just one of you. Not going to be much to see now. Best if you just let the process take its course, if you want my advice.

Ben was coming forward to volunteer, but his part in this subplot was done. Jim Williams stepped up again, out of the arms of these two women, out of their generosity, because who else could go? His uncertain, wordless gesture of assent — he raised a single finger, as though he were inconspicuously bidding at an auction — emerged from him without thought. Janey and Sandy and Elena let him go. He climbed into the back of the ambulance, and the driver climbed back into the driver's seat.

And then the car wouldn't start. They had run the radio too long. Maybe. Or it was just one of those days. The engine coughed roughly several times, but nothing. Elena heard them swearing inside the ambulance; they had just started it, it had no history of problems.

They jumped the engine off the police car. The state employees stood around scratching their heads, looking for the cables. After a dull, impenetrable quarter hour — Jim getting in and out of the back — ignition was achieved. The police took everyone's name and number.

This quarter hour was the last time when the Hoods and the Williamses would be this close, when their stories would be so easily told together, when, if there was going to be conversation on the subject of those keys and that party, or about dry-humping and teenaged drinking, or about the misshapen affection that bound these people, such talk should have taken place. They would be neighbors for a while yet. Look, Elena knew that apology was the impossible paragraph, its words were like the secret names of God. Simple apology, simple acknowledgment. *That stuff, all that stuff that happened, it's all forgotten. It's history*. Simple, right? They were all forgiven and free, unshackled, liberated to go and unravel the narratives of their lives. They were free to take up their fates, to take up their nameless destinies. So why didn't apology come to Elena's lips? Or to Benjamin's? Elena wanted to say all this, to say impossible, ancient words of confession and absolution. And she knew that if she didn't, she was condemned to watch the blunders of the past come around again for a revival, an encore presentation. So she did her best. She reached out for Janey and whispered to her a few unsatisfactory words, pittances. *Oh, Janey, oh, Janey, I'm so so so sorry. Oh, I am so sorry*. Their embrace was brief. And then Benjamin caught them at this moment and he wanted to be part of it. He touched his wife's shoulder and then Janey's shoulder. Neither seemed to notice. He stood awkwardly there. And then he turned toward the kids. Wendy and Sandy were facing away, toward the woods, toward the security of fallen trees, plotting the next ten years.

They were transfixed, the Hoods and Williamses, by the spectacle of a lost future. It brought them together and it drove them apart but maybe this parting was inevitable anyway. Soon the car was jumped, and the police were gone, and Jim Williams, in the ambulance, vanished into the underworld.

Wendy Hood's bedroom. (They had walked Sandy and Janey over to the Steeles' house, to wait for Jim, and then they had walked home, in single file.) Worn, balding teddy bear tossed aside on the corduroy bedspread. On the walls: posters of David Cassidy, the *Dark Side of the Moon* record sleeve, a peace symbol. Bumper sticker — *Impeach Nixon* — on the back of the door. All-in-one Magnavox record player with a warped copy of Neil Diamond's *Hot August Night* resting on it. Side four, including "Mother Love's Travelling Salvation Show."

Wendy was sprawled diagonally across the bed with her face stuffed into the folds of a crumpled feather pillow. She was sad and frightened. There was a malevolence lurking in the postelectrical silence of her house. And Mike. She imagined death coming for him, death riding on her town's rich, privileged winds, death as witches, single women with cats, coming for him and carrying him past the window where she, Wendy, dallied with his brother. No, she imagined Mike was alone somewhere, that the hereafter for him featured aloneness, just like he had been alone at the moment of his death. Power lines, they said.

She couldn't follow a single thought to its conclusion. She couldn't distinguish between Mike and Sandy, as she lay there on the bed. She saw Sandy in the basement with her, instead of Mike, or she suddenly believed that she had spent the night with Mike and that now Sandy was dead. Sex and death were all confused in her. Everything was all confused. She didn't know what to do to console herself, if she even deserved consolation. She wanted to sleep in the bosom of the good people of New Canaan. She wanted to forget, to ride the pendulum away from this weekend and its bad luck.

But she had other impulses, too. She pulled the soiled garter belt out of the front of the jeans she had changed into and it emerged like the handkerchief of cheap legerdemain, that endless handkerchief of changing colors and styles — which reveals, in its ultimate fold, a gray and diseased pigeon. She had begun to mythologize this garter belt in the last hour or so. Its rank sea smell — tuna salad with mustard-honey dressing — mingling with the intoxicating smell of her own unwashed body. Its black, sultry shape, alluring and violent.

Wendy had to try it on. She didn't make this decision, really, she just yielded to it. The river flowed in one direction and she paddled along with it. Flow. First she inhaled the human fumes of that garment. She cradled it. She had read in one of Paul's cheap pornographic magazines — *Oui* — that semen was both a good conditioner and a fine skin lotion. The smell of Mike's lost progeny — the hint of the family he might have had — was thick upon her. This was what memory was like — it was all fingerprinted with desire. So, reveling in the good ideas falling away from her, Wendy began to unzip her jeans. Had the electricity been on, she would have played weepers on her Magnavox. She would have played death ballads on old, scratchy forty-fives.

With the hooks available, she locked the garment around the spot where her hips were beginning to blossom. She looked with horror at the precise fit of the thing. She stumbled, jeans and panties around her ankles, back onto her bed; she could see where her downy, blond pubic hair would vanish soon and give way to the thick, coarse tangle of womanhood. It sickened her. What had happened to Mike? What had she done to him? A few more years and she wouldn't even be a kid anymore. She would bind her breasts tautly against her. She would preserve her chastity, starve her menses; she would keep herself free from wants. But even as she vowed these vows, she felt in herself the oblique stain of arousal. Wendy wiggled her hips on the bed, in Mike's mother's garter belt — as she was now sure it must be — feeling grief and need mixed up together.

In the thrall of the moment, her jeans knotting her ankles together, shivering, her ass — tickled by the straps of the garter belt — exposed to the chill air, she reached into the drawer of her unsturdy bedside table and found the Wilkinson double-bonded razor she had liberated from her parents' bathroom.

She pulled up the sleeves of her turtleneck sweater. A tear appeared at the edge of her eye — from the pain — as she tested the blade on her wrist, delicately. A small test cut. It was just a scratch really, nothing like the fountain she deserved, the fountaining of blood you might get from a hair shirt, say, or from an undergarment fashioned with nails and tacks, each tipped with special preparations to attract insects and vermin. Wendy clenched her jaw. She raised a cold sweat on her brow. She pulled at clumps of her blond locks. And then she panicked. She could imagine cutting down to the bone, parting sinew and nerve and what fatty tissue was lodged there. She could imagine grappling with her own shiny bones, wresting them apart and scattering them on the carpet, but then she was begging Mike to pardon her, telling Mike that she couldn't do it, that she was gonna have to stick around, *Charles*. She just couldn't. Poor Mike, solitary ghost. Solitary ghost of New Canaan.

With jeans still twisted around her ankles, with a wrist presented as if in some kind of religious rite, Wendy waddled out into the hall and then into the bathroom.

There was no running water, because of the flood, but a bucket of cold water sat on the floor of the bathroom — for flushing the commode. Wendy plunged her wrist into this bucket. The cold water stung. The scratch on her forearm turned the water the color of a cranberry spritzer, the color of those transfusions of cranberry and ginger ale her mom used to give her when she was out sick from school. She hobbled toward the door, the blade still in her left hand. She squirmed to the edge of the staircase.

They rarely used the living room, except for company. But Elena and Benjamin were camped there now, guests in their own home. Each nursed a lukewarm cup of Sanka. And they had changed their clothes — they were clothed in many layers. They were prepared. Their voices were soft and low, like lover's voices. The leak in the wall, while it hadn't subsided entirely, had slowed, and since Benjamin had shut off the water at the valve down in the basement, there would be less trouble when the pipes refroze that evening. The fire in the fireplace sputtered: it was on its way out.

— Well, someone's going to have to go into town for the plumber, Benjamin said quietly. And to get some supplies, some food. I'll be happy to go. You could come along if you like. Maybe we all need to get out and have a little activity. Maybe that would be just the ticket. If we can get the Firebird started. The station wagon wouldn't. . . . I can understand that you're upset, honey. I'm upset too. But it would be better if we could just get this all out in the open. That's all I'm asking. I'm sincere about this, about my part.

Elena whispered, as though whispering to herself. Some inaudible murmur of equivocation.

— No one can know when he died, Hood said. He might have died instantly, or he might have just fallen unconscious and frozen to death. That's not for anybody to know really. They'll make up some scientific horseshit. You never know. So you were just doing whatever you were doing. Everyone's going to feel bad. That's just what something like this is like. But this sort of second guessing. . . . Well, that's just baloney.

They sipped.

And Elena said, suddenly:

— Oh, and your conscience is clear.

Then:

— Well, where were you anyway? Were you up to anything better? Where did you spend the night if your conscience is so clear?

— I didn't say anything, Ben said. I made no judgment —

— So high and mighty —

— I was on the bathroom floor. Rob and Dot's bathroom. If it makes you happy . . . to know that. I was goddam passed out on the floor of a goddam bathroom. And I'm not saying, if that's what you think I'm saying, that spending some time on their water bed — your spending some time there — is the worst thing, even if it makes me feel —

Elena grew quieter still:

— It doesn't make me happy. It's predictable is what it is. It's just predictable, and that doesn't make me happy. I've seen more drunkenness in this marriage. I've seen a lot of awful stuff. There are more *vomit stains* around this house —

— I know, I know, I know, Ben said. I've said I'm sorry. I know. I've apologized until I'm blue. . . . I'm going to —

— Sorry is a nothing word, Ben. It just takes up air. You're going to have to —

— Well, what can I offer you then? We took these vows, remember? I want to talk about that now. We said these words, you said them, too, and I'm trying to stick by them —

— In somebody else's arms. That's how you —

— Trying to *restore them* is what I mean. You haven't improved the situation either by. . . . Listen, I'm upset about poor Mike. I don't want to . . . I'm not going to . . . even if Jim's kids are out all hours of the night, I can see that he's doing the best he can with them. I know it's hard to raise kids —

— Like ours are not? Elena said. Look at our own children —

— Just let me speak for a moment, honey. Just let me finish what I'm trying to say. A terrible thing like this . . . and let's remember that I was the one who found Mike's body. I found it —

Benjamin's face twisted into grimace.

— I was giving him . . . what do you call it? Mouth-to-mouth. Blowing air into his lungs. And it didn't matter that

I always thought he was a little shit. It didn't matter. And what I mean is that this ought to make it plain, you know, how a family ought to be. That's what I want to tell you: we have trouble with the house, we have trouble with the kids, I have trouble at work, but we can still work it out.

— What? What trouble at work?

— Well, it's. . . . You know. It's just not going all that well. You know that.

— No, I didn't know that. Because you don't tell me these things.

— I just . . . I just haven't felt good about myself at work. I need —

Elena didn't say anything.

— *Stop looking at me that way,* Ben said. I don't want to raise my voice. I don't want to have to put Wendy through all this again. This conversation should take place in private, that's what I'm asking. I'd like to suggest, Elena, that the trouble at work — which is more difficult than I've wanted to admit even to myself — well, I'm in a situation where I can try to make a new start here.

— Come on, Ben. What makes you think that's the way I'm thinking about it?

— Goddammit, *that's it,* Benjamin said. You think you're not part of the problem here, but you are. Let's face up to that for a second. Let's talk about the sorts of problems you bring to this room. That you are a remote person. You're a remote, difficult person, and for someone who's always made a lot of noise about community, about the community of the Unitarian goddam faith and all that balderdash, about psychiatrists and psychologists and all that, all that community of overpriced mental-health quackery, you don't seem to have a lot of concern for this community right here, in this house, and the decision you made seventeen years ago and the people who are part of that decision with you.

Elena said, almost whispering, not looking him in the eyes at all, looking instead at the fire:

— It wasn't just this free and easy choice, you know. You don't know how it works. Later, I don't know how I make these decisions, how I *made* them. I don't have any skills, and I never did. I'm no worker. I woke up breast-feeding one morning. And I don't feel like there's much dignity in it, that's what I mean. So what am I supposed to do?

Hood got up to poke at the fire.

— So what are you saying? You're saying this was just some arrangement?

— I'm not saying that . . . I'm saying you're not looking at the other angles. . . . There are points of view here.

— You were just coerced into this marriage by the social climate and all that: Carl Rogers or Carl Jung or somebody says women of the fifties were coerced into marriage. And they need Virginia Slims or something. And meanwhile I've neglected the family. I'm the neglecter. The villain.

He crouched down low and inserted a balled-up piece of newspaper under the last unconsumed transverse of Duraflame log.

— So you think it's best if you leave, he said.

— That's right, Elena said.

Then:

— Well, this is the era for it, Benjamin said.

Elena said nothing.

Benjamin watched the fire.

Their remorse was peaceful.

— Should we tell the kids now? Is that what you want to do?

He set down the bellows.

— And that reminds me, he said. Where the hell is Paul, anyway?

— What?

— Paul, our son, Paul. Did you call the city to see if he stayed over with his friends?

— I thought you did.

— You mean you. . . . Oh, great, this is great. This is great.

— Is it my sole responsibility to look after the children? Elena said. It's a holiday weekend — you're here.

— Well, I'm glad I won't have to listen to this shit for the rest of my life, because I couldn't take it. Did you *happen* to talk with Wendy about Paul's plans, whether she knew anything about it?

The answer arrived right then. The drawing room doors — a pair of antique sliding doors whose period feel had once made Benjamin Hood feel good — parted. Wendy entered, like the buried woman breaking the surface of the earth, coming up for air. She looked nothing like the Wendy that Elena remembered, the exasperating and charming little girl who had to be the center of attention. The little girl whom everybody loved, waiters, doormen, conductors, passersby, all of whom had to talk to her. That girl had vanished entirely, and though Elena recognized this apparition, she recognized it from some more distant register of memory. The generations seemed to have collapsed into Wendy, because Wendy looked exactly like Elena's own mother, coming downstairs, her mother frightened by the implications of another long afternoon. Wendy, with her arm stretched out in front of her. Her jeans partly hiked up, partly unzipped, over a black lace garter belt, straps clearly visible, zipped into the zipper.

The huffing sobs coming from her daughter like a backward language. Elena heard her mother's cries, heard the ghost of her own mother, and she saw her own place in the ladder of madness and desolation. She felt that she, too, would be locked away, locked into Silver Meadow and visited only on weekends. The two of them encircled their daughter.

— Oh, baby doll, Benjamin said. What the hell. Oh, lord.

Hood saw, with horror, the familiar garter belt.

— It's okay, darling, Elena said to Wendy. And then to her husband: — It's okay, it's just a scratch. This isn't too bad. It'll close up fine. It's not a . . .

Elena held Wendy's doll body close, and then, reciting incantations known only to mothers, she unhooked the garter belt, the way some teenaged smoothy could undo a complicated support bra backwards in the dark. She fastened up Wendy's pants and set the crusty garment aside.

— Are you sure? Benjamin said. What about tetanus? Shouldn't we . . .

— Wendy, Elena said. What did you use to do this?

Wendy mumbled:

— Wilkinson double-bonded . . .

— A new one? A new blade?

Wendy nodded.

— Take better care of those things, Elena said to her husband. Lock them away. And where did you get that . . . that lingerie?

— Williamses', Wendy said.

She sank to the floor, wilted, and her two parents sat down with her, on the damp, fungal carpet. The garter belt lay aside like some strangely essential family gear. Elena knew all about the rococo ornamentation of grief and so she didn't try to comfort Wendy. Not right away. No hug was going to do the trick now. But Benjamin tried the laying on of hands. Where he had been penurious as a dad before, he suddenly recognized necessity. He wrapped his arms around his daughter. And Elena wasn't impervious to the sight of it. She wasn't impervious to the way embraces were a sort of cardiology. So Wendy lay in her father's arms, asking what happened, what happened to Mike, where was he now, refusing, so far, to be the bearer of his memory. Refusing, therefore, to let him journey away. All these losses were sutured up in Wendy now, like when she and Paul found Benjamin's father in the basement one weekend, when they heard his oddly practical voice calling out to them, *I've lost the use of my legs.* That stroke weekend. Like when Elena's father had died in the spring. All Wendy's losses were one. And so were Elena's, and Benjamin's, and Janey's, and Jim's, and . . .

—Darling, Elena said. Did Paul happen to call last night?

Between hyperventilating gasps:

—Said he was going to take the last train.

—Trains won't be running, Benjamin mumbled. Can't be.

—Maybe we should drive out to the station anyway, Elena said. Let's just go take a look.

—You don't think you should stay here? With her? What if they. . . . What if the telephones start working? I could go . . .

—No, I'd rather. . . . If there's going to be any trouble. I'd rather.

And then Elena smiled:

—It's got a heater, too. The car.

—Would that be okay? Ben said to Wendy, quietly. Do

you think you could come with your mother and me while we drive down there? I'd rather you came with us, sweetheart.

It was almost noon when Benjamin got back with the Firebird. They packed Wendy in, her wrists sleeved in a Handi Wipes, that rag from the convenient plastic container. She had a glass of Tang with her. And a space blanket. The dog was huddled in the back seat. Up against her.

The temperature had dipped again. The unrestrained sun of the morning was gone. They headed down past the Silvermine Arts Guild and the Silvermine Tavern, where a cereal commercial had recently been filmed, and in doing so, they traveled across the latitudes of ancestral New Canaan. Here John Gruelle had first drawn his famous Raggedy Ann; landscape artist D. Putnam Bradley had painted his sweet pastorals; here Hamilton Hamilton had pen-and-inked, and Childe Hassam had gallicized a little verdant scene. Among writers Padraic Colum, Irish-born poet and folklorist, and Robert Flaherty, Arctic explorer, lived here, and William Rose Benét and Maxwell E. Perkins. Perkins, maybe, while editing *Look Homeward, Angel:* "We had a grand winter at New Canaan. Skating on most of the week-ends and hockey, and over New Year's, for three windless days, the whole three-mile lake, a sheet of flexible black ice."

Over this history they drove, over decomposing Canaan Parish. Before long the Hoods would move. Half of the family would move and the other remain. Maybe in the years that followed, they would spend their weekends, like the Williamses, arranging the complexities of visitation. Benjamin Hood would drop his daughter off or find his daughter waiting in the driveway of her mother's house, in

Wilton or Westport or East Haven or Darien. He would see his wife through the rustle of drapery. Benjamin Hood would leave his daughter alone for the afternoon at R-rated films, or he would go with her, exhausted, to the Red Coach Grill or McDonaldland. And Elena would be doing a telemarketing job offering subscriptions to *Club,* or she would have a photocopying job, and she would be secretly dating. Like Benjamin. But they wouldn't be dating the Williamses.

At the train station in New Canaan, that little end-of-the-line train station, they were told that the 11:10 had never made it to Stamford. It had been disabled somewhere around Greenwich.

The three Hoods crowded around the ticket window. Three blossoms on a thorny stem. They barked questions.

— Good news is, said the man at the window, they restored the power not long ago. On the New Haven line. The trains are running now. Probably your boy is in Stamford right now. Catching a taxi.

— If he has any money, Benjamin said.

The two men tried to force a laugh.

So they set off for Stamford, driving slowly. In the midst of all this personal trouble, what did a little history matter? What difference did snapshots make, or bronzed shoes? Who cared about those plastic cubes full of snapshots? History was cheap trophies and misspelled school newspapers, and it was also the end of town meetings in 1969, and it was also the guy in New Canaan who remained a *voluntary slave* for years after the Emancipation Proclamation, and it was the driving off of the Sagamores in the seventeenth century, and the pristine quiet of the region before the first English settlers. History's surveillance was subtle and enduring and its circular shape caught the

Hoods, the Nixons, and everyone else. You could pay Arthur Janov to teach you to scream about history, or you could learn prayer or a mantra, or you could write your life down and hope to make peace with it, write it down, or paint it, or turn it into improvisational theater, but that was the best you could probably do. You were stuck.

FUCKING FAMILY. Feeble and forlorn and floundering and foolish and frustrating and functional and sad, sad. Fucking family. Fiend or foe. Next month: the end of the Fantastic Four. The Fab Four. The Fetishistic Four. Family was all tricks with mirrors. Flimflam. Back through the generations, back forefathers and forefathers and forefathers, it was a mantle he didn't think he could hold up. All flummery. Paul Hood, the flame, the torch, burnt out. Burnt at both ends. He wished he could forget them, wished he could put this trip behind him, wished he was still eating with a bib, making models of stock cars, four on the floor, wished he was back in the arms of some girl. Missed Libbets. On the platform in Stamford. He wanted to run, to flee fathers, forefathers, fornification, femmes fatales, and all that stuff. He wanted to flee friends.

The night had been really, really long. Hours scribbling pictures on a scrap of newspaper he had found under the seat, hours frigid in the dark, really long that night, so long that he was starting to believe the dumb lies he'd told. Starting to believe dumb, little stories about his family. Believing in familiar comforts. Scribbling pictures and writing crumbling sentences. Free-verse trash and quotations from *Thick as a Brick*. Practically hallucinating. He actually believed his family would be waiting for him when he got in. They would be waiting there — while the rapist on the train hotfooted it back to his leopard skin–blanketed, water-bedded crash pad — and they would be terribly concerned and they would hug him and they would think up new nicknames for him and they would drive him directly to the largest possible bowl of shrimp cocktail.

Nah, it wasn't like that. Family values. The Carpenters were family values. And Nixon making Elvis an honorary drug enforcement agent. Family kept the doors open for alcoholism and incest and battery and ignorance; it ensured the passage of racist bullshit and bigotry from one generation to the next. His parents were gene-splicers, genetic engineers, implanting him with the same grim diseases they had suffered. He was a flash fire waiting to happen. He was fucked up and friendless and his chances were about fifty-fifty.

So the train had started moving again sometime around dawn, inching along at a speed no quicker than footsteps. Messing with Paul's unsteady pictures, with the stories he was making up, stories in which he hadn't done all the stupid things he had done in the last twenty-four hours. The train had been reduced to some prior kind of train, a steam engine bearing them through cow country. They arrived in Stamford early in the morning and all these people, all these other losers, asked Paul if he needed a ride, if anyone was going to meet him. All these people talking to him. All this kindness. But he said, no no no, not to worry, and he had been dragging his ass around the train station ever since. He had fought some babyish response to all this, he had pasted a smile on his mouth — yeah, my parents are coming for me. Asked a cabbie if this money, these last few crumpled bills — were enough to take him to New Canaan? Yep, the money was enough, but the roads were impassable. Have to wait till they cleared them off.

Anyway, Paul knew about these long waits. His mother was always late. He wasn't surprised to be reduced to this. He would start walking soon, except that he wouldn't walk home, he would walk back to school. He would walk until he could hitch and then he wouldn't stop until he was way up in the North. He wouldn't stop until he was so far north there were no deciduous trees, until granite bubbled up underneath every lawn. Glacier country.

He moved from the old waiting room with its congregation of bad-luck types, back out onto the platform, up and down the platform, kicked some newspaper vending machines, hoping for spare change. He paid ten cents to get into the pay toilet and washed his face. Back to the waiting room. Back out onto the platform.

He knew that he wouldn't come to a bad end, though, because he knew how comic books ended. They never ended. Comic books never ended. There was always more character development. Always another wrinkle in what had seemed to be unchanging and permanent. Every time the Thing left the F.F. he came back. His pain and rage receded and he was bantering jocosely with Stretcho and Sue and Johnny. He was back. Nobody ever died, at least not forever, and nobody ever disappeared, no quarrel was devastating, no closure was entire. The good moments, when the light outside was just right and everybody agreed — these moments came back again and again. Franklin would be resuscitated. Sue would take Reed back. And Dr. Doom, whose ashes had been scattered in subspace, would menace them again. He'd impersonate their landlord or their accountant or something.

So, after spending an hour stripping the emblems off of expensive cars in front of the train station, Paul Hood wasn't surprised to see his family's red Firebird ease into the parking lot. The Firebird. His face flushed. His heart was stuck up in him somewhere where he couldn't ignore it. He had a heart. When his mother got out of the car, he remembered that time — when he was a kid — when they had gone away for a week and left him and Wendy with a battle-ax whose only defense for her cooking was that her husband, rest in peace, had had no sense of smell. Paul saw his mom and he remembered when they had finally come home, when Daisy Chain wouldn't shut up for half an hour barking and climbing all over the furniture. For a couple of hours everyone had been laughing.

His dad climbed out of the car, and Wendy pushed forward the bucket seats, with the dog slobbering behind her, and they were all standing out there smiling these strange half-smiles. His family. His mom was his mom and his dad was his dad and he was stuck with that, whatever became of them. Like Darien was stuck with the Long Island Sound, like the Cambodians were stuck with the Mekong, like Concord was stuck with the Merrimack. It was better than spending the rest of your life on Conrail. Home was where they had to take you in. Language was for praising home, for praising home and God and rivers. God and language and rivers and home were elastic. Everything stretched around the surface of family.

But these weren't smiles, really. His family wasn't smiling. Smiles were cheap jewelry. They were looking down, his family, scuffing the snow and ice in the parking lot. It wasn't as good as all that. It wasn't a romance. It was enough that he dropped the emblems. Just unloaded those elaborate bits of chromium right on the cracked pavement there. He threw his arms around his puffy dad. And then he threw his arms around his icy mom. Kissed Wendy. Kissed the dog.

— Well, we are glad *you* are okay, his father said. How long have you been here?

Paul just threw up his hands.

— Have a lot to tell you, Benjamin said.

Everyone tried to laugh.

— And it's not all good.

It was all quiet again. They buckled themselves into the car, heat on high, as if they had all been deprived of heat lifelong. Daisy Chain scrambled over Wendy's back to get his humid dog tongue all up in Paul's face.

Then Paul's dad just put his head down on the steering wheel and sat that way for a while. This went on for a long time. And then he started to choke or something. Paul had never heard anything like it. He thought it might be a joke. Or a medical emergency. He didn't know what to do. His mom's gloved hand wavered in the air at his father's back as though she were going to set it there. She didn't. His father turned back to look at him, to look at Wendy, smiling, not saying anything, his cheeks shiny with some dew.

— Something I have to tell you two, he said.

And right then there was a sign in the sky. An actual sign in the sky. The conversation stopped and there was a sign in the sky and it knotted together everything in that twenty-four hours. Above the parking lot. A flaming figure four. And it wasn't only above the parking lot. They saw it all over the country, over the Unitarian Church of Stamford, over New Canaan High School, over the Port Chester train station and up and down the New Haven line, over emergency vehicles in Greenwich and Norwalk, over the little office where Wesley Myers was trying to write the next day's sermon, for the first Sunday in Advent. In halls devoted to public service, in private mansions and dilapidated apartments. The heavens declared: the flaming figure four.

They saw it from the Firebird. They did, and it stayed with them all that fall, that apotheosis.

Or that's how I remember it, anyway. Me. Paul. The gab. That's what I remember. And this story really ends right at that spot. I have to leave Benjamin there with that news, with a wish for reconciliation that he will bury in himself; I have to leave Elena, my mom, whom I have never really understood; I have to leave Wendy, uncertain, with one arm around the dog, and I have to leave myself — Paul — on the cusp of my adulthood, at the end of that *annus mirabilis* where comic books were indistinguishable from the truth, at the beginning of my confessions. I have to leave him and his family there because after all this time, after twenty years, it's time I left.

Finis.